The Fortune of Carthage

By: William Kelso

Visit the author's website **http://www.williamkelso.co.uk/**

William Kelso is the author of: The Shield of Rome

The Fortune of Carthage

Devotio: The House of Mus

Caledonia – Book One of the Veteran of Rome series

Hibernia – Book Two of the Veteran of Rome series

Britannia – Book Three of the Veteran of Rome series

Hyperborea – Book Four of the Veteran of Rome series

Germania – Book Five of the Veteran of Rome series

The Dacian War – Book Six of the Veteran of Rome series

Armenia Capta – Book Seven of the Veteran of Rome series

The Fortune of Carthage

Published in 2012 by FeedARead Publishing – Third edition

British Library C.I.P.

A CIP catalogue record for this title is available from the British Library.

Chapter One - Armageddon - Spring 146 BC

The city of Carthage was on fire. The flames had turned the night sky crimson. Bostar could feel their heat. He stood on the walls of the Byrsa staring down towards the naval harbour. In the streets below him the desperate, ferocious fighting went on. Rubble from collapsed buildings lay strewn across the once pristine streets. Corpses lay everywhere, their stench creeping into his nostrils. Screams filled the night. The killing was like no battle he had ever witnessed and he was certainly no stranger to war. This was something different. Everyone knew. Everyone knew that these were the last days of Carthage, ancient, glorious Carthage. There was no more food. There were no more weapons. There was no longer any hope. The seven-hundred year history of the city he loved was coming to an end. The house to house fighting had not ceased for six days and six nights, not for one single moment. The Carthaginians had barricaded themselves into their tall, five and six storey apartment blocks and had contested every floor. The fighting had gone on until the defenders had been forced up onto the roofs where they had pelted the attackers with anything they could find. Both sides had not taken prisoners. People had been buried head first, their legs sticking up into the air whilst others had been buried with only their heads above ground. Horses had galloped over them and crushed their skulls. The fury with which the Carthaginians defended their homes was astonishing. The dogged, grim determination of the Roman Legionaries, as they fought their way from apartment block to apartment block and from floor to floor was terrifying. The last defenders of Carthage were not young men trained for war but the old, the infirm, women and children. Anyone with enough strength and capable of throwing something. If only his old commander, Hasdrubal, could have seen this sight he thought.

Bostar gripped his wooden staff. He was in good health for an eighty- one-year old although he was always hungry. His other hand rested on the shoulder of an eleven-year old boy. His great grandson was staring at the burning buildings below them. He looked terrified. The two of them were the last survivors of their entire family. The men had died years ago when the siege had first begun and the women had refused to leave their home and flee to the relative safety of the Byrsa, the citadel and heart of the city of Carthage. They were down their somewhere in the tall apartment buildings fighting the Romans with roof tiles and stones. Probably they were already dead. Bostar knew he would never see any of them again but the boy had not accepted that yet. Bostar closed his eyes and tried to picture what the women of his family looked like. His wife had died of starvation a few months ago. His daughter had followed her within weeks but the others, the younger ones, to whom he and his wife had given most of their food rations had resolved not to surrender.

"When will it stop?" the boy said turning his face away from the burning streets.

Bostar opened his eyes and glanced down at his great grandson. Then with his hand he forced the boy's head back to face the inferno.

"Look at it," he said sternly, "Look at the end of our city. You must look at it. You must remember. You must remember us. You must remember who we were. That is your duty. Do your duty now."

4

The boy said nothing. Bostar sensed his fear. The boy wanted to run away and hide but there was nowhere to run to and no places to hide. The Romans, after a siege lasting three years, had finally broken into the city, stormed the naval and civilian harbours and had sacked the temple of Apollo. Now they were methodically fighting their way up the streets towards the hill on which stood the last Carthaginian stronghold, the Byrsa. The hill upon which Queen Dido had founded the city. Bostar looked up at the night sky. When the sun rose in the morning, it would be the last sunrise that Carthage would ever know. The fifty thousand people who had sought refuge within the Byrsa had decided to surrender in the morning. He turned to look up at the temple of Aesculapius, the god of healing. The temple rose high above the Byrsa. On its narrow and solitary rocky plateau it resembled an eagles nest. He smiled as he remembered the day upon which he had been appointed a priest of Aesculapius. That was more than thirty years ago. Now he was the high priest. That was why he was here and not down in the streets below fighting on the roof tops. The few within the Byrsa who had opposed surrender were going to retreat into the temple at dawn. There they would fight to the death.

"Are we going to die?" the boy said.

Bostar didn't reply. It was nearly time he thought. Nearly time to do the thing he dreaded most. His fingers gripped the boy's shoulder. There was so much he would have liked to have told the boy but there was no time, nor did he have the strength. Hunger had made him weak. And once I was such a handsome, strong young man he thought. The memory brought a wry smile to his face. He'd been eighteen years old when he had joined Hasdrubal Barca in Spain, sixty-three years ago. His skill with a sword had caught the General's eye. Hasdrubal had requested

5

that Bostar become one of his bodyguards. The honour of being chosen for this position was immense. He had spent two years with Hasdrubal, Hannibal's younger brother. He had been involved in countless skirmishes and battles but most of all he had come to know his commander. He had known Hasdrubal far better than any man in that army. He had remained loyal to Hasdrubal. He was the only one to have witnessed Hasdrubal's last words. He had been there when Carthage had a real chance to win the war and avert the fate that now pressed so fiercely against the walls of the Byrsa. Yes, despite the intervening decades, the memories were still quite clear. Probably he realised, he was the last man in the city to remember those days, the days when, instead of Rome, Carthage could have become mistress of the Mediterranean.

Bostar sighed with sudden melancholy. Around him the city burned and the demonic cries and sound of fighting went on unremitting. If only he could be young again he thought. What would he give to be there, riding behind his commander, staring up at the snow-covered peaks of the mighty Alps. Seeing the African elephants plodding along through the snow. Hearing the unmistakable and haunting sound of the Gallic Carnyx, battle trumpets. What days they had experienced. What things he had seen and heard. The glory that could have been. Bostar blinked. Then despite the circumstances he started to laugh. It was all Marcus's fault. All this, everything around him, the destruction of his beloved city, it was all Marcus's fault. Bostar had been taken prisoner by the Romans. He'd become a slave and had been given to a Roman farmer called Marcus as a reward for that man's valour. He had worked on Marcus's farm for fifteen years as a slave before the Roman had freed him and he had been allowed to return to his home at Carthage.

Bostar's laughter faded. He glanced down at the boy. It was time. He leaned his staff against the parapet and with both hands he grabbed the boys shoulders. He looked down at his great grandson, fighting back the sudden surge of emotion.

"Listen, listen carefully to what I have to say. You are the last of our family now. You must survive. Your duty is to live, do you understand?"

The boy was staring up at his great grandfather in bewilderment. Then tears sprang from his eyes.

"Survive this, survive all of this," Bostar said harshly. "It doesn't matter what you do but just survive and remember us, your family. Remember how we once were. There is nothing more precious than that."

The boy was staring up at him his face wet with tears. He nodded bravely.

Bostar looked at him struggling with his own emotions. Then he reached inside his tunic and withdrew a bundle of papyrus scrolls bound together by the last of his wife's hair. He pressed the bundle into the boy's hand and closed his fingers over the boy's hand.

"Join the people who are going to surrender tomorrow. Protect these scrolls. Don't lose them. The scrolls must survive. Do you understand?"

The boy looked down at the bundle in his hand. Then he looked up again and despite his tears he nodded.

Bostar patted the boy on his cheek and smiled.

The boy was too young and frightened to understand. Bostar sighed. Rome, the victor would now write the history of Carthage. Roman propaganda would hide the glory of Carthage and distort everything she had ever achieved in seven hundred years. The Roman hatred of Carthage was implacable and her scribes would be as vindictive as her soldiers. He had experienced that himself. The scrolls were a final act of resistance. On the papyrus he had recorded every detail that he could remember about the year in which Hasdrubal had marched on Rome. The year in which the greatest war of the ages had hung in the balance.

"Are you not coming with me?"

The boys question caught him off guard. Bostar looked away. Then he smiled and drew the boy to him in a hug. For a moment the old man and his great grandson clung to each other, both unwilling to let go.

"Go now, join the others down below and when they go out in the morning you must follow them," Bostar said.

The boy clung to his great grandfather, sobbing silently. Bostar ruffled his hair.

"It's alright, it's alright," he said quietly.

The boy loosened his grip and bravely he stared up at his great grandfather.

"I will remember you," he said.

8

Bostar struggled to contain himself. Then he took the boy's hand and started towards the stairs leading down from the walls.

***

Bostar quietly climbed the sixty steps up to the great doors of the temple of Aesculapius. Every step was an effort and drained him. Hunger was as much an enemy as the Romans in the streets below. It was morning and to the east the sun was rising on its journey through the sky. Finally, in front of the doors he turned to look back down into the city. Palls of black smoke hung over the remaining buildings and the harbours but the sound of fighting was dying away. In the Byrsa itself the thousands of weary, dispirited people were beginning to surrender. The peace envoys who had carried olive branches had returned. Terms had been negotiated. The Byrsa and the fifty thousand people inside would surrender and in return have their lives spared. The three-year siege of the city of Carthage was ending at last. The first of the multitude were already filing out through a narrow gate in the walls. Bostar turned away from the sight and gripping his staff he shuffled through the doors. The anxious Roman deserters who made up the majority of those refusing to surrender let him pass. A few of the younger men looked at him. They were all terrified, there could be no surrender for the deserters, only death and they knew it. The few who looked at him seemed to be silently imploring his help as if he could make the gods intervene in the affairs of man. Bostar ignored them contemptuously. The moment when they could have saved their skin had long since passed. Bostar was the last man to walk through the doors. As he made his way into the temple, his beloved temple, the great doors were closed behind him and barricaded.

***

Bostar stood on the roof staring down at the Byrsa below. Behind him a section of the temple was on fire. The flames roared and crackled, black acrid smoke poured upwards but the wind was merciful and blew it away and out to sea. The fire had been started on purpose. The Roman deserters were killing themselves. Hundreds of bodies already lay littered throughout the temple. A small clutch of Carthaginian's had joined their high priest on the roof. It was the only place left where they could escape from the smoke. The Roman Legionaries had finally entered the citadel but they had not stormed the temple. The reason was clear. In the Byrsa below him, Bostar could see the handsome and dignified figure of the Roman commander in chief, the Consul Publius Aemilius Scipio. Scipio was sitting on a chair looted from the temple of Apollo. At his feet sitting on the ground, like a small child before his parent was the Carthaginian leader and commander of the city. The sight filled Bostar with disgust. Their leader had abandoned them at the last. He was begging the Romans for his life. Was this then how the end of Carthage would be recorded? The Carthaginian leader imploring Rome for mercy? How different a fate this was to the one that Hasdrubal, his old commander had chosen. Hasdrubal would never have stooped so low. This was making a mockery of Carthage. This was making a mockery of the memory of all those brave men who had died for her. Was the Carthaginian commander going to decorate a Roman triumph? Bostar gripped his staff with growing fury.

At his side the clutch of Carthaginians suddenly parted and allowed a woman to move to the front. She was clad in fine robes and jewellery and on each side of her, holding their hands, she led her two young sons, no more than children, to the edge of the roof. Bostar bowed his head in respect but the lady did not notice him. The wife of the Carthaginian leader was staring down at her husband. Her cold furious expression needed no explanation.

"Husband," she cried, "I see now what a worthless wretched creature you are." Then she turned to look at Scipio. "For you Roman, the gods have no cause for indignation for you are exercising the right of war. Upon this man, this betrayer of his country and her temples, of me and his children, may the gods of Carthage take vengeance, and you be their instrument."

There was no reply from below. The Carthaginian commander looked utterly defeated and miserable. He refused to look at his wife. The Romans were silent and the only noise was the growing roar of the flames. The wife of the Carthaginian commander was staring at her husband. On each side of her she gripped her son's hands. Her contempt was palpable. "Ah, what punishment you shall receive from the man at whose feet you now sit," she cried. Then before anyone could stop her she turned and pulling her young sons close she leapt with them from the roof and into the fire.

Bostar was staring at the figure of Scipio. There were tears in the Roman's eyes. Then Bostar glanced up at the sun and smiled.

"I have fulfilled my duty to you Lord Hasdrubal," he said quietly. Then he too turned and jumped into the raging fire.

***

The boy filed out of the Byrsa along with thousands of other survivors. No one paid him any attention. He was just another lost child without family, home or country. He didn't know what to do. Follow the others his great grandfather had said. The Roman soldiers lined the street down towards the harbour. The destruction of the city was shocking and the Roman faces hard and brutal as they stared at their defeated foe. The long column of wretched survivors shuffled along, making their way through the ruins of their city. Smoke hung heavy in the air and the cries of the wounded still filled the burnt apartment buildings. At the circular naval harbour the slave traders were waiting for them. Men and women were separated. Long lines of exhausted and starving people, chained together by their ankles, sat amongst the rubble, awaiting what their new masters had in mind for them.

A man beckoned to him. He was a Roman. The boy complied and as he did so the man forced open his mouth with his fingers.

"Good teeth, this one," the slaver shouted to his comrades.

Another slaver walked up to the boy and turned him round, examining him with a critical, experienced eye.

"He's strong and healthy, they need slaves like him in the mines. Put him with the others in that category."

Then the slaver frowned and patted the boy's tunic. "Well what have we here," he said pulling the bundle of scrolls from the boy's tunic.

The boy did not understand what they were saying. Desperately he tried to grab the scrolls from the slavers hand but the man held them out of reach. With mounting horror the boy looked on as the slaver unrolled the papyrus. The man glanced at the writing and shook his head.

"Punic rubbish, I can't read it," he said to his comrade.

The slaver glanced down at the boy, "If the boy can read and write he will fetch a higher price. I have changed my mind. Put him in the educated group. He will be a household slave."

Then without another glance at the boy the slaver tossed the scrolls into a nearby fire where the flames greedily consumed them.

Chapter Two - One day

Spring 207 BC

Marcus stood by the open gate staring down the muddy track that led away from his small farm. He looked worried. Why had she run away? The sun had just risen and beyond the boundary fence of his farm he could see pigs rooting around in the fields. There was no sign of anyone at this time of the morning, but Marcus had found her footsteps in the mud. They were hers alright, small, shallow and fresh. Why had she left? He gripped the wooden fence and a pained expression appeared on his rugged face. He had first realised that something was wrong when he'd noticed that her room was empty.

He was always the first to rise, even before his slaves had lit the hearth and prepared his breakfast. His neighbours had laughed at him and told him to relax and let the slaves do the work but Marcus could not let go of old habits. It was after all, how life had been in the old days before the northern wars of conquest had brought an influx of cheap slaves.

She was not coming back some instinct told him. She had been his slave girl for fifteen years and now without explanation or warning she had run away. Why? He sighed and there was a hint of sadness in the way his shoulders drooped. The girl was valuable. Slaves were valuable. He couldn't afford to buy another girl. He would have to find her and bring her back and teach her some discipline and respect. Then with a shrug he threw off his worries and turned to survey the damage. The girl had left the gate open and his whole herd of pigs had escaped in the night. Had she done that on purpose? A final bitter parting gift from a disgruntled slave? He grunted in disapproval, it was going to take the whole morning to round up all the pigs and get them back into their enclosure. Time was money and there was already so much work that had to be done that day.

He closed the gate and turned to examine his small farm. It was only sixty-five acres, much smaller than the farms his neighbours possessed, but it meant everything to Marcus. Five generations of his family had worked this land and now it was his turn. He still remembered the pride he'd felt when he'd inherited the place from his father. "Make her flourish," had been his father's final parting words. His fingers tightened their grip on the wooden gate. He had done his best but his father had never had to farm with Hannibal rampaging through Italy, nor had the old man had to cope with spiralling war taxes and the general lawlessness that had dogged the countryside since Hannibal's invasion eleven years ago. The worried look returned to Marcus's face. Farming had become a lot harder since war had broken out and not a day passed by now when he did not worry about his home and his family. The war had changed people he thought. The old ancestral code and manners that he'd known and which had been passed down generation after generation were disappearing and as the strain of war continued year after year, people were becoming harder and crueller. Marcus had tried to stay loyal to the old ways but it was difficult. Whatever the cost he thought, he had to keep his farm and he had to keep his family together and survive.

He was a well built, clean shaven man of forty-five with black hair that was greying fast. He was dressed in a plain white woollen tunic with short sleeves. The tunic ended just above his knees and on his feet he was wearing a pair of leather sandals which enclosed his toes. His skin was deeply tanned and his

15

hands were the rough hands of a farmer used to hard labour. His quick, intelligent eyes took in everything, checking to see if the slave girl had damaged or stolen anymore of his property. The wheat fields that surrounded his farm house like the waters of an ocean were only interrupted by the muddy track and a copse of Cypress trees that surrounded the well. It was here beneath the shade of their branches that all his ancestors were buried. The farm animals, two oxen and some cows stood dumbly in their pens. The two asses used to pull his wagon were eating and his horse whinnied quietly in her stable. Behind the farm house and out of sight he could hear his dog barking. Smoke had started to rise from the chimney. He grunted. The cook would be up preparing his porridge breakfast. At last he seemed satisfied. Apart from the runaway slave girl and the escaped pigs everything looked as it should.

He glanced across the courtyard to the two cottages he had built for his Gallic slaves. He'd given them some extra resting time after yesterday's hard labour but the slave girl's disappearance had changed all that. It was time he woke them up and set them to work rounding up the pigs. It was also planting season and they would be out all day in the fields, planting the wheat that he would harvest in August. He strode towards the cottages. Apart from the runaway slave girl he had eleven Gaul's, two entire families, six men and boys capable of working in the fields, four women to help his wife around the farm and one toddler, born the previous spring. They were sullen people, who liked to keep themselves to themselves, tall and brawny and when they thought he could not hear them, they would speak in their own language which Marcus couldn't understand. But they were strong and efficient workers and Marcus valued their knowledge of farming. Marcus had heard of other farms suffering slave rebellions but the only sign of

16

unease he'd experienced was nine years ago when news had come of the terrible slaughter of Romans at Cannae.

Round the back of the farm house, with its white washed walls and red roof tiles his dog was still barking. The smell of fresh bread being prepared in the oven wafted across to him. He stomped up to the first cottage and with his fist banged on the door, "Wake up, work!" he cried. He moved on to the next cottage and repeated the action. Inside the buildings he heard people stumbling around. He stood outside waiting impatiently. Across the courtyard Flavia, his wife poked her head out of the doorway of their home. Seeing her he called out, "Livia has gone. She has runaway and let the pigs escape. I am going to round them up now."

"She's gone, where?" Flavia looked shocked.

"I don't know," he shouted, "When I am done with the pigs I shall go and look for her. She can't have gone far."

Flavia took a few moments to take in the news. She was dressed in a traditional, long and flowing, white Stola, dress that covered her arms and ankles and was fixed by a belt around her waist.

"Do not be cruel to her Marcus, I want her back unharmed, our daughter needs her," she called out.

Marcus looked annoyed but he was careful to hide it from his wife. He had never mistreated his slaves. He had always thought that honest labour deserved fair treatment but as father and head of his family, by law and tradition, it was he and he alone that should decide such matters.

17

Why was that damned dog still barking?

Marcus frowned with a sudden sense of foreboding. Leaving the cottages he crossed the stone courtyard and strode around the side of his home. At the back of the building, on a gentle rocky slope was the pride of his farm, a small vineyard that had taken him years to cultivate and that now produced a quality wine. But Marcus paid it no attention. His eyes were on the dog. The beast was chained to the wall and was still barking.

"Be quiet Brennus!" Marcus commanded.

The dog whined and padded over to its master. Marcus was about to give it a pat on the head when he saw the figure stumbling across the fields towards his farm. He squinted as he tried to make out who it was. The man looked out of breath. He struggled along as if he had been running for a long time. As he caught sight of Marcus, the figure raised his arm and cried out nearly tripping over himself. Marcus felt the hairs on his back start to stand up. Something was wrong. He could sense it in the man's actions.

As the figure lumbered up to him Marcus recognised the young man and his heart sank with a mixture of disgust and anxiety. It was the partner of his eldest son, Publius, who lived in Rome, three miles away. Marcus did not approve of the lifestyle that his eldest had chosen. The boy followed the Greek practice of having sex with other men. He even claimed to love them. That may be all good and well for the Greeks, Marcus thought, but it was not the way a true Roman should conduct himself. He had tried to talk to the boy but it had been no use, nor had threats and in the end the tension in the household had become such that Publius had moved out and gone to live in the city where he

18

had found work as an actor. An actor, Marcus thought scornfully, what kind of profession was that? Actors were on a par with prostitutes!

The young man, whose name he faintly remembered as Dorian came to a halt before him. He bent over trying to catch his breath. He was wearing a tunic with long sleeves. It was then that Marcus noticed the tears in the man's eyes.

"Well, what's all the rush for?" Marcus exclaimed sternly.

"Sir," Dorian cried, "Its Publius, your son. He has been murdered."

Chapter Three - Marcus Vibius Pansa

The two of them sat at the oak dining table in the long room of the farm house. Dorian had his head in his hands, his elbows leaning on the table. Marcus sat staring out of the window. Across from them, kneeling on the floor in front of a wall shelf on which stood the Lares, the statues of the household gods, his wife Flavia was murmuring prayers. Marcus's gaze was fixed on the copse of Cypress trees. He had never expected to have to bury his son. It was something that no father should ever have to do. He'd had his differences with Publius. He had despised him even, but Publius was still his son and now that he was dead, Marcus felt the loss. He wanted to tell his son that everything was alright, but now it was too late.

At last Marcus wrenched his eyes from the Cypress trees and looked at Dorian. The young man was in a bad way. Slowly Marcus got to feet, walked to the cabinet beside the hearth and poured three cups of wine before handing one to the young man. Dorian threw the contents down his throat in one go. On the floor Flavia was staring at the Lares, her face pale, her eyes red, her lips moving but no sound came from her mouth. Marcus left her cup standing on the table and returned to his seat. As he sat down he noticed a little face peering at him from the half-closed kitchen door. It was Laelia, his seven-year old daughter. The girl looked frightened.

"It's alright little one," Marcus said trying to give her a reassuring smile. "Go back to your room."

The face vanished. Marcus glanced at his wife but she had not seemed to notice the exchange. Laelia had nearly killed Flavia.

The girl had come out the wrong way and it had taken all the skill of the doctor and the midwife to save both mother and daughter. Laelia had been born deformed, her face was different and she couldn't speak properly. The priests had told Marcus that she would forever remain a child. They had said that the girl was cursed by the gods and had told Marcus that he should kill his daughter. It was tradition but as he had looked down upon the baby's face Marcus had known that he could not do that.

Marcus cleared his throat. "Tell me again what you found?"

Dorian lifted his head from his hands and looked up at the ceiling where a dark oak beam ran the length of the room. He swallowed nervously and his eyes refused to meet Marcus's gaze.

"Like I said. We were both invited to the house of Marcus Livius Drusus, the Consul. It was a long-standing invitation. We had been hired as entertainment." Dorian's face blushed lightly as he spoke. "I last saw Publius at the Consul's party, we did our act, were paid and then he went home, everything seemed fine." Dorian suddenly grew thoughtful, "although," he murmured, "Publius was a bit tense last night. I put it down to nerves ahead of our performance." Dorian turned to look straight at Marcus, his eyes widening. "How stupid of me, I nearly forgot," he exclaimed. "Publius said that he wanted to speak with you. I got the impression that it was urgent. He was going to come here today!"

Marcus's face remained unreadable. "What did my son want to speak to me about?"

But Dorian shook his head, "I don't know, he didn't say."
"So then what happened?"

"He went home", Dorian shrugged helplessly. "I saw him leave the Consul's house. That was the last time that I saw him." Dorian paused. "It was murder you know," he said solemnly, "Publius was happy with his life, he would not have killed himself. I am sure of that."

"Did he go home alone?" Marcus interrupted.

Dorian hesitated for a fraction of a second, "Yes he was alone when he left the Consul's house," he nodded.

Marcus paused to scrutinise the youth. "Then what?" he said.

Dorian lowered his eyes. "I had arranged to meet him later. We share the same room. When I arrived home the door was open. There was blood on the floor and someone had gone through all our belongings. The room was a mess. I walked in and there he was lying on his bed with a knife sticking out of his chest. I left him there just as I found him and ran all the way from Rome to tell you. I didn't know what else to do. I am sorry, I am such a coward."

"Why did you not go home together? The act was finished as you said."

Dorian blushed and his eyes avoided Marcus's gaze. "I…I had some other business that I needed to take care of," he murmured.

Marcus looked away. He could imagine what this other "business" was and it filled him with disgust but now was not the time for such emotions. He leaned forward, "Who did this Dorian, who killed my son?"

Dorian trembled and Marcus suddenly realised that the boy was frightened.

"I must go," Dorian said rising to his feet. "I shall come again for the funeral."

Marcus let him go. When he was alone he glanced at his wife. Flavia was still kneeling on the floor uttering her silent prayers. Marcus sighed and rose stiffly and scooped her up in his arms, burying her face into his shoulder. He felt the tension in her muscles and then the wet warm tears as they trickled down his arm.

"Who did this to our boy?" Flavia whispered hoarsely.

"I don't know," he said gently stroking her hair, "But I think Dorian is lying. There is something that he is not telling us."

***

Marcus and Flavia sat silently around the large oak table. Marcus glanced at the empty chairs. There had been a time when the long room had been a lively, cheerful place, filled with children's voices, toys, activity and laughter. They had always taken their family meals here. He'd sat at the head of the table with Flavia opposite him and the children and Livia in between. It was here that Flavia had taught her boys to read and write. She had created a profitable enterprise by writing short stories
23

for children, which she sold to families in Rome. The war news was always depressing and the stories had been designed to cheer the children up. She had found a ready market for them in Rome.

But now everything had changed. Publius was dead and Livia had run away. Marcus's eyes wandered back to the window and the Cypress trees outside. His younger son was serving abroad with Scipio. Marcus had not heard anything from him for nearly two years. It was not unusual for news travelled slowly but it didn't stop him worrying about the boy. The casualties from the fighting had been horrendous and he didn't know of any family that had not suffered a loss. In the spare time that he managed to get, Marcus would take his horse and ride the fifteen miles to the port of Ostia. There he would frequent all the taverns, accosting any soldiers or sailors who had just landed, asking for information about the fighting and whether they had heard any news about his son. But there had been no news, nothing at all.

"Master, visitor," one of his Gallic slaves said in a thick accent. Marcus looked up. He had not noticed the slave enter the house. He rose and followed the man outside. By the gate leading to the muddy track a man dressed in a white tunic with a broad purple border and a toga draped over the top, sat on a horse waiting patiently to be allowed to enter the farm.

Marcus recognised him. It was Numa, a Senator and close friend. He gestured for the slave to open the gate.

"I came as soon as I heard the news," Numa exclaimed as he dismounted and handed the reins to the slave. His coloured shoes sank into the mud. He strode across the space that separated them and embraced Marcus. "This is truly terrible news. I grieve for you, how is Flavia?"

"Thank you, old friend," Marcus tried to smile, "Flavia is holding up but I think she has not fully accepted it yet. Come inside."

The two men entered the farm house. Numa was a tall man and he had to stoop slightly as he went through the doorway. The two of them had known each other for eighteen years. Numa had been a young Patrician from a wealthy family who owned a seat in the Senate. Marcus and he had been called up for service in two hundred and twenty-five BC and had both served under the Consul Aemilius at the battle of Telamon. Numa had been a Decurion in charge of thirty horsemen and Marcus had been one of his riders. In the battle Numa had saved Marcus from being killed by a Gaul and the two had remained friends ever since.

Flavia acknowledged their guest with a small nod. Marcus poured Numa a cup of wine and the Senator took it gladly. His eyes swept around the room as if he was searching for something.

"What have you heard?" Numa said as he sat down and glanced at Marcus.

Marcus cleared his throat and told Numa about Dorian's visit. Numa listened in silence. Then when Marcus had nothing more to say he stirred.

"So that was all the actor could tell you?" he inquired sharply.

"They didn't find anything else? Publius didn't mention anything?"

Marcus shook his head, "That's all I know. I asked him twice."

Numa seemed to consider the news. Then he glanced at Flavia.

"If you need my help you just have to ask," he said. "That is the reason why I have come here. I am sorry for your loss. Publius was like a son to me. I shall pray to Jupiter."

"Thank you," Marcus murmured.

"So what are you going to do now?" Numa asked.

Marcus opened his mouth to reply but he was interrupted by his wife. Flavia had risen to her feet and the expression in her eyes made the hair stand up on Marcus's back.

"Marcus Vibius Pansa," Flavia spoke with a tightly controlled voice, "you will bring back the body of my boy and we will bury him in his proper place. You will go to Rome and bring my boy home. Then you will track down the person responsible for his death and we shall see justice done."

Flavia's eyes were fixed on her husband. In his seat, Numa blushed and lowered his head. Marcus's face was unreadable. Then slowly he turned to his guest and nodded. "The pursuit of justice is my responsibility alone," he said quietly. "It is the family that must seek justice for no one else will. I will go to Rome and find out who did this and once justice has been done, Publius will rest in peace."

The room fell silent. Numa was staring at the floor tiles. The silence lengthened. Then the Senator raised his head and there was a weary expression on his face.

"There is something that you need to know," he said. "I too was at that party last night. Livius is an old friend of the family and yes I spoke with Publius, he seemed happy but his friend, this Dorian..." Numa sighed. "Dorian is a Nepenthe addict and I think he has introduced the drugs to your son. I certainly saw Nepenthe, Opium being used at that party. You know what the drug of forgetfulness does to your mind. It's disgusting. The Senate should ban its use."

"What's your point Numa?" Marcus interrupted.

"My point, old friend is that a man called Mamercus is the main supplier of Nepenthe. Mamercus is a parasite, he operates out of the Subura neighbourhood and he knows people everywhere. He's a dangerous and powerful man. Have you heard of him?" Marcus shook his head.

"Well Mamercus happened to also be at this party last night. I can't say for certain because I did not hear their exact conversation but Publius and he seemed to have had an argument last night."

"Why would Publius have an argument with such a man?" Marcus frowned.

Numa shrugged. "Who knows, maybe it was about an unpaid bill or a loan. These youths who use Nepenthe don't ask their parents for permission but they probably do trade on their parent's credit. If you are going to seek justice for Publius, I would start by investigating that man. He is rotten, Marcus."

Chapter Four – Wild flowers

Little Laelia sat on top of Livia's shoulders, her hands clasped around the older girl's neck as the two girls made their way down the country path towards the small woodland half a mile away. Laelia's feet dangled onto Livia's chest and she was humming a happy tune. Livia looked relaxed. In her hand she was holding a small wicker basket. It was morning and the sky was blue and bright but far to the east a line of grey rain clouds were gathering.

Livia was sixteen with jet black hair that she'd tied in a ponytail and fixed with a bone hair pin. She was wearing a palla over her simple, brown sleeveless peplos dress which was fastened by two fibula, pins at the shoulder and a belt around her waist. On her feet she was wearing a couple of worn out sandals.

"Flow...ers," Laelia said suddenly pointing at some wild flowers that were growing along the edge of the path.

"Do you want them?" Livia replied but Laelia shook her head.

Livia paused to shift the seven-year olds weight to a more comfortable position. Then she started walking again. Livia could remember when Laelia had been born. The farm had filled with tension as all had waited to see whether mother and daughter would pull through and survive. The doctor and midwife had given Flavia a fifty percent chance of living. But they had survived and Livia's main duty from that day on had been to look after little Laelia, little deformed and handicapped Laelia. Livia could still remember the sheer fear in Flavia's eyes as she had waited for Marcus to decide on whether to accept his new daughter or not. If Marcus had refused to accept the baby, Laelia would have been left to die. What a stupid custom that was Livia thought. She had resented her new task at first but as Laelia had grown older the two of them had formed a surprisingly strong and close friendship. Livia was the only friend that Laelia had and Laelia was the only friend she had. The cursed cripple and the slave girl. They were natural allies.

The woodland was full of wild flowers and as they reached the trees, Laelia indicated that she wanted to get down. Livia lifted the little girl over her head and lowered her carefully to the ground. They had come to the woodland because Laelia had said that she wanted to make a crown of flowers which she would wear on the journey into Rome later that morning.

"Flow...ers," Laelia exclaimed again as she looked around.

Livia took the little girl's hand and the two of them made their way deeper into the woodland.

"That...one," Laelia said pointing at a pale yellow Primrose. Livia stooped and picked the flower and placed in the small wicker basket.

As they slowly meandered through the woodland picking the colourful wild flowers that Laelia wanted, Livia thought about Marcus, her owner. She has a Gallic streak in her face, the posh folk who sometimes visited the farm had said. We don't know where she is from, Marcus had always replied. He'd spoken the truth. Livia bit her lip. Marcus always spoke the truth and it annoyed her. The truth was that she didn't know who she was or where she had come from. Livia had no identity. She didn't know on what day she had been born. She wasn't even sure of her real name. Her parents had abandoned her at birth and left her as a baby on the road between Ostia and Rome. She couldn't remember a thing about it of course but apparently it was Marcus who had found her and brought her back to his farm. It was Marcus who had named her Livia. It was Marcus who had insisted on treating her like a slave, long after the rest of the family, Flavia, her two sons and Laelia, had started to want to treat her like a daughter and a sister.

When Marcus had brought her back to his farm, all those years ago, she had become a slave, such was the law, but maybe, just maybe she hadn't been born a slave. Idly she reached up to her neck and felt the small terracotta phallus that hung there on a thin bronze chain. The phallus was a charm intended to ward off evil and it had been around her neck when Marcus had found her. It was the only thing that she had that connected her to her biological parents. Many a night she had sat examining the charm thinking about who her mother and father could have been and why they had abandoned her. There were two letters engraved on the charm. VF. She had no idea what they meant or stood for.

The basket was nearly full and Livia could sense that Laelia was getting bored.

"Sing, sing," Laelia cried suddenly her eyes shining with excitement. Livia smiled at the little girl's enthusiasm. She placed the basket with flowers on the ground. Then she cleared her throat, took a step backwards and facing Laelia, she bowed like she had once seen Publius do to the audience on stage. Laelia giggled and clapped her hands. Then quietly, Livia began to sing. Her voice rose steadily and powerfully and her Latin melody seemed to fill the woodland with a beautiful haunting
31

sound that seemed to turn nature itself melancholy. When at last she finished Laelia clapped her hands in delight and tried to bow in return. Livia laughed at the little girl's antics as Laelia too seemed to be trying to impersonate her elder brother.

"Why don't you come over here and sing for us darling?" a man's voice suddenly said.

Livia whirled round. She had been so focussed on her singing that she had not noticed the two young men approaching. The two men looked around eighteen and one of them had a dead fox slung over his shoulder. They were staring at her with broad smiles that had nothing to do with friendliness. As she stared at the intruders she felt their eyes sliding across her body. She blushed. Then she turned to Laelia. Despite the age difference, it was the little girl who decided what they should do. Livia after all, was her slave girl.

"Bad, bad," Laelia said reaching up for Livia's hand. "Home," the little girl said.

Livia grasped Laelia's hand and with the other she picked up the basket of flowers. She blushed again as she felt the boys eyes feasting on her body. The farm hands on the neighbouring farms always noticed her. They called her beautiful and were always trying it on. She knew that men were attracted to her, she noticed their looks, their smiles and comments but she had never allowed the attention to go to her head.

"If you change your mind, you know where you can find me," one of the young men cried as the two girls walked away back towards the farm. His words were followed by hoots of laughter. Laelia gripped Livia's hand tightly but the two girls did not talk.

They were half a mile from the farm when the gang of children appeared on the path up ahead. Catching sight of Livia and Laelia, the gang pointed and cried out. Then they were coming towards the two girls. There were seven of them, four girls and three boys. Livia knew them all and her heart sank. The children were all aged between ten and sixteen. The group had been trying to bully Laelia for years. The deformed and handicapped Laelia had been a natural target on which to pick and nothing it seemed could stop the cruel delight the gang took in mocking and taunting the little girl.

The gang halted before them blocking the path.

"I saw you in those woods," one of the girls cried out staring accusingly at Livia, "what were you doing there with those boys then?"

"Are you a slut?" another of the girls cried.

"Ofcourse she is, she's always out there in those woods," a third girl chipped in with a nasty look on her face. "My mother says slave girls like that are whores."

Livia ignored the barbs and holding Laelia's hand tightly she tried to push her way through the group but the eldest boy stretched out his hand and pushed her back.

"Look at her, she's so strange," one of the other boys said staring at Laelia in disgust. "My father says it's not right that she was allowed to live. My father says that she doesn't have a future. She's going to die young."

"Leave her alone," Livia snapped.

"Or what?" the eldest boy said taking a step towards her and raising his chin. The boy was slightly taller than Livia and the same age.

At her side Livia sensed Laelia's fear. Then before she could open her mouth, the little girl burst out crying.

Laelia's crying was met with an outburst of laughter and hilarity.

"Look at the thing," the boy who had blocked their way exclaimed as he gave Laelia a push, "Look it can actually cry."

"Don't touch her," Livia snapped.

"Or what?" the boy snarled giving Laelia another shove.

Livia released her grip on Laelia's hand and swung her fist into the boy's face with all her might. The boy staggered backwards with a howl of pain, his hands clutching at his face. Livia raised her fist in the air and turned on the children.

"Anyone for anymore!" she cried ferociously.

Livia stood trembling on the path, her fist shaking with rage. She had never felt so angry before, it was as if a red mist had descended upon her and the fury seemed to give her super human strength. She had never known that she could be so angry.

"Bitch," one of the girls hissed but none of them dared to approach her. Livia suddenly realised that the children were scared of her. Then grasping Laelia's hand, she pushed through the gang, past the boy she'd hit and on towards the farm.

Chapter Five - The runaway

Livia's fury seemed to slip away as they approached the farm. She didn't like her violent self but she could not pretend that it wasn't there. Laelia was still crying and her face had turned red. Livia halted, turned and bent down to wipe the tears from the little girl's face.

"Please, stop crying," Livia whispered trying to smile at Laelia. If they showed up at the farm like this, Livia knew, she would get into trouble with Flavia who would want to know why her daughter was in such a distressed state. Telling the truth would only make things worse for Flavia was fiercely protective of her handicapped daughter. She would scold Livia for not having seen the children earlier and for not taking a different path back to the farm. That was her duty, to look after Laelia and if the girl came home crying then she had failed in that task.

"Please," Livia implored again, ruffling the girl's hair.

Laelia sniffed and looked up at her slave. Then she sniffed again, blinked and rubbed her hand in her eyes. The crying had stopped.

***

Flavia was sitting perfectly still on a chair in the long room of the farm house. One of the Gallic slave women had just finished doing up her mistress's hair and was fitting Flavia's plain ear rings when Livia and Laelia appeared. Another woman stood patiently behind Flavia holding a Palla, ready to slip it over her mistress's shoulders. Flavia was going into Rome to sell her children's stories to a new client and she wanted Laelia to accompany her. Flavia had never shied away from showing her daughter the sights of the great city, despite the stares and looks that the little girl solicited. Flavia's determination to treat her daughter like any other daughter had won her Livia's respect.

Flavia looked up as the two of them came in. She frowned as she saw Laelia but she said nothing. Livia sat down on a chair beside the oak table, placed the wicker basket on top and began to twist the flowers that they'd picked into a round crown. As she did so she felt Flavia looking at her.

"Is something the matter Livia?" Flavia asked.

Livia shook her head and continued with building the crown.

"We are ready to go mistress," the slave woman said dipping her head respectfully.

Flavia stood up and the second slave placed her Palla around Flavia's shoulders. Livia looked up and caught the cold glance of one of the slave women looking at her. The Gallic women didn't like her and the feeling was mutual. Livia had always been kept separate from the other slaves. Her room had been in the farm house and she had taken her meals with the family as if she was one of them, which she knew she was not. The other women had resented her closeness to Flavia and had taken every opportunity to remind her that she was a slave too. It was just jealousy but it had meant that she had no friends amongst the Gaul's.

***

The four women walked the three miles from the farm to the gates of Rome. Flavia strode ahead followed closely by one of the Gaul's carrying the satchel that contained the children's stories. Behind them came Livia. She was carrying Laelia tucked under her arm and the little girl had her hands clasped around Livia's neck as she twisted to look around. The crown of colourful flowers sat gaily on her head.

"For...tune...tell...er," Laelia said suddenly. Then she repeated the word and then again.

Livia stiffened as she remembered what that horrible boy had said to Laelia. My father says that she doesn't have a future. She's going to die young. She glanced at Laelia and shook her head but the girl ignored her.

"For...tune...tell...er."

"They are charlatans, tricksters, don't waste your money on them, darling," Flavia called out in reply.
But Laelia would not take no for an answer. She shook her head violently so that the crown nearly fell off.

"For...tune...tell...er."

The three women strode on through the gates of Rome in silence as Laelia kept repeating the word over and over again until at last Flavia seemed to grow tired of the conversation. At the door to the new client's house on the Quirinal, a smart but otherwise ordinary neighbourhood of Rome, Flavia turned to look at her daughter and sighed.

"Livia, take her to the old Sybil on the Long road." Flavia said pressing a few coins into her hand. "Come back here right away when you are done."

Livia nodded dutifully and taking Laelia's hand the two girls walked away down the street. The Sybil's shop was a simple two room building. A wooden sign advertising her wares and skills hung above the entrance door and beside it, scratched into the wall was the faded letters of a shopping licence. The shop itself took up the front room. A curtain of beads hung in the doorway that separated the front from the back room. Livia stared at the rows of terracotta charms, clay pots containing coloured potions and the statues of a hundred different deities, that lined the shelves against the far wall. Livia and Laelia were the only customers.

The old Sybil wore a blond wig and the woman looked impossibly old.

"Well ladies, come to have your fortune told have you?" she said glancing at Laelia with a curious look.

Laelia nodded happily and eagerly extended her palm. The Sybil laughed and turned to Livia.

"Did your mistress give you any coins with which to pay me?" she snapped.

Livia handed over the coins and stepped back. That was part of her duties, to become invisible when it was required and that was often. The Sybil took Laelia's hand and seemed to go into a trance. Her eyes rolled around in their sockets. Then the smell of Incense suddenly wafted into the shop as she swayed to and fro muttering words that the girls had never heard before. Livia wanted to laugh but she kept quiet. She would only upset Laelia if she laughed at the show that was being performed before them. Instead, cheekily she leaned to one side, when the Sybil's eyes were closed and slightly parted the beads in the doorway. A boy in the back room was pressing down furiously on the pump that was pushing the incense into the room.

Laelia had her fortune told and when it was over the little girl emitted a happy grunting noise and clapped her hands together.

Livia leaned forward to help Laelia out of her chair and as she did so, the phallic charm around her neck slipped out of her Peplos dress and into plain view. She tried to stuff it back but a bony hand stopped her. The old Sybil's face had utterly changed as she had stared at the charm, turning it round in her fingers. Then the old woman looked up and Livia saw a sudden wisdom in those old grey eyes.

"A child abandoned on the side of the road," the Sybil said as if she was in a trance, "a girl with a father's gift and a brother in Placentia, I do not think she knows. He will need her before the year is out. I must tell her, I must."

Livia blinked in astonishment. Then she ripped the charm from the Sybil's fingers and as she did so the old woman seemed to come back to herself. "What are you talking about? I have a brother. How can that be true? How can you know such a thing?" Livia cried struggling with a rising tide of emotion.

The Sybil was staring at her as if she had just seen her for the first time. Then Livia scooped Laelia up into her arms and fled from the shop.

39

***

It was late in the afternoon when they returned to the farm. Flavia was in a good mood for the client had purchased all her stories. Laelia too seemed in a good mood for she was humming happily as Livia carried her back home. Livia however was not paying any attention to her companions. Her thoughts were miles away. She felt physically sick. The Sybil's words would not go away. On the contrary their hold over her seemed to be growing, nibbling away at her resistance. On Marcus's farm she had eaten at the same table as the family, she had grown up with his two sons, she was Laelia's best and only friend and Flavia treated her almost as a daughter but Marcus; Marcus always managed to remind her that she would never be really part of his family. Marcus managed to remind her that she was a slave, that she was different, that she was not their equal. His attitude hurt her and there were many nights, alone in her room, when she felt so lonely, as if she was back again by the side of the road, an abandoned child. Would she be like this forever? Would she be lonely forever? Would she be forbidden from marrying and raising her own family, forever? She had tried to avoid those questions because they only led to that terrible dark place where she didn't want to go. But now something had changed. There was another way out. If she had a brother in Placentia, wherever that was, then maybe she had other family too? Maybe she would finally meet her real mother and father. The thought had lodged itself so firmly in her mind that she couldn't think of anything else. If she had a brother then she needed to find him. If she didn't then she would spend the rest of her life wondering about what could have been.

***

It was the middle of the night and the rain clouds that had been building up in the east all day had finally moved west and released their rain. Livia could hear the rain pattering on the roof tiles of the farm house. She was glad for the noise had masked any sounds that she may have made. The farm house was asleep. She stood in the doorway of her small room, fully clad in her brown Peplos dress. Her Palla was pulled across her shoulders. Over her head she was wearing a hood and on her back she was carrying a leather bag containing a little food she'd taken from the kitchen and all her worldly belongings. She glanced around her room for a final time. Her heart was thumping wildly in her chest and she felt as if she would scream with tension and nerves but there was a determined look on her face. A runaway slave was an outlaw, with no rights and no protection. Marcus could have her put to death if he knew what she was about to do. But she had to do it.

With a last glance she stepped silently through the doorway and down the long corridor along which were the bedrooms of Marcus's family. She could hear snoring coming from one room. That would be Marcus. As she passed Laelia's room she paused and closed her eyes. She couldn't ever explain to the little girl why she was leaving. She wouldn't understand but if anything were to hold her back it would be Laelia. Livia bit her lip. Then she turned and stepped through the doorway of Laelia's room and knelt beside the bed. Laelia was asleep, her chest rising and falling with a steady rhythm. Livia forced back a tear from her eye. Then she bent down and kissed the little girl lightly on the forehead. She couldn't leave without saying goodbye to Laelia.

Outside the rain was heavier than she had expected. Livia wiped the water from her face and strode through the mud

41

towards the gate. Then she glanced in the direction of the pen that held Marcus's pigs. If she let them out it would stop Marcus from coming after her right away. It would only buy her a few hours but it was all that she would need.

"Good luck rounding up your pigs," she whispered as she opened the gate to the swine herd pen. Then quickly she strode across the courtyard, through the main gate and into the wet night.

Chapter Six – The second son of the Thunderbolt

Hasdrubal Barca sat on his horse staring down into the green valley that stretched away far below him. The high alpine mountains were at his back. He had finally made it into Italy just like his brother, Hannibal, had done ten years before. Hasdrubal smiled and the soldiers clustered around him grinned at their general, not bothering to hide their relief. The treacherous mountains, with their avalanches, crevasses, deep gorges and bitter cold were behind them and the rich fertile land of Italy was within reach.

Hasdrubal glanced back up the mountain pass along which his army was still coming. What a journey they had had. Their adventures could keep a bard busy for a week. Was it really eleven months ago since they had left Spain and plunged in to the heart of Gaul and the unknown? It had been a brave and bold move but Hasdrubal had been planning it for years. Scipio, that brash young man who thought he could measure himself against anyone had failed to stop him this time.

The sun reflected off the white snow-capped peaks and boulder fields and tried to dazzle him. His splendid peaked Thracian helmet glinted as he looked up at the blue, welcoming sky and allowed the sun's rays to warm his face. The sun reminded him of Africa. How long ago had it been since he had last seen Carthage, since he had last seen Hannibal and Mago, his brothers. It was eleven years he realised. He had last seen them eleven years ago. Hasdrubal sighed and turned his eyes back to the green valley below.

He missed Hannibal and Mago and for years now he had dreamt of seeing them again. How wonderful it would be to speak with them, to relive the happy, robust youth that they had shared under their father's guidance. Hannibal had been the oldest, there had always been something untouchable about Hannibal, Hasdrubal thought. It was as if his elder brother was something apart, unflinching, unflappable and unstoppable. Mago and he had tried to compete, they had tried to outdo their brother, the three of them had always competed fiercely with each other but it had been an honest struggle and at the end of the day they had known they were brothers and had loved each other for it. Their father had insisted that they share the hardships of the ordinary soldier and the years living in army camps had toughened and hardened the brothers. Hamilcar, their father had taught them everything he knew and his sons had lapped it up and had grown hungry for more. Yes it would be good to see Hannibal, Hasdrubal thought. Eleven years ago, on the eve of Hannibal's march towards Italy the brothers had agreed that Hasdrubal would follow within a year with a new army. That had been the plan had the Scipio's not thwarted him. Hasdrubal shrugged. It didn't matter. He had made it at last. He was about to fulfil the promise he had made to his brother all those years ago.

"Bostar," he called out in his native Punic tongue, "can you record this picture for me with your pen?"

One of his young Punic bodyguards by his side, shifted in his saddle. "Yes General, I can do that."

"Good man, tonight come to my tent and we will speak some more about the history that you are writing for me," Hasdrubal said without looking at him.

44

Hasdrubal turned to examine his men as they passed on down the track that led down to the valley. They looked weary, thin and hungry and he wondered what their morale would be like. He'd taken twenty thousand Iberians and Africans into Gaul eleven months ago and now his officers reported that barely fifteen thousand men were still with the colours. It didn't matter, he thought. Hannibal had had not many more men and had nearly singlehandedly brought Rome to her knees. Hasdrubal spat onto the ground. When he joined forces with his brother the two of them together would be invincible. When that happened, nothing that the Romans did would be able to stop the two sons of Hamilcar from marching on Rome. With Rome conquered this long war would be at an end. That at least had been the plan eleven years ago.

"General," a voice cried out in Punic. Hasdrubal saw a young cavalry captain urging his horse up the track towards him.

"I am here, what's going on?" Hasdrubal cried.

The young captain steered his horse through the stream of men descending the track and came to a halt beside Hasdrubal. He looked flustered and his face was covered in sweat.

"Trouble Sir," at the front of the column, the army is coming to a halt."

"Why, what's holding us up?" Hasdrubal snapped.

"I don't know," the officer looked exasperated, "I can't understand a fucking word that these Iberians say, but they wanted you. They kept repeating your name Sir."

Hasdrubal grunted and he turned to look down the mountain track but his advance guard were out of view. Damn, he would have to go. He turned to his bodyguard. "Follow me," he roared.

Led by the young captain the small troop of horsemen cantered down the track alongside the slow plodding infantry. Hasdrubal was not a tall man but he was well built and clad in splendid Greek style armour that had been made for him by the finest metal smiths of Carthage and as he rode down the rocky track his men recognised him. It started with a single cheer that grew and grew as the horsemen descended alongside the column. The cheers grew until it seemed the whole army was cheering their commander. Hasdrubal could barely supress his delight but he kept his face stern and paid his men no attention. As they passed six of his elephants, their keepers halted the great beasts and raised their fists in salute. One of the animals, maybe startled by all the noise, raised its trunk and vented a great trumpeting roar that echoed off the distant mountains. Hasdrubal allowed himself a quick smile, here then was the answer to the question of his men's morale. It was high, it was a good sign and it filled him with new hope and energy.

"Sir, look, up ahead," the young captain pointed.

The track had widened into a small plateau and along its southern edges were the first trees that marked the beginning of a huge dark green forest. His advance guard, comprised of Iberian cavalry had come to a halt and stood in a tense extended line facing the forest. Their spears were lowered as if ready for attack. Hasdrubal peered beyond them into the forest. It was not hard to see what was holding them up. Blocking the mountain track that led down into the trees was a solid band of Gallic spearmen, their weapons pointing at the Iberians. A lonely figure with a white beard and clad in a green cloak stood to one side.

The commander of the Iberians rode up to Hasdrubal and saluted. The officer looked annoyed and ready for a fight.

"They didn't move when I told them to", he said. "Shall I order the attack? My men can take them easily enough."

"They didn't move because they can't understand you," Hasdrubal snapped using the Iberian language he had learned in Spain. Hasdrubal glanced down the line of horsemen. "Order your men to stand down."

"But General…," the Iberian officer protested.

"Now," Hasdrubal growled, "don't you understand. They are Gauls. They are going to be our allies you fool."

Then without waiting for an answer Hasdrubal pushed his horse through the line of Iberians and rode up to the front rank of spearmen. The man with the white beard did not move, nor did the spear points and Hasdrubal felt a pair of shrewd eyes watching him. The man had to be druid. He'd met similar men during his stay in Gaul. Slowly he dismounted from his horse and removed his helmet. The Gauls watched him impassively and not a man made a sound.

"I am Hasdrubal, brother of Hannibal and I have come to ask for your help." Hasdrubal said glancing at the druid. He spoke in the Gallic tongue reciting the words he had learned for just this occasion.

His words were followed by silence. Then at last the druid shifted on his feet.

"We have been waiting for you Hasdrubal, brother of Hannibal. You and your men are welcome." The druid spoke using the Iberian language.

Hasdrubal nodded in gratitude but he knew that the conversation was not yet finished.

"I have many men, I have gold and I have brought the great war beasts from Africa," he postured raising himself to his full height, "but my men need food and some time to rest. Then when we are done, we shall move south and fight the Romans. Your tribesmen are welcome to join my army."

The druid nodded solemnly, "Yes we know this, but what about plunder. Your brother promised us the gold and bounty of the Romans but then when we were on campaign and far from our homes, he forbade the plunder of Roman lands. This is not very popular with our warriors."

For a moment Hasdrubal looked uncertain. He turned to look at his horsemen arranged in a wide semi-circle around the band of spearmen. Had Hannibal really handled it in that way? The druid's words confirmed that his brother had exercised a tight discipline over the thousands of Gallic volunteers who had flocked to his army and some instinct was telling Hasdrubal that he should do the same and yet...

"Your people shall be free to take from the Romans what they want," Hasdrubal said grandly spreading his arms wide. He knew it was against all the advice but his army was too depleted and he needed all the Gallic support he could get.

The druid examined him sternly and then his face cracked into a grin and he cried something to the war band that Hasdrubal did not understand. A moment later the spear points were raised and the Gauls let out a great cheerful cry and rushed forward to touch Hasdrubal. The Carthaginian stood his ground as the Gaul's swarmed around him in their eagerness to touch his beard, his armour, his face, his sword and even his feet.

"How close are the Roman armies from here?" Hasdrubal cried as he managed to catch the druid's eye.

The white bearded holy man looked triumphant. "There is not a single Roman army or consul between here and the town of Placentia on the great river. They were not expecting you until later in the year."

"Not a single Roman army between here and the Po," Hasdrubal repeated the words to himself and as he realised their significance, a huge grin appeared on his face.

His invasion of Italy had begun unopposed.

Chapter Seven – Rome

There was only light traffic on the Via Salaria, the old salt road. It was noon and the dark grey rain clouds that had laid siege to the city all morning had finally moved off to the west. Marcus sat at the front of his wagon which was pulled along by his two asses. Beside him, holding the reins was the eldest of his Gallic slaves and in the back with his legs dangling over the side of the cart was the man's son. The men were silent as the wagon jolted and rattled along the rough track.

Up ahead Marcus could see the sun reflecting on the walls of Rome. The great yellowish blocks of stone, rising to a height of ten yards, looked formidable as they snaked away across the hills. No invader had ever breached those walls, not even the invincible Hannibal had dared take them on. Along the sides of the road, the silent tombstones of the dead seemed to mock the progress of the old rickety cart and its occupants. You will never find out who did this. He is ours now, not yours. Go back and forget about your son. Marcus glanced across at the head stones. Here then was Rome's welcoming committee he thought.

The Colline gate loomed up before them. The sentries on duty recognised Marcus and waved him through without a word. They passed under the gatehouse and into the city. The elder slave guided the wagon down the Alta Semita. The street was narrow, crowded and noisy and their progress slowed as people pushed past on either side. No one paid them any attention. The asses brayed nervously and one of them squirted a jet of urine onto the paving stones. The wagon pushed on deeper into the city. Washing lines had been hung across the street between the tall buildings and from the numerous workshops that lined the street came the sounds and smells of industry and business, the hammering of the blacksmith, the advertising calls of fish mongers, butchers and bakers, the rows of newly made sandals, the putrid smell of Garum, fermented fish sauce and the rowdy laughter from the taverns.

Marcus glanced around him. He had been coming to Rome for nearly forty years and he knew her streets nearly as well as he knew his own farm. Rome had changed for the worse since the war had begun he thought. Thousands of refugees, fleeing the fighting and devastation in the countryside had fled to Rome. The city was bursting with people and it was a miracle that she could cope. Homelessness, robbery and violence had gone through the roof. As to prove his point they passed by a narrow alley along which he saw a long line of men and women, sitting on the ground clad in pathetic blankets and torn pieces of clothing. A man was handing out free soup from a large barrel. As Marcus stared at them, a rat shot across the alley, disappearing into a hole in the wall.

The slave urged the asses onwards and they turned into the Vicus Longus, the long road. Around them the four storeyed Insulae, apartment buildings seemed to crowd out the sun. On the corner an old hag dressed in a blond wig emerged from her shop and seeing Marcus called out to him, "A copper to tell your future Sir."

Marcus ignored her and as the wagon passed by he heard her mocking laugh follow him up the street. "Afraid are we, what the gods have in store for you?"

The wagon rattled and jolted along the street as they plunged deeper into the heart of the city. Then abruptly the elder Gaul pulled on the reins and the two animals came to a halt. Silently the slave turned to look at his master. There was a strange look in the man's eyes that Marcus had not noticed before.

Slowly Marcus got down from the cart and turned to look down the alley in front of which they had stopped. People pushed passed him and further down the street a woman cried a warning before emptying the contents of a toilet bowl out of a window.

"I am going to go inside. Come and help me when I call you," Marcus said turning to the elder slave, "Leave your boy to guard the wagon. If there is any trouble he is to call us, understood?"

The slave nodded silently and muttered a few words to his son.

Marcus turned to look down the alley again and his eyes found the small window on the second floor of the three-storey apartment block. The building was badly constructed, filthy and in dire need of repair. If a fire broke out the place would become an instant death trap. He sighed. This then was where Publius, his son had chosen to make his home. Marcus had only visited the place once. That had been a year ago. Publius had been so proud of his few square yards. He had been so proud that he was paying his own rent and standing on his own feet. Marcus's hand tightened its grip on his belt. Then he stepped across the street and entered the alley. His nose wrinkled at the smell of excrement and stale urine. He ducked into the entrance and found himself in a small, dark and cool room with a narrow stairway leading up. A man was sitting on a stool, his back leaning against the wall, dozing.

"Wake up! Are you the caretaker of this building?"

The sudden noise startled the man and he stumbled backwards in alarm. The stool tipped over onto the floor. It took the man a moment to recover.

"I am. What do you want?"

"I have come for my son's body. He lived on the second floor." The caretaker stared at Marcus. Then the blood seemed to drain from his face.

"Yes, and who are you?"

"His father."

The caretaker sniffed and glanced up at the stairs. "The door is open, I haven't touched anything but the boy owes rent, are you going to settle that?"

In response Marcus reached for a bag of coins in his tunic and dropped them on the floor. Then he turned to go up the stairs.

"When I come back down I have some questions I would like to ask you," he said.

The caretaker made no reply.

***

Publius' body lay on his bed beside the wall just like Dorian had said. His eyes were open staring sightlessly up at the ceiling. A knife had been stuck into his chest and the blanket, mattress and wooden floor were stained red with a large pool of blood. He was naked. Marcus stood quietly in the middle of the room. Then he bent down and closed his son's eyes, gathered the blankets together and wrapped them around the corpse. When he was done Marcus muttered a short, silent prayer and bent down to kiss his son's forehead. Then he sat down at the end of the bed and turned to look around. The room was a mess. Clothes, pottery and food littered the floor and by the window a wooden cabinet had been upturned. Marcus glanced at the bed opposite him. That had to be Dorian's. Someone had cut open the mattress and the contents were strewn across the floor. Whoever had caused the mess had not only killed Publius, Marcus frowned; they had been looking for something.

He rose to his feet and examined the room in closer detail. The door looked undamaged. Whoever the killer had been, he or she hadn't needed to break down the door. Did that mean that his son had known the murderer? He stooped and began picking his way through the mess on the floor but after a few minutes he gave up. The murderer or murderers would not have left anything valuable there. He sighed and wandered over to the small window and looked out. In the main street he could see his wagon and the Gaul's.

What had Publius wanted to talk to him about? They had rarely talked since his son had made his home in the city. What could have been so important? Marcus suddenly looked lost in his son's room. The only thing he and Publius seemed to have had in common was a love of boxing. Boxing was the only thing they could talk about after Publius had left the family farm. The realisation brought on a sudden sadness. Marcus turned his back on the window and stared at the room and as he did so a thought occurred to him. When Publius was still a boy and living on the farm he had taken a secret delight in writing poetry. The boy had known that he Marcus would not approve of such idle past times and so he had hidden the sheets of poetry in the door to his room. Marcus knew because that was where he had found the poetry. Doors, for some reason he didn't fully understand, had always held a special significance for his son.

Of course! His eyes widened as he turned to look at the door. Quickly he crossed the room, closed the door and took a step back into the room to examine the wood. It was an old composite model made of various pieces of wood. In a corner someone had scratched their name and a rude message. Marcus ignored it as he continued his search but there were no more written messages. Quietly he raised himself onto his toes and started at the top, rapping his knuckles lightly on the wood. It was a minute later when he found it. The wood in this section sounded hollow. He peered closely at the offending spot and gently pressed his fingers into the wood. With surprising ease a long thin segment of wood no wider than a finger nail loosened. He prized it clear and peered inside the cavity. The hole was small and shallow but resting inside was a tightly rolled piece of parchment. He nudged it clear and it fell neatly into his hand. Placing the strip of wood on the floor Marcus slowly sat down on the bed.

Was this what the murderer had been looking for? There was no wax seal and gently he unrolled the parchment and held it up to the light with both hands. It looked like a letter. Marcus frowned. He couldn't understand a word. The script and letters were utterly alien to him. Whoever had written this had not done it in Latin. He stared at the letters and then at last, defeated, he shook his head. He rolled the parchment up again and stuffed it into his tunic before turning to look at the corpse on the bed. What had his son gotten himself involved with?

He remembered that he should be asking some questions. Standing up he left the room and went back down the stairs. The caretakers stool stood in a corner but the man himself had vanished. Marcus poked his head out of the main doorway but there was no sign of him in the alley. Damn, he thought, he should have asked his questions when he had arrived. He went back up the stairs and knocked on a door on the first landing. The mess in his son's room must have caused a huge amount of noise and someone must have heard something.

The door was opened by a woman but as he started to explain who he was she slammed it shut in his face. He knocked again but she refused to talk to him and none of the other rooms opened their doors to him either. He moved on to the third floor and here he had some luck. A disabled man, a veteran soldier was willing to talk to him.

"Yes I heard the noise," the man muttered as he stood in his doorway. "The walls and ceilings are thin in this place. I hear everything." He paused and scratched his arm. "You don't go down to see what it's all about though. You understand what I am saying. People keep themselves to themselves."

Marcus nodded, "Yes I know but did you see anything, anything at all? It would help."

The man sighed and turned to see if they were alone. He looked weary. "I saw this," the man said quietly, "I saw Mamercus and his Subura scum come here yesterday afternoon. They went into your boy's room and stayed there for a short while. I think they were here for money, that's the main reason for Mamercus to leave his lair. Mamercus threatened your boy alright. He said he would cut him open. I don't know why, does anyone need a reason these days? Then they came out and left. That's all I know."

"This was yesterday in the afternoon?" Marcus inquired.

The veteran nodded, "Your boy was alive when they left. I saw him go out a few minutes later."

"What about my son's friend?" Marcus pressed, "My son shared his room with another man. Did you see him at all?"

"The Nepenthe addict," the veteran replied scornfully, "No didn't see him but I heard him come back this morning. That was after the commotion downstairs; heard him run away too."

Marcus opened his mouth to speak but the veteran was already closing the door. Instead he turned and started back down the stairs. He had gotten all the information he was going to get. It was time to take Publius home.

As he came down the stairs he caught a glimpse of a man standing in his son's room.

"Heh," Marcus called out.

The man turned and ran. He was across the landing before Marcus could react. Then he was thudding down the stairs. Marcus jumped the last couple of steps and raced after the figure yelling for him to stop. The stranger was fast and he was out of the main door before Marcus had a chance to see his

57

face. Marcus burst from the building and into the daylight still yelling for the man to stop. The fugitive had reached the end of the alley and was just about to turn the corner into the Vicus Longus when the elder Gaul took him down with a tackle that sent both men tumbling to the ground. When Marcus reached them, the Gallic slave had the runner in a firm arm lock.

Marcus stared at his slave in surprise and the man stared back at him and Marcus suddenly noticed the pity in his eyes. He wrenched his attention back to the stranger. The man was face down, squealing and struggling to get free but the Gaul was too strong for him. In the street people stopped to stare but no one said anything, nor did they intervene.

"Well done," Marcus said to his slave, "Haul him up. I want to see his face."

The Gaul did as he was ordered and Marcus took a step back in surprise as he saw who the man was. It was Dorian.

"What are you doing here, why did you run?" Marcus cried angrily.

The Gallic slave dragged Dorian into the alley and held him up against the wall. Dorian's face had gone bright red.

"I don't know," he whimpered miserably.

"I hear that you are a Nepenthe addict. Did you get my son involved too?" Marcus cried. He didn't know why he was so angry. The young actor was clearly terrified.

"Publius refused to touch it, that's the truth. I am sorry, I should have told you." Dorian blurted.

"So what did this Mamercus want with him then? He came here yesterday and threatened Publius."

But Dorian shook his head violently. "No, he didn't threaten Publius, he threatened me. I owe Mamercus money. Publius was in the room when it happened."

Surprised Marcus closed his mouth unsure of what to say. Then his anger seemed to fade a little.

"This Mamercus was at the party last night." Marcus said lowering his voice. "I heard that he had an argument with my son. Did you witness this?"

Dorian shook his head. "Mamercus was there yes, but I didn't see anything."

"Really," Marcus looked doubtful, "and this special business that you had to take care of, the special business that meant that my son was alone in his room at the time of the murder, did this involve Mamercus by any chance?"

Dorian swallowed and for a moment he looked embarrassed. "Mamercus wanted me to provide him with some…favours. He asked me to stay behind."

"You are a prostitute, aren't you?" Marcus snapped in sudden disgust. "What about my son, did Publius ever sell his body?"

Dorian seemed to have calmed down. He shook his head and for the first time he looked up at Marcus with dignity. "Yes, I sell my body and I survive like every other man and woman in this city. That's who I am. Publius did not agree with me. He hated what I did. We quarrelled about it of course, but he too was not perfect. I know. How do you think he really made his money, by acting, really…?"

"You tell me?" Marcus snapped.

But Dorian shook his head, "I don't know, I really don't," he said and Marcus knew somehow that the boy was speaking the truth.

He looked away and then gestured for the slave to release his grip on Dorian. The old veteran who lived on the third floor had been right about the threats but wrong about the victim.

"I think it is time that I went to see this Mamercus," he said.

Chapter Eight – A copper for your future

Livia plunged on into the night not pausing for anything. Her face was a mask of determination. The darkness and rain may have put off most travellers but she knew where she was going. It was three miles from the farm to the city walls of Rome. She had done the journey many times, but never alone.

The rain began to ease. Soon she would be in the city. On the side of the road she noticed shapes in the darkness. They would be the tombs and mausoleums of the dead. Instinctively she tightened her grip on her Palla. With her free hand she rummaged in her pocket, making sure that the few coins she had prepared were still there. It was dangerous for a young single woman to travel on her own. The money, she hoped, was to pay off any unforeseen dangers.

It was sunrise when she finally reached the Colline gate. The night watchmen were alert and a soldier stepped forwards to bar her way into the city. Seeing that she was un- accompanied he grinned and placed his hands on his hips.

"Going anywhere in a hurry?" he asked.

"To have my fortune told," she smiled sweetly. She had learned to smile at men in authority. Somehow it made things go smoother.

"I go off duty in an hour," the soldier grinned, "where can I find you?"

"Oh I don't know," she said as she pushed past him, "What, I wonder would your wife make of that?"

She kept on walking expecting the soldier to order her to a halt but no such order came and then she was through the gate and into the city. She had guessed right.

***

The Sybil's shop was closed but she banged on the door until she heard muffled movement inside and then a croaky voice that sounded like it had drank too much wine called out.

"What do you want?"

"I have money," she replied.

For a moment the shop was silent. Then she heard the lock being undone and a moment later the door opened a tiny fraction. Without waiting for an invitation Livia barged inside nearly knocking the Sybil to the ground. In the middle of the shop she turned on her heel and raising her arm, pointed a finger at the old woman.

"Remember me," she said feeling the emotion in her voice.

The Sybil looked startled but she recovered quickly. Closing the door she folded her arms across her chest.

"Yes, you came here yesterday. I am sorry but I don't do refunds."

Livia's finger trembled. "You told me that I had a brother living in Placentia. How can you know such a thing?"

The Sybil stared at her for a moment. Then the woman sighed and stumbled back to the couch upon which she had been sleeping.

"I know many things child but if you want to know about your brother it will cost you."

"This is all I have," Livia placed her coins on the table with a bang.

The Sybil stretched her neck to check the money. She seemed satisfied.

"That charm that you wear around your neck child and those letters," the woman said slowly, "The design is very rare, I should know, I have peddled enough of these things in my time, but I have seen this one only once before, your brother has the same charm, same letters and he looks like you. His name is Titus but he does not like to be called that."

"If you know who my brother is then you must know my parents!" Livia' voice quivered unsteadily.

The old woman shook her head sadly. "No, never met them."

"You said that he would need me before the year was out? What does that mean?"

The Sybil stretched herself out on the couch. "I am sorry child. I can't remember everything that I say. It just comes to me sometimes."

"Are you my mother?" Livia said.

The Sybil laughed and her laughter was so genuine that Livia found herself blushing.

"Dear child; that is the funniest thing anyone has said to me in a very long time. If I was your mother then you must be a child of the gods for no man has touched me in over twenty years."

Livia swallowed. "I have run away," she said. "I am not going back. I am going to find my brother. Will you help me?"

The earnestness in her voice made the Sybil sit up and look at her.

"Oh child that is a brave decision. Some may call it foolish. You leave your master's house with just the hope, just the hope of finding a brother that you don't even know really exists and you come here. If your master were to catch up with you he could have you put to death. You are still his property."

"Will you help me?" Livia said stubbornly.

The Sybil sat very still for a moment. Then she sighed. "I am getting too old for this," she muttered. Then she smiled displaying a toothless mouth.

"Go to Placentia then and find your way to the house of Getorix the druid. He will know where you can find Titus. Tell Getorix that Drusilla remembers him. There that should see you on your way."

"But how do you really know that Titus is my brother?" Livia pressed her.

The Sybil smiled to herself.

"You will know when you see him?" she said.

Chapter Nine - Field Hospital Number I

Tarraco on the coast of Spain

The screams of the wounded soldier filled the square courtyard. "For the god's sake, keep him still," Gaius snapped at his two orderlies who were pinning the man down on the wooden operating table. The arrow still protruded from the man's chest. Gaius, his hands covered in blood worked quickly, loosening the shaft by rocking it to and fro. It was important that he retrieved the arrow head. The metal must not remain in the body. It was too close to the heart. Slowly he pulled the shaft clear. The arrow came out of the body making a sucking noise. More blood welled up from the wound. He had the arrow head. He could see it coming out. On the table, the man's screams had stopped. Gaius looked up in alarm. The man's eyes were closed and his head lolled to one side. One of the orderlies pressed his fingers into the man's neck. Then he looked up at Gaius and shook his head.

"What, what happened?" Gaius cried angrily. The orderlies avoided his gaze. Gaius turned to stare at his patient. The man was dead. He had been so close to saving his life but the gods had snatched him at the last. In frustration Gaius hurled his scalpel onto the pavement stones and stomped off into the ward. He had failed to save another one. Had he made a mistake? He knew he had made mistakes before and that it had cost men their lives. The problem was that he didn't really know what he was doing. He didn't understand enough about the human body, it's working and the cures and how he should go about treating the wounded. That realisation had been one of the most depressing thoughts he had ever had to endure.

As he stepped into the ward with its long line of wounded men laying on mattresses on the floor a hand touched his shoulder. Gaius saw that it was Soranus, the Greek doctor and principal, whom Scipio had put in charge of the field hospital. Soranus was a tall man, bearded and he had a sympathetic look in his eyes.

"You can't save them all. Sometimes the Gods make their decision and we are not allowed to interfere."

Gaius nodded and his frustration seemed to slip away. "I shall keep trying my best," he replied. "Practice will make me improve."

Soranus nodded, patted him on the shoulder and strode away down the ward. The eyes of the wounded seemed to follow the doctor's every move as if his presence alone would heal them. The Greeks were undoubtedly the finest doctors and surgeons in the world, Gaius thought. They certainly knew more than he or any other Roman about the human body and how to treat it. There was no formal military hospital system in the Republic but Scipio, supreme Roman commander in Spain had, at his own expense, hired Soranus and provided the funds for field hospital number I. The very existence of the hospital was therefore only down to Scipio's generosity and concern for his soldier's welfare. The rising star had even found time last month to visit his wounded men.

Gaius was a young man of twenty-two with broad shoulders but slightly shorter than the average man. Over his white woollen army tunic he had draped a linen cloth to prevent the blood from staining his tunic. He'd been in Spain for two years now. When he had been called up, the lot had assigned him to Scipio's army. He'd started out in the Hastati, the youngest and fittest of the three classes in which the Roman army was divided. The Hastati always formed the front line and their casualties were therefore high but if he survived that, then in a few years he would be promoted to the Principes, the second order, men in the prime of their lives and if he survived that, then when he was a true veteran of proven ability, courage and toughness, he could have expected to be admitted to the Triarii. The Triarii were the rock upon which many Roman armies had rallied and turned the battle in their favour.

But the fates had had something different in mind for Gaius. Soon after Scipio's assault and capture of the Punic city of New Carthage in which Gaius had taken part, he had watched his closest friend die from a minor wound. It was nothing more than a simple cut but his friend had died within three days. So when the Centurion came round asking for volunteers with medical experience Gaius was the first to raise his hand. It wasn't right that brave and good companions should die from such small trivial wounds. The gods were having a laugh. Whilst his medical knowledge was limited to watching the animals live and die on the farm on which he had been raised it was certainly more than some of the men who also volunteered. Within a week he was promoted to surgeon, packed off to the Roman HQ in Spain at Tarraco and given his first patients.

He strode back into the courtyard and the burning Spanish sun and retrieved his scalpel from the ground. The two orderlies had wrapped the corpse in a blanket and were carrying it away to the morgue. He ran his finger gently down the side of the knife. It was sharp, razor sharp and a thin line of blood appeared on his finger. Gaius stared at the red blood trying to understand its purpose. What did this red stuff do, why could a man not live without it?

"Doctor, next one," an orderly called from across the courtyard. Gaius looked up and nodded. In the clear blue sky the burning sun warmed his face and the light reflected from the white hospital walls. He sighed, gathered himself together and walked back to the operating table.

A moment later the orderly appeared and behind him came two men. One was a Roman soldier, still armed and clad in his armour and wearing his conical helmet with a raised central knob. The man had a cruel looking face and his head swung from side to side staring at everything with barely concealed suspicion. The other man was older with thin white hair and a bald patch and he was grimacing in pain. The man shuffled ahead of the soldier, his left arm hanging limply at his side. Gaius blinked in surprise. The man's ankles had iron chains around them. He didn't look like a soldier.

Seeing Gaius, the Roman gave his captive a shove.

"Get moving you lazy bastard," he growled.

Gaius, trying to read the situation, stared at both men.

"Afraid he's going to run away are you?" Gaius said folding his arms across his chest. He had taken an instant dislike to the Roman soldier.

The soldier grinned, showing a mouth that had gaping holes where teeth used to be. "He's worth a lot of money, this one," the man replied, "and he belongs to me. I am just looking after my property."

Gaius glanced at the man with the limp arm. The man looked foreign and Gaius guessed that he was in his mid forties. The slave was staring at the operating table.

Gaius turned his attention back to the soldier and shook his head.

"This is a military hospital, I only operate on soldiers. Go to the temples, the priests may be able to help you."

"It's all been arranged doctor," the soldier replied. "I spoke with the principal here. He has given me permission to bring my slave. Check if you like."

Gaius felt a surge of irritation. He had been overruled. No doubt, somewhere some money had exchanged hands. Reluctantly he gestured for the two men to approach the wooden table. An orderly was trying to clean away the blood that the previous patient had left behind.

"How come he's worth so much? That left arm of his looks useless." Gaius replied laying out his instruments.

"He's a Carthaginian POW. See this gold ring," the soldier said raising his hand. "He was wearing this. This is a Roman senator's ring. This bastard must have taken it from the battlefield at Cannae."

Gaius looked up sharply and stared at the slave. "A Carthaginian," he snapped, "since when does Scipio's hospital look after the enemy?"

"Since this morning," the soldier said.

Gaius muttered something under his breath. It was clear why the soldier had brought his slave. He was making sure that his investment remained alive. Reluctantly he peered at the ring, it looked genuine.

"Or he obtained it afterwards in Carthage, he doesn't look like a soldier," Gaius replied. The Carthaginian was silent, his eyes staring at the operating table.

"Caught him as he was fleeing to Gades, Cadiz. I inflicted that wound on him myself," the soldier said proudly. "I captured him so he belongs to me. He doesn't speak a word of Latin but his family in Africa will pay good money for his release when they hear of his misfortune. I am going to be a rich man."

Gaius glanced up at the Carthaginian. "Alright, get him onto the table and I will take a look at his arm." He picked up his scalpel as the soldier shoved his slave forwards. "Get on the table," the soldier cried.

"If you are going to cut me with that knife," the Carthaginian said suddenly in crisp, perfect Latin, "then I want it washed in boiling water first."

The soldier jumped back in surprise as if something had bitten him. Gaius froze in mid movement. Then slowly he looked up at his patient. "And why should I do that?" he said.

71

The Carthaginian was suddenly examining him with calm intelligent eyes. "The boiling water will stop your instruments from infecting the wound," he replied.

"How do you know that?" Gaius challenged him.

The Carthaginian smiled in amusement. "My name is Hanno, young man and I am the finest tutor in Carthage. My rates are reasonable and I speak six languages and have knowledge of geography, mathematics, medicine, literature, astronomy and the female body. And yes you are right, I purchased that ring in Carthage, seven years ago."

Gaius stared at his patient in disbelief. "Boiling water," he muttered at last. He had never considered that.

"You bastard, you lied to me," the Roman soldier stepped forward and smacked his slave over the head with his hand.

Hanno took the blow in silence. The soldier was about to strike again when Gaius' hand caught his arm.

"Enough," he cried, "this is my hospital."

The soldier glared at him but then slowly lowered his arm. Gaius turned to his orderly. "Fetch some boiling water and have my instruments cleaned." He turned to Hanno. "Fine, we will do it your way, it's your arm after all."

He lifted the Carthaginians arm in the air. The man emitted a soft painful groan. Gaius peered closer at the wound which was just below the shoulder. Then curiously he poked at with his finger.

"Can you use your muscles? Can you do anything with your fingers?"

Hanno shook his head. "I can't do anything. It's lame."

Gaius looked thoughtful for a moment. "I think," he said cautiously, "that's it's going to have to come off."

"You want to cut off my arm?" the Carthaginian exclaimed.

Gaius nodded, "If I don't the gangrene will spread. If you want to live, it's the only way I know of saving you."

"He wants to live, doctor," the soldier interrupted. "Do it, cut off his arm."

The Carthaginian looked glum. Then he closed his eyes and seemed to resign himself to his fate. "One arm is not so bad," he muttered to himself, "but if I die, young man," he said fixing his eyes on Gaius, "because you are a fool, then that will be very bad news indeed."

Chapter Ten – Riddles

Marcus buried Publius that evening below the Cypress trees in a grave next to those of his ancestors. The corpse, carefully shrouded in white linen was carried on a simple bier by four of the Gaul's in silent procession. Preceding them were Marcus, Flavia and little Laelia. Flavia was dressed in a dark cloak draped over her Stola. The small party of mourners halted by the well and the body was laid on the ground beside the freshly dug grave. Marcus's family had always buried their dead instead of cremating them. The mourners were silent. Then Marcus gestured to one of the slave women and the girl handed him the jug of wine. Marcus looked down at the corpse and then out across the wheat fields that surrounded his farm. A cool breeze was blowing inland from the distant sea and the wind swirled around the trees in playful delight.

Marcus lifted his head and spoke. "Today we bury my son, Publius Vibius Pansa. He lived twenty-three years, six months and eight days. He was a descendant of illustrious Atilius, who was his forefather, Aedile in the year of Rullianus and Mus. Publius was a member of the college of actors and made his family and our ancestors proud."

Marcus paused. Then he raised his head again and spoke offering a sacrifice to Ceres, the goddess of the harvest. When he was finished he slowly and carefully poured the wine onto the ground around the grave. Then he handed the empty jug to the slave and stepped back. It was done. His son was with the Manes now, the spirits of the dead and he would never again be able to eat at and visit the family table.

From the corner of his eye he saw Flavia stifle a tear. Then his wife looked up at him and Marcus had to look away.

"Bury him," he said turning to the slaves. Then he marched off.

As he strode back to the house he noticed a lone figure standing by the gate. It was Dorian. The young man had fulfilled his promise to be there at the funeral. Marcus changed course and approached the actor. The young man was wiping his eyes with his hand.

"Thank you for coming," Marcus said quietly.

Dorian nodded but said nothing.

Marcus fished around in his tunic and produced the strange parchment he'd found in Publius' room. He held it up for Dorian to see.

"Recognise this? Can you read it?"

Dorian glanced at the parchment and the strange script but he didn't seem interested. He shook his head and his gaze returned to the copse of trees in the field where the slaves were filling in the grave.

Marcus looked disappointed. Then he gripped Dorian's shoulder in understanding but the two of them did not exchange any further words. There was nothing more to discuss. Marcus turned and strode back to his farmhouse leaving Dorian to his grief. He'd shown the parchment to his Gallic slave on the way back from Rome but it had produced the same result. No one it seemed could read the damn thing. On impulse he shouted to one of the Gallic boys.

"You, go and fetch the Greek tutor from Numa's villa and bring him here at once. You know which house I am talking about?"

The boy nodded and without a word he dropped his spade and sped away. Numa had several houses, most of them in Rome but one of them, a sumptuous villa was not too far away, just a couple of miles up the Via Salaria and it was here that his young children lived. His friend was rich enough to employ his own tutor for his children but the Greek was more than just a tutor, he was the best educated man Marcus had ever known. If anyone could read the parchment, it would be that man.

***

It was getting late that evening when Marcus heard his dog barking and the nervous whinny of a horse being led into the courtyard. He rose from his seat in the long room and grabbing an oil lamp from the wall stepped out into the night air. In the torch light he could make out his slave boy and his visitor. The Greek tutor was a man in his early thirties and he didn't look too pleased.

"Greetings Arkadios, come inside," Marcus said raising his lamp. The Greek stiffly dismounted from the horse and the slave boy led the beast away into the darkness.

"My patron is visiting the house tomorrow," Arkadios said with a hint of resentment in his voice, "I must prepare for his arrival. Will this take long?"

"Not very long," Marcus said reassuringly. He led them through the house and into the long room where one of the slave women had just lit the fire in the hearth. The fire crackled and spat as it devoured the wood. Marcus gestured for the Greek to sit down at the oak table. Then he called to the slave girl to bring them two cups of wine. After they'd had a few sips and Marcus had politely inquired about his friend's children it was time to get down to business.

"I have a problem," Marcus said carefully, "something that I was hoping you could help me with." From his tunic he produced the parchment and laid it on the table. "No one seems to be able to read this. I was wondering whether it means anything to you? Will you give it a try?"

Arkadios sighed wearily, rubbed his eyes and bent forward to study the parchment and the strange writing that it contained. As he did so his face seemed to become transformed and as he read on his eyes widened and a furious blush appeared on his cheeks.

"What is it? Can you read it?" Marcus looked excited.

Abruptly the Greek stopped reading and looked up. He looked agitated as he rose unsteadily to his feet banging his knee against the table.

"I am sorry I can't explain what it says," he whispered. "I must go. You had better find someone else who can read it better than I."

He was halfway to the door before Marcus could react.

"What is this? You can read it?" Marcus exclaimed rising to his feet.

Arkadios was already at the door with his back turned to Marcus. "As I said I can't fully understand what it says. Find someone else!"

"What language is it written in?" Marcus' voice was no longer civil but that of a man barking an order.

In the doorway, the Greek hesitated. "It's Punic," he hissed.

Then he was gone.

By the time Marcus had stepped out into the courtyard, Arkadios had vanished into the night. Marcus looked alarmed. The man had even left his horse behind. He would have to get the slave boy to return the beast tomorrow. Alarm gave way to contempt as he stared into the darkness into which the Greek had disappeared. What strange behaviour.

In the long room he sat down and frowned at the parchment. What on earth was his son doing with a letter written in Punic?

Chapter Eleven – The house on the Caelian

Marcus emerged from the Alta Semita Street and entered the forum. It was late in the morning and the sky was a brilliant blue. The forum was the beating heart of the City of Rome. It was here that Rome's bankers, lawyers and traders did their business. It was here that the Republic had its official seat of government, the Curia Hostilia, the Senate house and looming over them all was the great temple of Jupiter on the Capitoline. Marcus knew the Forum well. He'd come here nearly every week, on market day to sell his wares to the city dwellers. As he picked his way through the throng of people surging down the Sacred Way, the traders tried to entice him to come and look at their stalls. The noise was tremendous. Bankers shook bags of coins in a bid to attract customers, lawyers called out their names and the number of court cases that they had won, soothsayers predicted doom and deliverance, traders promised the highest possible quality goods and unseen and unheard, the gangs of pickpockets prayed on the unwary.

Marcus cast an idle glance at the temple of Jupiter checking to see if the great doors to the temple were still open. If the temple doors were open, it meant that Rome was still at war. The temple doors were open. He hadn't really expected them to be closed. They hadn't been closed in over eleven years. He'd come to the city alone but on the right-hand side of his belt he had fastened his old gladius, the trusted weapon that had safely seen him through two pitched battles and sixteen campaigning seasons. He didn't normally walk around armed but today he had sensed he may need to.

He pushed on, past the Senate house and the speaker's platform, the Rostra and up the Sacred Way. His destination was a house on the Caelian. As he passed the circular temple of Vesta he noticed that a crowd had gathered around a young man with wild unkempt hair. The man was standing on a barrel, shouting and waving his arms in the air. Marcus's face darkened in disgust. Men and women like him had become an all too common sight lately. They could be found on nearly every street corner. The strain of war was telling on the city and the people had begun to turn to all kinds of quacks, imposters and oracles. The populace had begun to lose faith in the traditional saving virtues of their gods and ancestors and was turning to anyone who promised a brighter future. Marcus turned to look round at the Senate House in dismay. The building was hardly a hundred paces away. How could the Senate tolerate such madness on their very doorstep? He should speak to Numa about it. Maybe his friend would be able to have the issue discussed.

Leaving the forum behind he climbed the street that led to the Caelian. The Caelian was a well to do neighbourhood where many equestrian families had their seats. As he passed on up the narrow, twisting street, a long funeral possession passed him going in the opposite direction and in a house further up he heard the unmistakable noise of women in mourning. Had we lost another battle? The news from the various fronts where seven Roman armies were engaged in fighting against Carthage, over one hundred and fifty thousand men in all, had been bad for so long that people had become cynical and sarcastic. The latest blow had come when it became known that the Consul Marcellus, nicknamed the Sword of Rome and one of the cities stoutest champions had been killed in a skirmish with Hannibal. Marcus had attended the funeral. He had known Marcellus.

Marcus didn't know exactly where to find the house he was looking for but its position was given away by the Lictor's, strong looking young men who clustered around it's entrance. The twelve young men were armed with short swords and in their hand's they each held a rod made of bundled sticks, tied together with a piece of red leather. The rods had an axe head protruding from its middle. Marcus had seen the Fasces before and he paid them no attention. The Lictor's looked as if they had prepared themselves for a long journey. Marcus strode up to the nearest of them.

"I wish to speak with the Consul," he said.

The young men fell silent as they turned to look at Marcus. The young man he'd addressed regarded him sceptically.

"He's busy citizen, come back on another day."

Marcus paused and glanced at the other Lictor's who had gathered around him.

"If I don't get to speak with the Consul," he said quietly, "I will have it all over town that your boss allows his house to be used by prostitutes and Subura scum."

The Lictor looked uncertain. He glanced at his comrades and then back at Marcus. "Wait here," he said at last.

He was back a few minutes later with a curious expression.

"You have five minutes of his time," the Lictor announced.

***

Marcus Livius Drusus, Consul of Rome glared at Marcus impatiently. The Consul was dressed in a white toga with a purple border. He was a tall stern, authoritarian looking man of around fifty with grey hair and a hooked nose. They stood in the atrium of the house. In the centre of the room a rectangular basin designed to catch the rainwater from the opening in the roof above it, had been sunk into the floor. A fine colourful mosaic, made up of thousands of small stones depicting battle scenes glinted beneath the water in the basin. Marcus stood to one side of the basin and the Consul glared at him from the opposite side. Two of the Lictor's had accompanied him into the house and now stood behind the Consul holding their Fasces with both hands. In the rooms around the atrium Marcus could see and hear slaves scuttling to and fro and the sharp urgent voice of a foreman.

"Honoured Consul," Marcus dipped his head respectfully, "I have come to seek justice for my son. I am here to ask for your help."

Livius stared at him with sharp, penetrating eyes. "What has this to do with me?" he snapped.

"My son, his name was Publius. He was here, two nights ago, at your party. Yesterday he was murdered." Marcus paused and proceeded to describe what Publius looked like.

Livius raised his eyebrows. "Publius, Publius," he repeated the name to himself. "No I don't think I know him. There were many people here on that night. You should speak with my foreman. He will have the guest list."

"Sir, I believe the murderer was at your party," Marcus stood his ground. "My son was not a guest. He was an actor, your entertainment. You hired him."

Livius regarded Marcus carefully. "Citizen," he said at last, "I don't know if you have heard the news but Hasdrubal has crossed the Alps. I am leaving for the north today. I do not have the time to investigate all your questions. If you don't have anything else to say then I must bid you farewell."

"Mamercus," Marcus raised his voice, "Lord of the gangs of the Subura, Nepenthe dealer and a man who has no qualms about inviting prostitutes into other men's houses. He plied his trade and had sex here in this very house not two days ago. Now why would a Consul of Rome wish to be associated with such a man?"

Livius' face seemed to pale just a fraction. "Mamercus is a business partner of mine. That's all you need to know," he replied sternly.

Marcus understood and it filled him with scorn. He may be a small farmer but he was a citizen too and he took a keen interest in how his government worked. The Consulship was a public office for which the senators competed furiously each year. The honour of holding this office was very great indeed. Recently, the elections had begun to be held on the Ides of March but upon the death, last year, in battle of the two Consuls, Marcellus and Crispinus, it had been necessary to bring the elections forward. The Consuls were elected by the Comitia Centuriata, the assembly of the Roman people. Often, Marcus had known, the elections had been rigged and the people bribed. Maybe just maybe, Mamercus with his influence and power had helped Livius into his current position.

"I did not ask for my office," Livius replied sharply as if reading Marcus' thoughts. "The senate is filled with self-serving idiots. They are small men with narrow minds. They convicted me once on a charge that I did not commit. But now they have recalled me together with that pompous, overweight prick, Nero. They want me back. They have no one else to lead them against Hasdrubal."

"Sir," Marcus said, "Mamercus had an argument with my son. My son was one of the two actors you hired. Did you witness what was said?"

Livius looked annoyed and he glanced beyond Marcus to where his slaves were packing up.

"Yes I remember the two actors, they were awful, amateurs," he snapped. He turned to look at Marcus and his expression had become hostile. "One of them, your son I suppose, did have an argument yes, I saw him, but it wasn't with Mamercus. It was with one of my fellow senators, a man named Numa."

Chapter Twelve – Into the Subura

Marcus looked back at the Consul's house, his brow creased with concern. He didn't understand. Had Numa lied to him or was the Consul trying to protect his business partner? Was Numa somehow involved? He didn't believe it. He had always known Numa to be an honest, honourable man. The two of them had been friends for eighteen years. Livius had clearly been annoyed by his visit. The Consul was known to be a hard, bitter man who never forgave even the smallest slight against him. No wonder the Senate had convicted him of embezzlement all those years ago, even if they had later pardoned him. The man was a total arse Marcus thought as he started on down the street.

He paused at the top of the road and his fingers touched the pommel of his gladius. Half a mile away he could see the dense, towering apartment blocks of the Subura. The neighbourhood was one of the worst in Rome with its badly and illegally constructed apartment towers, some five stories high and death traps for their occupants should fire break out which happened regularly. The dark, narrow twisting alleys that connected the buildings were a mugger's paradise and no sane person ventured into the Subura at night. No sane person without a very good reason ventured into its labyrinth of alleys during the day. Marcus had been to the Subura before of course. Now and then his business had taken him there but he had never enjoyed the experience. The Subura was a concrete underworld that housed all the stinking, miserable, rotten scum of the earth. The Subura was not the Rome he knew. It was an alien place and he was always relieved to leave it behind.

The stink was the first thing he noticed. It came mainly from the Cloaca Maxima, Rome's main sewer which ran underneath the neighbourhood but the grime, shit, urine and rotting rubbish was everywhere. He pushed on down the narrow, twisting alley. In the doorways and shop fronts life seemed to be going on as usual. A beggar looked up at him with imploring eyes and held out his hand, two old women cloaked entirely in black stared sullenly at him from a doorway and a group of small children darted and danced around him like flies offering him all kinds of services that they were too young to understand. He ignored them all and pushed on. At an intersection of three alleys he halted. This was a good a place as any he thought. As he paused, a prostitute stepped out from a doorway and came towards him. She smiled. The woman was wearing a long blond wig and heavy makeup but no jewellery of any kind. Her toga had been so cut to reveal her breasts. She ran her fingers across Marcus's chest.

"Wife boring you?" she said. "Want to fuck?"

Marcus lifted her hand from his chest. "Mamercus," he said simply.

The woman looked disappointed. "You will have more fun with me," she replied.

"Where can I find him?" Marcus opened his hand and showed her the two copper coins that lay there.

The prostitute took them and pointed down one of the alleys.

"Down there, fifth doorway on your right."

Marcus left her standing there and moved on down the alley. As he did so he got the strong impression that he was being watched. They didn't want him here. The Subura belonged to its inhabitants and to no one else. The population had always been suspicious of outsiders. They liked his money and his goods but he, Marcus thought, he was a foreigner in this place.

He reached the fifth doorway. A couple of men in short tunics and knives in their belts were reclining outside, eating apples from a bowl at their feet. As he approached one of the men moved to the other side of the alley. Marcus sensed movement behind him. He glanced back and saw that a third man was blocking the alley he'd just come down. He too was armed. Trapped!

"Mamercus," he said turning to the men by the door. "Tell him Marcus is here to seek justice for his murdered son."

The thugs looked at him. They weren't frightened. They knew that they had him cornered.

Without a word one of the men ducked his head inside the doorway. "Mamercus," he cried, "Someone here to see you."

"Tell him to fuck off," a voice shouted, "I am busy."

"Fuck off," the thug said turning back to Marcus.

Marcus took a step forwards and his foot connected with the apple bowl sending it and the apples flying off down the alley. As the nearest thug lunged at him he caught the man's arm, twisted it upwards and brought his knee up into the man's crotch. The thug screamed in pain and collapsed to the ground.

87

Marcus was aware of the other two closing in on him. He pulled his gladius from his belt and pointing it straight at the face of the man before him, he started forwards with such speed that he drove his opponent backwards.

"What's going on here?" a voice boomed from the doorway.

A fat man with a goatee beard and grey thinning hair stood in the doorway to the tower block. He looked to be in his mid-thirties and was dressed in a black woollen tunic with short sleeves. Slowly Marcus lowered his sword. The man behind him hesitated and on the ground the thug he'd struck was on his knees, groaning. Marcus turned to look at the fat man.

"Are you Mamercus?" he said.

"I am Mamercus," the fat man replied glaring at Marcus.

"I have come to talk with you," Marcus said.

Mamercus stared at him, examining Marcus carefully. There was craftiness and cunning in his eyes that seemed to warn Marcus not to underestimate this man.

"Who are you?" Mamercus growled.

"My name is Marcus. I have come to seek justice for my son."

Mamercus raised his eyebrows. On the ground the thug was still groaning, his hands pressed into his crotch. Mamercus spat on the man in disgust.

"So the father has come to seek justice for his murdered son," he said turning to look at Marcus. "His name was Publius, was it not?"

Marcus struggled to hide his surprise. "How do you know that?"

"I make it my business to know many things," Mamercus replied. There was a sudden interest in his eyes. "Not here, inside," he snapped.

Marcus stepped through the doorway and into a dark, cool room. A table stood in its middle and two couches lined the walls. On one of then sat two completely naked girls of around eighteen. They looked up at Marcus in amusement. Mamercus gestured for Marcus to sit down. One of the thugs followed them inside and stood by the door his arms folded across his chest. He gave Marcus a spiteful look.

Mamercus sat down opposite Marcus and placed an arm around one of the naked girls. "Well, seek your justice," he declared.

Marcus glanced around the room. Then his eyes came to rest on Mamercus.

"Two days ago my son was murdered in his bed. He'd just returned from a party at which you were present. A witness says that you had an argument with my son. I want to know the truth."

Mamercus stared at Marcus. Then he glanced at the girl beside him and smiled at her. "Marcus wants to know if I killed his son," he said. "Isn't that what you are asking me?" There was something cold and ruthless in Mamercus' voice as he turned to look at Marcus.

"Well did you?"

The room went very still. Marcus sensed the sudden tension in the thug at the door. The two naked girls were staring at him. The silence lengthened. Then Mamercus's booming laughter filled the room. "What have we here," he exclaimed leaning forwards, "You come alone into my world, with all my men around me and you calmly accuse me of murdering your son?" Mamercus looked incredulous. "What is this? Some kind of joke, do you have a death wish?"

"Did you kill my son?" Marcus repeated.

Mamercus's laughter faded away. On the couch one of the naked girls rose to her feet, crossed the room and sat down beside Marcus and began to run her fingers lightly across his chest and arm.

"Who told you that I was responsible? Which mother fucker is dragging my name through the sewers?"

"A Senator, Numa is his name, he was at that party. He told me that you had an argument with my son."
Mamercus looked startled. It showed for just a split second. Then his face darkened. "Numa, you prick, you boneless prick..." he snarled.

"You know the Senator?"

Mamercus ignored the question. He glanced at the girl beside him. She giggled. "Marcus the farmer," Mamercus said in a mocking tone, "Marcus is a man from the past, child, a dutiful man who remains loyal to his land. Marcus believes that family is at the heart of everything. He is a man who will do what it takes to protect his family and his property. Men like him once made Rome great."

"If not family, what then?"

Mamercus looked at Marcus with a mocking expression. "Power is at the heart of everything," he replied. "It doesn't matter whether I am wrong or right as long as I have the power to impose my will. Vae Victis, Woe to the vanquished, isn't that what Brennus the Gaul said when he sacked Rome? The man who possesses power will prosper but the man who doesn't will fail and be forgotten. It is men who seek power who will write the future of Rome, not small dutiful farmers clinging to dying traditions."

Mamercus eyed Marcus shrewdly. He seemed to be enjoying himself. Again the room fell silent. Then at last Mamercus stirred. "I didn't have any argument with your son and I didn't kill him," he said, "but I do know who did."

On the couch the naked girl leaned forwards and licked Marcus' arm. Silence descended once more.

"Who killed my son?" Marcus said quietly.

But Mamercus shook his head and raised his voice. "You are a business man Marcus and so am I. This is not a fucking charity shop. If you want to know who murdered your son, it's going to cost you ten thousand Denarius."

Marcus stared at Mamercus in disbelief. Ten thousand Denarius! It was a huge sum of money which he didn't have. If he sold his farm and all its contents, if he sold his slaves and his children, then maybe, just maybe he would be able to raise the money. Beside him the girl took his hand and placed it on her breast. Across from him the other girl giggled.

"Well now," Mamercus said, "this is interesting. I think we are about to find out how far Marcus the farmer will go for his justice."

Marcus rose to his feet. "I will return with the money," he said, "and if it turns out that you have been lying to me, I am going to cut off your balls and stuff them down your throat."

"You can try," Mamercus chuckled as Marcus went out of the doorway.

***

Marcus looked troubled as he strode the last couple of miles back to his farm. It was early evening and few people were about. He didn't know what to make of what the Consul and Mamercus had told him. Who was right? Had Numa really lied to him and if so why? Could he really trust the Subura gang master? He'd wanted to grab the man by his neck and shake the answer from his lips but if he'd tried that he would have been dead.

He thought again about the money. How was he going to raise such a colossal sum? Marcus had always avoided debt. Should he sell the farm, the farm on which five generations of his family had lived? He couldn't do that but what else could he do? As he agonised and mulled it over he noticed two horsemen coming towards him down the road. They seemed to be heading for the city. As they drew closer he saw that they were wearing long riding cloaks with hoods which concealed their faces. That was strange.

"Marcus Vibius Pansa," one of the men called out.

"That's me," Marcus replied looking puzzled.

The riders trotted towards him and then one of them raised a spear from where he'd been concealing it and pointed the weapon at Marcus. The projectile flew through the air towards him. With a cry Marcus flung himself flat onto the ground and the spear missed. A pair of boots landed on the ground with a thud and one of the hooded riders came at him holding a knife in his hand. Marcus had no time to draw his gladius. He caught the man's knife arm and the two of them wrestled for control. A horse whinnied and Marcus knew he had to act before the second rider came for him. With a deep throated roar he drew back and smashed his forehead into his attacker's face. The rider screamed in pain and staggered backwards dropping his knife. Marcus drew his gladius and as he did so a second spear whistled past his head. He stumbled backwards in fright. The wounded rider had made it back to his horse and managed to mount the beast. Then the two riders were away, galloping past him, down the road that led to the city. Marcus bent forwards, panting for breath and retched onto the hard ground.

Chapter Thirteen - Master and servant

Gaius leaned forwards on his chair, his chin resting on his hand as he listened to the Carthaginian. It was evening and he was off duty. Hanno, lay on a mattress in the ward recovering from the operation that had removed his left arm. Gaius had managed to stem the flow of blood and the stump was now heavily bandaged. Hanno's legs were still locked together by an iron chain and his owner sat at the end of the long corridor beside the only door, dozing.

Hanno spoke in a low voice anxious lest he disturb the long line of wounded soldiers. He'd come to Spain he explained, to tutor the sons of Hasdrubal Gisco, one of the Carthaginian generals but he'd never reached his destination. His boat had been ship wrecked in a storm off New Carthage and he'd come ashore alone and having lost all his possessions. Knowing that the city of New Carthage had fallen to Scipio he'd tried to make his way to Gades, the oldest Phoenician colony in Spain but on the way he'd fallen foul of a Roman patrol who had captured him.

Gaius regarded Hanno with a frown as he mulled the idea over in his mind. It had come to him shortly after he'd cut the man's arm off. Hanno seemed genuine enough but he was still the enemy and Gaius wasn't sure how people would react. There were other problems too he thought glancing at the dozing soldier by the door. At last he made up his mind.

"Will your family pay the ransom for your release?" Gaius interrupted.

Hanno's face became pensive and uncertain. He glanced down the corridor at his owner. "I fear not," he said at last, "I had our family fortune with me when I was shipwrecked. There is nothing left."

Gaius gestured towards Hanno's owner. "If he finds out he will probably send you to the silver mines, a man like that has no need for such an expensive mind."

Hanno stared up at Gaius quizzically. "What do you mean?"

"I know such men," Gaius said, "he lives for the weight of the gold in his purse and for the feel of his dick in his hand. You mean nothing to him."

A glint appeared in Hanno's eyes.

"And you?" he said carefully, "What about you?"

Gaius looked away. "I have a wife and a son," he said slowly. "My wife is local, a Spanish girl. She lives here with me in Tarraco. My son is seven years old and his education would benefit if he had a good tutor."

"Seven years is a good age for learning, " Hanno nodded solemnly.

"I have no money," Gaius said, "so the tutor would have to work for nothing but after two years service he would be free to return home, as a free man."

Hanno considered what had just been said. "It is fair," he said abruptly, "but I don't think it very likely."

95

***

Gaius sat in his tiny office twirling the point of his cutting knife on the table. He looked pleased. Gaining the services of Hanno was a real coup. Not in his wildest dreams would he have been able to afford such a man. His son would have an excellent chance to secure himself a better position in life. Education, Gaius knew was key if one wanted to climb societies ladder. Now all he had to do was spirit the Carthaginian away from his present master. That wouldn't be easy, Hanno's master, he sensed had that gut instinct for spotting trouble. He would have to act with extreme care.

He found himself day dreaming about his wife. He'd married her nine months ago and the girl was heavily pregnant with their second child. She'd been wed before and hadn't been a virgin but Gaius' hadn't minded. His wife had been married to his closest friend, the one who had died at New Carthage and in his will his friend had asked Gaius, demanded it even, that he take care of his widow and his son. It was not uncommon for soldiers to marry the wives of their fallen comrades. Gaius had asked her if she didn't mind and she had said yes right away. He had adopted her son and the two of them had got on surprisingly well. There was just one thing that overshadowed his contentment. He had never asked his father for permission to marry. The old man, by law and tradition, had to give his approval. If he found out, he could force Gaius to divorce and disown his young family.

"Gaius, you are needed," Soranus, the principal was standing in the doorway. He looked worried.

Gaius rose wearily to his feet. Had there been another skirmish? The wounded from the last one had only just been treated. "How many?" he inquired but Soranus shook his head. "No, Scipio has ordered us to come to him, it seems that the priests are complaining. They are trying to get their hands on our medical funds. I am going to put forward our case and I need you to come with me."

Gaius looked startled. "Bastards," he exclaimed grabbing his cloak.

***

Publius Cornelius Scipio, Pro Consul, supreme commander of Roman forces in Spain and the victor of the battle of Baecula looked amused. He was young for a man who bore so much responsibility but he carried the burden of command as if it didn't exist. His handsome features and noble demeanour never failed to impress those who came before him. He sat behind a table, dressed not in his army uniform but in a white toga, his hands resting lightly on the table.

Gaius and Soranus dipped their heads respectfully as they stepped forward. A few paces away the two augurs, priests, bowed low. Their eyes were fixed on the Pro Consul as if he was the only man in the room.

"Gentlemen," Scipio said glancing at each party in turn, "how am I going to resolve this dispute without offending you both?"

"The only party that you can offend are the Gods, Pro Consul," one of the priests, a tall man with a black beard said raising his voice. "These others, these so-called healers," he gestured
97

irritably at Gaius and Soranus, "they are soldiers, they are under your command, you can order them to do what you like, but the Gods, no one can give orders to the gods."

Scipio leaned back and nodded, his face unreadable. Then he glanced towards Soranus and Gaius.

"Sir, it is true, we are soldiers," Soranus began, "but the field hospital does good work and many wounded men are put back on their feet. These soldiers can and do return to their units. The hospital must survive, Sir."

"Pro Consul," the bearded augur interrupted. "Have you seen how many people come to our temples? Have you seen the popularity of our Gods? Your funds would be better spent in a donation to us. In this way the people will know that you honour their gods and they will approve of you, the more."

"We are talking about men's lives here," Soranus cried angrily turning to stare at the Augurs. "My hospital saves lives! What would you do instead? You know nothing of medicine. You believe that the Gods will heal the wounded. They won't. Only we can do that, with scalpel, hooks and bandage. You are charlatans who fornicate with temple whores, the lot of you!"

The sudden outburst caught Gaius by surprise. He had never known Soranus to be angry or to raise his voice.

The augurs refused to look at them. Instead they kept their eyes on the Pro Consul.

"Blasphemy, blasphemy," the bearded augur hissed, "you deny the existence of the gods!"

Scipio looked down at the table. His hands were clasped together. Then he looked up and the amusement in his eyes had faded.

"You," he pointed at Gaius, "I remember your face. Where have I seen you before?"

Beside him Gaius sensed Soranus stir in surprise.

"I was the fourth man over the wall at New Carthage," Gaius replied quietly. "You commended me after the battle."

"Fourth man over the wall," excitement shone in Scipio's eyes. "I am sure that you wished you had been first?"

Gaius shrugged, "It was not meant to be, Sir. Sextus Digitius was the first man over the wall. He deserves his golden crown."

The corona muralis was a golden crown that was traditionally awarded to the first man to breach the enemy walls.

"Yes", the amusement had returned to Scipio's eyes, "although the Centurion from the Fourth, Quintus Trebellius claims it was he who was first over the wall."

"The Centurion can claim what he likes," Gaius responded, "but Sextus was the first man over the wall, Sir."

Scipio laughed in delight. "Maybe it was so," he said grandly, "and that is why I gave both of them a Golden crown." The Pro Consul paused, "So what would you advise me to do about our current situation?"

At his side Gaius felt Soranus tense. The priests opened their mouths but Scipio held up his hand for silence.

"Our hospital is not only about healing wounded soldiers Sir," Gaius replied looking up at the Pro Consul, "I have spoken with many of the men, they have all heard about what we are doing. The hospital is good for morale. The soldiers know that someone at least will try and help them if they are wounded. Take that away and you will batter the morale of your army, Sir." Scipio leaned back in his chair and stared at Gaius. His face was unreadable. Then he looked down at the table.

"Soranus and you," Scipio said looking at the bearded priest, "will remain behind. Everyone else will leave."

***

Gaius paced up and down outside the room nervously. The augur who had followed him out of the chamber sat silently on a stone bench staring away into the distance. It had been ten minutes Gaius thought. Then with a creaking noise the doors finally opened and Soranus emerged. He strode straight down the hall, his lips tightly pressed together and he avoided Gaius' questioning gaze. Gaius caught up with him as he was half way down the hall.

"Well what did he say?" he exclaimed.

Soranus looked straight ahead. "The hospital is saved," he said, "thanks to your intervention, no doubt."

"But?" Gaius interrupted seeing his principal's expression.

"But you are being shipped out," Soranus said, "Scipio has ordered you to return to Rome. You will be sailing with the next convoy of wounded men."

Soranus halted and turned to look at Gaius with sudden sadness. "I am going to lose a good doctor but it's the price we must pay for saving the hospital. Thank you friend for what you have done."

"Back to Rome," Gaius muttered.

Chapter Fourteen - A new destiny

Gaius strode down the ward of his hospital. The wounded men lying on their mattresses eyed him hopefully but he ignored them. The news that he was to return to Rome had shaken him. It had been more than two years since he'd been home but that was not what worried him. He would be taking his wife and son with him of course and then he would have to introduce them to his family. He could not keep them secret any longer. Stop being scared of him he thought scornfully. He would have to face his father and explain himself.

He paused beside the mattress upon which Hanno was lying. The Carthaginian was asleep. Gaius glanced at the stump but the bandages looked good. He kicked the Carthaginian and Hanno woke with a start. Gaius nodded and then glanced towards the Roman soldier who was still where he'd left him, dozing in the noon heat.

"It's going to have to happen tonight," Gaius whispered. "I am leaving for Rome tomorrow by sea."

Hanno blinked and then turned to look at his stump. "So soon," he muttered, "You know I think I can still feel the arm, even if it isn't there anymore."

"How?" Gaius said looking straight at Hanno.

Hanno glanced at his master down the corridor. Then slowly he looked up at Gaius. "I will poison him," he whispered.

Gaius looked uncomfortable, "I do not wish to have his blood on my hands," he replied. "It's not right."

Hanno looked bemused. "Alright I will make him really sick and leave the antidote here. He will be incapacitated for a long time. He deserves it."

"What will it take?" Gaius said.

"Three berries from the Nightshade plant, crush them into his porridge. The results will be spectacular," Hanno grinned.

***

Morning dawned over Tarraco. The laboured cries of workmen and the chisel of stone masons filled the streets of the city. The great fortifications that Scipio's father and uncle had started were still ongoing. Gaius felt a cool, refreshing breeze on his face. The wind was blowing out to sea. It was as if the gods wanted him to go home he thought despondently. He gripped his son's hand as he made his way down the street that led to the harbour. A few paces behind came his wife, her belly protruding prominently. A couple of slaves brought up the rear, guiding a cart upon which were piled the family's belongings. The wagon was pulled along down the narrow street by a single donkey.

The city of Tarraco nestled high upon the cliffs some hundred yards above the shore. Gaius strode down the steep harbour road. The wind was stronger here and he stared out across the brilliant, blue sea that shimmered in the morning light. Out in the bay a single bireme, its ponderous oars moving slowly and rhythmically like some strange insect, was heading for the

103

harbour entrance. Reinforcements or supplies or both Gaius thought. The ships were coming and going all the time. He peered down into the harbour below.

The harbour was still under construction but along the single mole which had been completed, resting at anchor were four biremes and a liburnian. A second breakwater was still being built and the straight line of tumbled rocks and stones only extended for a short distance into the sea. To prevent the new harbour from silting up, Gaius knew, the engineers had dug underwater channels through the existing mole and a second harbour entrance was being planned in the other mole. The free flow of water was vital to the harbour's functioning. As Gaius stared at the harbour works he noticed that no one was working on its construction. So much work was going on at Tarraco that there must not be enough labour to go round.

He turned to look at the ships. The biremes as their name suggested, had two decks of oars and a single mast. The ships were around twenty-five yards long and four yards wide. Their beautiful curved figureheads at their prows revealed their names.

"Mars, Minerva, Isis and Neptune," Gaius said with a smile.

"You can see which one they are by the figurehead on their prow."

"Which one is ours father?" his son cried out in excitement.

"Have a guess?" Gaius replied.

"Mars," the boy said immediately.

104

Gaius smiled, "Patience, son. We will find out soon enough."

The beach beside the harbour was busy. A long line of slaves and prisoners of war were coming down from the city carrying stretchers upon which lay wounded and invalided Roman soldiers. The galley captains had gathered together on the pier and were supervising the loading of the wounded men onto the ships. Going in the opposite direction and up the steep path to the city was a long line of slaves carrying sacks slung over their shoulders. One of the captains seeing Gaius, moved to intercept him. The seaman nodded conspiratorially.

"Everything is as it should be Sir," he said, "You will sail on the Mars, she's my ship. We leave when the loading is complete, I want to take advantage of this wind."

"I told you it would be the Mars," Gaius' son exclaimed in triumph.

"No," the captain shook his head. "Your family will be on the Isis with the other women and children."

"We are to travel on different ships?" Gaius looked up in alarm.

"Yes, the naval staff think it best," the captain nodded. "The rowers don't like to have women onboard and in the event that we are intercepted we will stand a better chance of being able to defend ourselves. Don't worry though, it won't come to that. The Punic sailors are too frightened to leave their harbours."

Gaius grunted in disapproval. Then he looked down at his son.

The boy looked disappointed but he'd put on his brave face.

105

"Fine," Gaius exclaimed turning to point the slaves in the direction of the Isis. He looked at his wife and gave her a sad smile. She had heard the conversation and her eyes betrayed her sudden fear and nervousness.

"It's alright," Gaius said, "Its only for five days if we have a favourable wind and we should be able to spend each night ashore."

His wife turned away without replying and gazed back up the cliffs to the city. She was leaving her home for the first time Gaius realised.

Then he turned back to the captain of the Mars and glancing around to make sure no one was watching them, pressed a bag of coins into his hand. "As promised," he murmured.

The captain's fingers closed around the bag without a word. Then he was away shouting at his men to hurry the loading.

Gaius stepped onto the gang plank that lay between the pier and the bireme. He was never entirely comfortable on a ship. The sea was an alien concept, unpredictable, terrifying and violent. He always felt so helpless on a ship. To take his mind off the sea he glanced around at the stretcher cases, inspecting those wounded and invalided soldiers who were already onboard. The men had served their time but now that they were useless they were being shipped back to Rome. Most of them looked pleased to be going home but some cast wary glances at the sea and the distant horizon.

Along the sides of the ship the rowers were relaxing by their oars. The men were not Romans and neither were they slaves.

Gaius could tell from their clothing and jewellery and from their strange foreign speech which he guessed was Greek. Most probably the rowers came from Massilia or the Greek coastal towns in southern Italy. The galley's sails were furled up by the mast and at the back of the Mars lay a man with a blanket covering his whole body and face. The man looked like he had recently died. Gaius's hand gripped the side of the ship and he stared out across the bay.

"We sail within the hour," he muttered.

From beneath the blanket there was a slight movement. "About time too," Hanno grumbled.

Chapter Fifteen - The wisdom of the Via Aurelia

Livia closed her eyes and felt the sun warming her face. It was morning and she sat leaning against a rock. Her first day on the Via Aurelia was behind her. It would be so nice to stay here for a while she thought, to relax and rest her weary feet and tend to her blisters. She didn't know how far she had come. It was only at dusk yesterday that she had noticed that the road had mile stones along it. She hadn't known where Placentia was. The Sybil had told her to follow the Via Aurelia northwards until she came to a town called Pisae. From there she would need to cross the mountains and enter the land of the Gaul's. Placentia was a Roman colony built on the southern bank of the great Pavus River, the Sybil had said. Then the old woman had shook her head and muttered that she was mad to try and undertake that journey. It would take her fourteen days alone just to walk to Pisae.

She had spent the night sleeping beside the road in a ditch. Sleeping she thought wryly, she hadn't slept a wink. The terror of sleeping alone, out in the middle of nowhere, with darkness all around her, had kept her awake for nearly the whole night. She'd felt terribly vulnerable. Every movement and noise during the night had been a potential animal just waiting to attack her. She'd realised that she had no weapons with which to defend herself. All she had were her fists and her wits.

She had left Rome through the Flumentana Gate and had crossed the Tiber heading north west towards the coast. Livia stirred and opened her eyes. She was hungry. All her life she'd had her breakfast in the kitchen. She turned and rummaged in her leather bag and took out a loaf of hard black bread. It was her last loaf. She bit her lip and stared at the bread. What was she going to do for food after it had been eaten? She hadn't thought about that. She bit her lip again as a sudden unease came over her. Was she going to starve? She took a bite from the bread and tried to think of something else. What would Laelia think about her now? Would the little girl be worried, would she be sad? Livia choked back a sudden tear. She missed Laelia, suddenly she missed her friend's company very much.

"Think of something else," she murmured to herself. But as she tried to think of something more cheerful the gloomy thoughts kept coming like a raging torrent. She was alone, she was all alone. No one was coming to help her. She didn't know how to hunt. She didn't have any money. She had no skills or goods that she could sell. She was a runaway slave. The Sybil was lying to her. The old woman was playing her for a fool. Titus didn't exist. Her brother was dead. Her brother had moved away. She would fail to find him. She was going to die young just like what that horrible boy had told Laelia. Marcus would catch her or some animal would come and devour her in the night. No one would ever know what had become of her. She had made a mistake. She should go back.

"No," she said furiously, "I am not going back."

She rose stiffly to her feet and clambered out of the ditch and onto the stone road. Then setting her jaw in a stubborn expression she started up the road once more. She wasn't going back. She wasn't going back to that lonely pointless life where all she did was exist. Where the future offered her nothing.

***

Livia sat beside the road trying to mend her broken sandal. The leather strap had snapped and her foot was covered in painful blisters. She had been on the road for three days now. Her face was stained with sweat and there were dark patches under her eyes. Livia was hungry. Yesterday she had been lucky to find some edible berries and roots in a wood. It was Flavia who had taught her sons and Livia which forest fruits they could eat and how to find them and Livia had suddenly been thankful that she had paid attention to the lesson.

A sudden pounding noise made her look up. Then she rose to her feet trying desperately to slip her foot back into the sandal. A man was thundering towards her, coming from the north, down the road on horseback. His black cloak was flying behind him. Livia struggled with her sandal. There was no time to run or hide. The man had seen her and was reining in his horse. Then he trotted up to her and his weary face creased into a smile as he looked down at Livia. A leather dispatch case hung from his saddle.

"Where are you going?" he asked.

Livia had managed to fit her foot back into her sandal. She didn't look up at the man. Instead she started walking up the road but the man turned his horse around and kept pace with her. The tone of his voice changed.

"Now what is a pretty young girl like you doing out here?" the despatch rider said glancing around to see if they were alone.

Livia kept on walking. She knew what that smile meant. Young unaccompanied women did not travel the road alone unless they were prostitutes. Flavia had warned her about the dangers that women faced. A woman out on her own was like lost cattle or salvage from a shipwreck. She could be taken and claimed by anyone. Men could simply take her and do with her what they liked. It was the family's responsibility to look after their own and Livia doubted very much that Marcus would come to seek justice for her if this man were to rape her.

"Stop, I am talking to you," the rider cried out suddenly. The man urged his horse forwards and turned to bar her way. Then he slid from the saddle. A sword hung from the belt of his tunic.

Livia's mind was racing. She could try and make a run for it but not in these sandals and the young man would be too quick for her. He looked too strong for her too. He was older than the boys who had usually come to taunt Laelia. Livia stopped and looked up at the young despatch rider. Her tongue hung a little from her mouth and her face was contorted. She twitched her shoulders in a spasm. It was the best impression she could give of a demented person. Then she opened her mouth and uttered a grunt and then another and another. She stretched her hand towards the man and started towards him.

The rider stared at her in shock. Then as her hand touched his shoulder he sprang back in alarm. His eyes widened.

"Get away from me you witch," he cried.

Livia stopped and slowly pointed a finger at the man and as she did so she began muttering and murmuring unintelligible words.

The rider staggered backwards in horror. His hand rose to clutch at a charm that hung around his neck. Then he swung

111

himself back into his saddle and with a cry he was off, thundering on down the road. As he galloped away the man turned to stare at Livia in horror.

When he had finally disappeared from view Livia let out a long sigh of relief. Her act had been solely based on seeing Publius play a demented witch on stage. The audience had loved it. They had loved it even more when the witch had been burned at the stake. It was Flavia who had told her that men feared women whom they thought were witches, for witches had the power to sap a man's strength from him. As she stared in the direction in which the rider had vanished, Livia began to chuckle and as the tension inside her started to come out, her chuckle turned into laughter. If only Publius could have witnessed her act.

***

In the distance Livia could see the town. She trudged wearily along the road towards it, singing softly to herself. She had been on the Via Aurelia for seven days now. The nights had been spent sleeping in woods and ditches along the road and she had lost her fear of being attacked by animals in the night. The soles of her feet had hardened. She'd washed herself in a stream and had survived on berries, the last of her bread and some porridge which she'd had to beg for from a group of merchants on their way to Rome. The food had been just enough to keep her going but not an hour went by when she was not hungry.

She looked up again at the town in the distance. The city walls were large and white and she tried to remember the name that the merchants had called it. Tarquinii, yes Tarquinii, that was it. Suddenly Livia stopped singing. Up ahead along the road,
112

leaning against a large rock was a boy. He hadn't seen her. The boy looked about the same age as her. He was staring vacantly into the distance.

Livia kept on walking and as she approached the boy turned to look at her. He smiled in a friendly way.

"Have you got any food?" Livia asked hopefully.

The boy was examining her. Then he got up off the ground and shook his head.

"I don't," he replied. "Have you come far?" he added.

Livia nodded and turned to study the country around her. It was time she rested for a while anyway and she could do with some company. The road was proving to be a very lonely place. She glanced at the boy again. He seemed friendly enough.

"Do you mind if I rest here for a while?" she said.

He nodded and sat back down on the ground twirling a long blade of grass in his fingers. Livia sat down beside him.

"What do you do?" Livia asked, "Is your home close by?"

The boy grinned. There was a dim lazy expression on his face.

"I don't have a home. I am a runaway. I used to be a slave but not anymore."

Livia blinked in surprise at the boy's candour. "So where do you get your food?" she asked.
113

"I steal it from the market," the boy gestured towards the town. "How long have you been doing that?" Livia said glanced at the city walls in the distance.

"A while," the boy shrugged. "But not always here. I am making my way to Rome. There will be some work for me in Rome. Where are you going?"

Livia sighed," I am on my way to Pisae."

"I don't see many girls out on the road on their own," the boy said.

"I don't come across many runaway slaves either," Livia replied.

The slave boy shrugged and twirled the blade of grass in his mouth. He was silent for a moment. "My owner was killed by Gaul's. They raided our farm and burnt it to the ground," he said at last. "I am glad they killed my owner. He was a beast. I hated him. We all did. He made us live in filthy conditions. He worked us till our hands bled. Till we were too tired to keep our eyes open. He starved some of us and sometimes he would pay us a visit during the night. He made all the girls scream in terror. He beat them too with that great big stick he liked to carry."

The boy glanced across towards the town. Then he rose to his feet. "I must go," he said with a farewell nod, "Have a good journey."

Livia watched him disappear southwards down the road as she mulled over the slave boy's words. Marcus had never beaten her, not once. He'd never leered at her like the farm labourers had. He'd been stern and strict, cold and unemotional but he
114

had never abused her. The slave boy's lot, it seemed, had been much harder than her own and the realisation brought a light blush to her cheeks.

***

Livia was hungry. She could feel the hunger in her stomach. She could think of nothing else but food. Her body felt weak and listless. But she had nothing. Her desperation had been growing all morning. She had tried begging from the travellers coming down the road but none had been in a charitable mood. She'd rooted around for forest fruits in the woods beside the road but had found nothing. She trudged wearily onwards. Had it really come down to this she thought? Would she have to sell her body for some food? The thought had sounded outrageous to her when she had first considered it a few days back, but now, now it may be the only option left her. She had to survive, she thought grimly, she would do what was necessary to survive.

Up ahead below a copse of trees she suddenly caught sight of a party of men and horses. The men were camped around a small fire over which they had placed a small copper cooking pot. She sniffed as she caught the scent of a meat stew. The men were laughing. They looked wealthy, well fed and smartly dressed. Livia crossed the road and stumbled into their picnic.

"Please Sir," she said, "Can I have some food?"

The men's laughter faded as they looked up in surprise. Then one of the men got to his feet and folded his arms across his chest. He was a handsome, confident looking young man of around twenty-five. He stared at her curiously, then he gestured to the pot. "Go ahead, there is plenty for all of us."

Livia rushed to the fire, fell to her knees and grabbed one of the plates beside the fire and using the wooden spoon she frantically labelled the stew onto the plate and then straight into her mouth. The food was hot and she burned her tongue but she didn't care. She wolfed down the first plate, then began spooning the food direct from the pot into her mouth oblivious to the bemused, startled faces around her. After she had finished half the pot though she suddenly felt a hand gripping her shoulder and forcing her up onto her feet. The young handsome man was staring at her sternly.

"You are a slave aren't you, a runaway slave. I can recognise them from a mile away."

Livia refused to look at him. She stared at the cooking pot and bit her lip. There was no point in putting up a struggle or trying to make a run for it. The three men were all of a military age and they had horses and weapons.

"Where does your owner live?" the man snapped squeezing her shoulder until his fingers began to hurt her.

"Rome," she muttered.

"What is his name?" the man's fingers were really hurting her now. Livia looked up at him and saw the cold, arrogant contempt in the man's eyes.

"Marcus Vibius Pansa," she murmured.

"Good," the man looked over at his colleagues, "We'll take her with us to Rome and find her owner. I am sure he will reward us well for bringing back his property. Bind her hands."

116

One of the men rose to his feet and moved around behind Livia. Then her hands were bound tightly together behind her back. The handsome man let go of her shoulder and clasped her chin forcing her to look at him.

"What will your owner do to you when I return you to him?" he snapped.

Livia glared defiantly back at him but said nothing. There was no point in talking to this man. To him, she was nothing more than some lost cow that he was returning to its cattle enclosure. The hot food had restored some of her strength and for the first time in days she felt the hunger in her stomach fade. Her rebellious and stubborn silence was rewarded with a slap across her head and then another.

"Answer me," the man cried.

Livia grimaced in pain but remained stubbornly silent. The man glared at her and then gave her a shove that nearly sent her tumbling to the ground. "She can walk all the way on a leash," he growled. "Let people see what she is, a runaway slave."

Livia stood motionless as one of the men bound a long rope around her waist. They were going to drag her all the way back to Rome as if she were a dog. The man finished tying the rope around her and tightened it with a couple of sharp tugs. Livia kept her eyes on the ground. The man's question had made her think. What indeed would Marcus do to her? She knew slaves were valuable, she had heard him say that many times but he also had the right to kill her. He had the right to put all his slaves to death for that was the custom, if one slave ran away then collective punishment was enforced. But Marcus was a farmer

117

she thought. He wouldn't kill his slaves, he wouldn't kill her, it would be bad for the farm. It was bad business and there was something else she suddenly knew. Marcus didn't have the heart, he didn't have that cruel heart to kill or torture her. The most she would get would be a lashing or a beating. A strange calmness seemed to come to her. The prospect of being returned to Marcus suddenly didn't hold the same terror it had once done. Maybe if she had talked to him, told him how she felt, he would have understood. Maybe then he would have changed his cold unemotional attitude and realised what she really craved. But it was too late for all of that now. She wasn't going back.

It was night and the three men were asleep around the glowing embers of the camp fire. All afternoon they had ridden south with Livia bound and leashed walking in between the horses. The men, she had discovered were professional slave hunters. There business was tracking down and returning runaway slaves to their owners. Livia silently cursed her luck. Of all the people's camps, she had to walk straight into a pack of slave hunters. The fates were laughing at her. She lay beside the fire pretending to sleep. Her feet had been bound together and her arms were still pinned behind her back. She opened her eyes and stared at the men but all seemed peaceful. Slowly she turned on her back and began to rub the rope that bound her hands against the sharp stone she'd noticed when they had first made their camp. She had deliberately sat down beside it. The movement was difficult and she kept glancing at the slave hunters but the men did not stir. At last after what seemed an age she felt the rope part. Her hands were free. Slowly and painfully she sat up and rubbed her aching shoulders. Then she started tugging on the rope that bound her feet. The rope came away quicker than she had expected. She glanced warily at the

118

men across the fire. What a pack of amateurs she thought with sudden contempt. Then her eye fell on the men's provisions. Silent like a cat she glided across the face of the fire and slipped one of the food pouches over her shoulder. Then she noticed that the handsome young man had placed his sandals neatly beside the fire. She bent down and swiped them. The shoes, even though they were too big for her, would replace her own sandals which were falling apart. Then she was away off into the dark night. The fierce elation of being free once more coursed through her veins.

Chapter Sixteen - The fifty third Colony

Livia crouched at the back of the raft as the pilot quietly guided the little vessel down the shallow, winding river. She shivered in the morning cold despite the new cloak that was wrapped around her shoulders. The raft was drifting through a gorge and on either side the sheer rock loomed high above her and plants and bushes clung to its sides peering down at the intruders. Upriver the peaks and summits of the Apennine mountains were covered by small green trees and undergrowth. The country was beautiful, rugged and wild. The small convoy of six rafts had been descending the Trebbia since sunrise and in the morning air the only sound that could be heard was the rush of the water as it found its way across great boulders, small whirlpools and white foaming rapids. The pilot of her vessel seemed to know the river well for he steered his craft calmly through the hazards. The man turned to look back at her and grinned as he saw her huddled up against the cold.

"We'll reach Placentia by night fall," he said.

Livia did not reply. Piled up around her and crammed into every inch of available space were sacks of wheat, amphorae and bundles upon bundles of arrows. In Pisae, ten days earlier she had found her way to the forum. It had been market day and the Etruscan farmers had come to town to sell their goods. She hadn't known the way to Placentia and on inquiry had been told that a supply convoy was heading to the town the very next day. The traders had warned her that it was dangerous to travel much further north for the Gallic tribes, who lived north of the Apennines were in a state of open revolt and news had now reached the town that Hasdrubal had crossed the Alps. Among the towns folk she had sensed a great amount of fear for no one knew which route south the Carthaginian invader would take.

In the food pouch which she'd taken from the slave hunters she had discovered not only food but also a small bag of silver coins. The money had been enough to buy her a new Palla, shoes and food. She had given the rest to the traders and they had agreed to take her along. The merchants had been ordered north with fresh supplies for Placentia as soon as the news that Hasdrubal had descended upon Italy had become known. The Romans it seemed were expecting their most northerly colony to be in imminent danger of being besieged. The convoy had left Pisae at sunrise the next day and the long column of mules, loaded with supplies, had started up the narrow, treacherous mountain tracks of the Apennine mountains. It had been a difficult journey. The merchants and the armed men they'd hired to guard the convoy had grown increasingly jittery as they had proceeded north. The Apennines north of Pisae were frontier country where Etruscan and Roman civilisation met and mingled with the Celtic traditions of the Gallic tribes. There was no love lost between the two peoples, even Livia knew that, for both sides had been more or less at war with each other for two hundred years.

At the town of Bobium the convoy had exchanged their mules for rafts and had taken to the Trebbia. It was too dangerous to continue by foot for beyond Bobium the farms and villages were Gallic and hostile. The only way to reach Placentia in relative safety was by river.

"He may be our enemy," the river pilot said suddenly, "But I can't help admiring Hannibal. No other man could do what he has done."

Livia did not reply. The man's words made her think about Marcus. She wondered what he was doing now? Would he have hired slave hunters to track her down? Under Roman law she would always be a slave. She would always have to be on her guard against those men who hoped to take her back to her owner. What kind of life was she going to lead? The stubborn, determined look on her face returned. She wanted to lead the same life as Marcus did.

It was just after noon when Livia caught sight of the Gaul's. Two men, clad in trousers but naked from the waist up were sitting beside the river, fishing. Their hair had been braided and hung lose around their broad shoulders and one of them had a drooping moustache whilst the other was wearing a torc, a neck ring. They rose to their feet as the Roman rafts came into view and Gaul and Roman stared at each other in stony silence as the little convoy passed on by. Livia gazed at the Gauls curiously. She had never seen men dressed like that before and it reminded her of something. She has a Gallic streak in her face. Wasn't that what the posh visitors to Marcus' farm had said about her? She wondered if she too had some Gallic blood in her. Maybe her father or mother had belonged to the Celtic tribes. Now that she was so close to her destination she felt a sudden excitement mixed with apprehension. Her long journey was coming to an end and soon she would know whether in had been in vain or not. The night before they had reached Bobium she had buried her last silver coin in the earth and offered it to Diane, the huntress and goddess of women, imploring her to guide her to Titus, her brother.

A few hours later the Trebbia had widened and the current had slowed. They had left the Apennines behind them at last and the land on either bank was flatter and above the dark green forest canopy she could see smoke swirling into the blue sky. A troop of Gaul's emerged from the forest and came up to the water's edge and stared at the rafts in the same sullen silence as the two fishermen had done. The Romans however paid them no attention.

"Don't look down into the water girl," the pilot exclaimed giving her a warning look.

"Why not?" she replied peering over the side of the raft.

"Don't you know anything," the man looked annoyed. "This is the spot where the Consul Sempronius Longus and his army were defeated by Hannibal eleven years ago. The bones of the dead litter the forest and the river bed. If you look carefully into the water you can see them. It will bring you ill fortune to gaze upon the bones of the dead. Their spirits still linger here. If a man is not properly buried he will wander forever and never find peace."

Livia peered into the water but she couldn't see anything. She looked up and examined the river banks.

"How long before we reach the town?" she said.

The pilot grumbled something to himself. "Soon," he muttered.

***

Rome's fifty third colony was only eleven years old and had not known a single year of peace since its foundation. Livia stood up to get a better view as the Trebbia flowed into the Po and the six rafts began to head for the right bank of the mighty river and a wooden jetty that served as the settlement's emporium and harbour. Placentia's location had been well chosen for the Trebbia bordered her on the west and the Po protected her to the north, placing her at a natural-cross-roads. Livia stared at the wooden palisade and ditch that protected the small settlement. Sections of the defences had been rebuilt in stone but the work was incomplete and for the most the wooden walls were the only protection that the colonists seemed to enjoy. High up on a wooden watch tower she noticed two men signalling the convoy and a moment later a trumpet bellowed out a mournful greeting.

"Are you sure you want to stay here?" the pilot said catching her eye. "Maybe you would do better to come with us. This is no place for a girl like you. We leave tomorrow, all the way down the Po and into the sea, then down the coast to Ariminum. I won't charge you."

Livia had her eyes glued on the colony. "I will stay," she replied, "my brother lives here."

"This place will be under siege within weeks," the pilot growled. "Haven't you heard the news, Hasdrubal is coming. Do you know what these Carthaginians do to a town once they have seized it? Be sensible girl."

"I am going to stay," Livia replied as she leapt ashore.

The river pilot raised his eyebrows, shrugged and then turned away.

The gates to the settlement were well guarded and Livia noticed more armed colonists patrolling the ramparts behind the wooden wall. The trees around the town had been chopped down until a space a hundred yards wide had been cleared. The bare tree stumps littered the earth and here and there someone had tried to dig them out. The colonists must have been trying to turn the forest into farm land but their efforts looked like they had been interrupted and she could see no crops. She strode on down the muddy path that led from the riverbank to the town. At the gates the armed men looked nervous and tense and for once their eyes didn't linger on her but were instead fixed on the supplies that were being brought ashore. No one asked her who she was and she passed on into the town without being molested. She'd had no idea what to expect but now that she had finally arrived she realised how small Placentia was.

The colony had been laid out in a rectangular grid like a Roman army camp which essentially what it was. From wall to wall the place measured no more than four hundred paces. She stopped just inside the gates and her fingers fondled the Phallic charm around her neck. Her heart was beating wildly in excitement but suddenly she felt nervous too. Look for Getorix the druid, the Sybil had told her. It wouldn't be too hard to find the man in such a small town she thought, but where to start? She peered down the unpaved street that ran the length of the settlement dividing the town into two. Wooden houses lined the road and many looked like they had been hastily erected. Smoke curled away into the sky from holes in their thatched roofs. The houses looked so different to those in Rome. She sniffed as she noticed the familiar smell of pigs, cattle and manure. Out of sight a dog was barking and a few paces away a man was pissing against a wall. He gave her a hard, challenging look as if to warn her to mind her own business. She looked away quickly and her gaze fell upon a building from which she could hear the rowdy voices of a crowd. It was a tavern. Without thinking she strode straight towards it.

Livia stepped inside the tavern and into a single large and dimly lit room. Opposite her a large fire burned in the hearth and over it roasting on a metal spike was a whole pig. A boy of around twelve, a slave stood beside the fire turning the handle of the spike so that the pig was constantly being rotated. In the fire the wood crackled and spat as the pigs juices dribbled down into it. Livia had never been into a tavern before but she had seen them from the outside when she'd been in Rome. Not the kind of place you want to go to, Publius had once told her with a smile. Now she stood in the doorway, unsure of what to do, staring at the crowd of men and women who sat on crude wooden benches drinking, eating, talking and laughing. In a corner two men were engaged in an arm wrestle and beyond them a couple were locked in a passionate embrace. No one seemed to have noticed her. How different things were here compared to the rural community in which she'd grown up.

She struggled through the crowd towards the bar where a fat, sweating man was serving cups of wine from a large barrel. He looked harassed.

"I am looking for the druid, Getorix, do you know where I can find him?"

He pretended not to hear her and she had to repeat the question. Then at last he looked up.

"Get out of here girl, no druids here."

Livia turned to look at the people in the tavern. "Are these town's folk? Maybe one of them will know where I can find the druid."

The fat bar man slapped a new cup onto the bar and stared at her as if she was stupid. "They're all Gaul's, Celts, can't you see," he hissed, "the Gaul's drink in here and the Romans have their own tavern at the end of the street. Have you just arrived?" Livia nodded and her cheeks coloured in embarrassment. "I thought the Gaul's were our enemies, aren't they?" she mumbled.

"Not these ones," the bar man replied, "these ones are on our side. Or at least I hope they will be for you never know what they do for a nice golden necklace. Go on get out of here and try the other tavern."

Livia looked up at the sweating bar man with an innocent, inquiring look and for a moment she saw guilt flicker in his eyes. Without a word she turned away from the bar and walked towards the fire and the roasting pig. The slave boy looked bored and in a world of his own. At the fire she turned to face the crowded tavern and then in a clear, strong voice she began to sing. Her voice rose powerfully and beautifully until it filled the entire room with her mournful, haunting song and as she sang the whole tavern fell silent and all heads turned to look at her. Livia had always liked to sing but she had only dared to sing in front of Laelia. Now her deep Latin melody seemed to change the very mood of the people and when she finally fell silent she could see that her voice had done its work. Every man and woman in the tavern was staring at her in stunned, silent surprise. Her song had turned them melancholy.

"I am looking for a druid called Getorix," she said. "Does anyone know where I can find him?"

The tavern remained silent. Then at the back, half hidden in shadows a man with a black beard and a green, white bordered cloak rose to his feet.

"I am Getorix," the man replied.

Chapter Seventeen - Gallia Cisalpina

Hasdrubal's tent was lavishly furnished. In a corner stood a Roman camp bed, a table with a jug of half-finished wine stood beside it and covering the floor were thick richly decorated bear hides. Skins belonging to cows, ox and wolves hung along the sides of the tent to keep out the cold night wind. In another corner arrayed on a crude wooden cross hung Hasdrubal's splendid Greek armour and weapons and underneath the bed were four large solid looking metal boxes containing the armies pay chest. Bostar, one of his bodyguards stood guard beside it, his eyes staring off into the distance as if he were a statue but Hasdrubal knew the young man. He'd picked him himself and ordered him to kill any man who tried to take or open the chests for without the fortune inside, Hasdrubal knew, he did not have an army.

Hasdrubal's thoughts were elsewhere however. He stood by the opening of the tent gazing out at the army camp. In the distance he could see the trees that marked the start of the great forest in which he found himself. The camp itself was a hive of activity. With satisfaction he noticed his men's progress. His Iberians and Africans looked fatter, healthier and stronger since they had descended from the Alps. It had all been due to the Gallic support he'd received. He glanced towards the entrance of the camp and noted with satisfaction the steady stream of Gallic warriors coming to join his army. Twenty-five thousand had joined him so far, doubling the size of his army in just a few weeks and more were on their way he'd been told. He wrenched his attention back to the siege engines that his men were building. It was with these machines that he would attack the walls of Rome and subdue that upstart city once and for all.

They would slow his progress southwards but they would prove their worth once they reached Rome.

"General?" a voice called him back into the tent.

Hasdrubal returned to the table that had been placed in the centre of the tent. Around it were gathered all his principal commanders and some of the Gallic kings of the Boii, the Cenomani and Insubres. He resumed his place at the table and looked down at the map of Italy that lay upon it. Small wooden counters beautifully carved to represent foot soldiers or cavalrymen had been placed on the map to denote friendly forces and the last known enemy army dispositions. Green for the Gallic tribes, yellow for the Carthaginians and red for the Romans. Hasdrubal was conscious that his men were waiting for him to speak. He stretched out his index finger and tapped the map around the town of Placentia.

"When the siege engines are completed we will advance on this place," he said staring at the map. "A quick victory here will bring the rest of the Gallic and Ligurian tribes over to our side. Look," his finger dragged across the map southwards until it came to rest on Rome, "there are two routes to Rome, one across the Apennine mountains and into Etruria and then down the western coastal road via Pisae and Telamon and the other," he dragged his finger slowly along the edge of the Appenines, southwards and eastwards towards the Adriatic coast, "is this route. Its longer but easier for we will not need to drag our heavy engines across the mountains." Hasdrubal looked up at his men. "Once we are in command of Placentia I will force the Romans to divide their forces to cover all the passes into the heart of Italy. I will keep them guessing as to what road we will take. It should give us enough of an advantage to enable us to meet and join forces with Hannibal."

Hasdrubal took a deep breath. It was time to reveal his plan. "This war gentlemen," he said," will be won by a single blow and we are going to strike it. It is clear that the Etruscans and Samnites will remain loyal to Rome. We cannot expect Rome' allies to desert her. That strategy is dead. So once we are in possession of Placentia we will advance towards Ariminum on the Adriatic coast. From there we will take the Flaminian Way and march southwards on Rome. The Flaminian road will speed our advance and there will be ample food supplies and loot to be found along the way." Hasdrubal paused and looked around at the eager faces. "Together with Hannibal, our combined armies are going to besiege and take Rome, gentlemen, we are going to end this war once and for all."

The generals were all staring at him.

"Where do you propose to meet your brother and his army?" the captain of the Iberian infantry asked.

Hasdrubal nodded, he had been thinking about that all day. He picked up the yellow and green counters and in a bold move slapped them down beside the town of Narnia in southern Umbria. Then he picked up Hannibal's yellow counters in the south of Italy and moved them northwards until every single yellow and green counter had been concentrated on Narnia.

"We shall meet him here," Hasdrubal said, "within seventy-five miles of Rome. My lord of spies says that Narnia was one of twelve Roman colonies which two years ago refused to provide any more men and money for the Roman war effort. Maybe we

131

will find sympathetic men amongst the population. From Narnia we will be at Rome's gates within five days."

"And crush them like ants," one of the Gallic kings growled.

"But how will your brother know where to meet us?" Hasdrubal's Numidian cavalry commander interrupted.

Hasdrubal nodded again. He'd thought of that too. "Tonight I will write a letter to my brother telling him what I intend to do and where I would like to meet him. Tomorrow six riders, trusted men whom I have selected myself will be given copies of these letters and told to ride southwards, find my brother and give him my despatch. That's how Hannibal will know where we are."

The generals nodded in agreement. It was the only way to get communications through these days now that the Roman navy controlled the seas and kept a close watch on all the ports and shorelines. The Carthaginian navy had ceased to exist in all effective terms now that it had lost all its naval bases in Corsica, Sardinia, Sicily and Spain.

"And once the junction between you and Hannibal is made," a man said in a calm voice, "my agents will be ready to strike."

Hasdrubal glanced up at the hooded figure who sat in a chair at the edge of the tent. The generals around the table did likewise. The man's face was hidden by the dark hood and cloak he was wearing. He'd taken no part in the discussion around the map and his very aloofness irritated Hasdrubal but he knew he needed the man.

"Gisgo," he replied raising himself to his full height, "I am glad to hear that. Why don't you inform us of your plans?"

But the figure in the chair shook his head with a chuckle.

"Secrecy is something I am very good at," Gisgo replied, "and our cause is best served by knowledge being restricted to but a few who need to know."

"We're all on the same side are we not," one of the Carthaginian generals snapped casting a contemptuous glance at the hooded figure.

"Ofcourse we are," Gisgo replied smoothly, "and you should be glad to have me on your side for if you were my enemy you would be dead by nightfall."

There was an angry stir amongst the Carthaginian generals but Hasdrubal was quick to intervene.

"I will trust in your expertise Gisgo," Hasdrubal said, "You served my brother well, you were with him eleven years ago and your reputation as lord of spies precedes you. Report to me as soon as you have made progress."

The hooded figure chuckled again. "If it hadn't been for your laziness Hasdrubal," he said sharply, "we could have been in this position four years ago and your brother would still be in control of Capua and Tarentum."

At his side Hasdrubal's hand clenched into a fist as the tent fell silent. There was nothing he would like better than ramming it down Gisgo's throat. The man could be so impossibly arrogant.

133

How dare he insult him, Hasdrubal, the general who had defeated and slain both the Scipio brothers? It was bad for morale to see that someone could insult their general and get away with it. But Gisgo knew he enjoyed Hannibal's protection and that single fact stopped Hasdrubal from having him flayed alive there and then.

"Yes I did serve your brother well didn't I," Gisgo continued, "and I very nearly singlehandedly brought the Romans to ruin after Cannae. I came closer to finishing off these Roman jackals than any of you. Fabius was lucky to survive, yes, the man they now call the Shield of Rome was a lucky man indeed to escape my assassin."

Chapter Eighteen - Tradition be damned

Someone wanted him dead. Marcus strode across the courtyard of his farm. His face was pale with anger.

"Boy," he shouted at one of the Gallic slaves, "Prepare my horse and armour."

The slaves who were in the courtyard tending to their duties seemed to shrink as they caught sight of their master's mood. Marcus paid them no attention. He barged into the kitchen of his house, startling the kitchen maid who yelped in fright at the sudden intrusion. Marcus slid his gladius from its sheath. The sword came away with a metallic ring. He placed it carefully on the table.

"Sharpen it," he ordered the maid. He stomped on into the Long room, his heavy sandals reverberating on the floor. Someone wanted him dead. The shock of the assassination attempt was still fresh. He'd been lucky, so damned lucky. Those spears should have struck him. How could his attackers have missed from such range? He should be dead. His forehead hurt from where he' d smashed it into his assailant's face. He'd heard something crack but he wasn't sure if had been him or his attackers nose he'd broken. Carefully he touched his face. He was bleeding from a cut to his forehead but apart from that everything seemed alright. Good he thought with grim satisfaction. One of the would-be assassins would have a broken nose. He cupped his hands into a bowl of water that stood on the table and splashed the liquid onto his face. Then he splashed some more onto his neck.

"What's happened?" Flavia stood by the door looking alarmed. She was dressed in her dark mourning Stola and her hair was undone.

Marcus half turned to look at his wife and as he did so she gasped as she saw the blood on his face.

"Someone just tried to kill me," he growled, "out on the old salt road."

Flavia raised her hand to her mouth and stared at him.

Without another word Marcus opened a drawer to a cupboard and pulled out a metal box. He inserted a key, opened the box and poured the contents onto the table. Flavia's jewellery, bracelets, ear rings and necklaces together with some gold and silver coins tumbled onto the wood. For nine years now the Oppian law had forbidden women from owning and displaying jewellery. The law had been passed in the dark years following the great defeat at Cannae, when it was thought prudent to ensure that the gold and silver resources of the state were not wasted on petty things like women's jewellery. Marcus stared at the small pile of jewellery and coins. It was all the money he had. Then with one sweep of his hand he scooped them up and dropped them into a leather bag.

"What are you going to do?" the alarm in Flavia's voice was rising. She took a step towards him.

Marcus stuffed the bag into his tunic and turned for the door without replying. She caught his arm as he was about to leave. "I met a man today in Rome," he said without looking at her, "who says that he knows who murdered Publius, but he wants ten thousand Denarius for his information."

"Ten thousand..." Flavia looked confused.

Marcus shook himself free and strode towards the door that led out into the courtyard.

"Marcus, no...you can't," there was a sudden fear in his wife's voice as she stumbled after him.

"Sword," he shouted as he emerged into the courtyard. From the stable the boy was half running towards him pulling his horse along by its reins. Another slave hastily trotted towards him carrying his chain mail armour and helmet and from the kitchen the maid appeared carrying his gladius.

"Marcus think about this, you can't."

But Marcus did not seem to hear his wife's words. He snatched his sword from the kitchen maid and ran his finger down its length. It was sharp. Then he lifted up his arms and the slave fastened his armour into its place.

Flavia stood by his side staring at her husband. Fully armed, he swung himself into the saddle.

"Where are you going?" a desperate note had entered Flavia's voice.

But Marcus did not reply as he urged his horse out the gate and down the track.

***

Numa's villa was a sumptuous place seven miles north of Rome. No expense had been spared in its construction. The square, two storied building stood on top of a steep hill which afforded it sweeping views of the neighbouring corn lands. The house itself was surrounded by a short brick wall a yard high, that served not to keep men out but to denote the extent of the owner's land. Wall plants had lodged themselves amongst the bricks turning the wall green. Marcus paused on the steep track that led up to the gate and gazed up at the white washed walls and the neat red roof tiles. The shutters beside the windows were closed and the house looked deserted but then it always did he thought. There was no farmland attached to the villa, this was purely a house in the country, a villa Urbana for Numa had no interest in farming. Marcus had always been curious to know how Numa's family had made their fortune but he'd never found out. Numa's family, it seemed had always been rich, since the very foundation of Rome.

He urged his horse up to the wooden gate. It was closed. He peered beyond it at the porch. Set in alcoves in the wall, the stone heads of four famous forefathers of Numa's family stared back at him from the Vestibule. One of them, Marcus remembered faintly, had helped to overthrow the last king to rule Rome and so establish the Republic. The house looked abandoned. Maybe he'd made a mistake and Numa had chosen to stay at one of his houses in Rome. He was about to turn away when his horse whinnied and from around the side of the house, hidden from view by an outbuilding he heard a horse whinny in reply. Curiously Marcus guided his horse off the track and along the low wall until he could see around the side of the building. Twelve horses stood in a line tied to wooden posts sunk into the ground. The beasts looked tired and worn out. Marcus frowned. That was unusual. What did Numa need twelve horses for?

"Yes," a voice said suddenly.

Marcus jerked backwards and stared at the man who had appeared from nowhere on the opposite side of the wall. The man was clad in a plain grey tunic and sandals and he was completely bald. Marcus relaxed. It was Numa's foreman, the man who looked after the house when its owner was not there.

"I have come to see your master," Marcus replied feeling annoyed at his own jitteriness.

"He is not here," the foreman replied and there was something cold and unwelcoming in his voice that made Marcus pause.

"Where can I find him?" Marcus replied at last.

"You can try in Rome," the man said. Then abruptly he turned on his heels and strode back towards the house.

Marcus watched him go in silence. Then a slight movement caught his eye and he looked up at the house. One of the shutters had moved and from the window a face was staring down at him. Marcus frowned as he recognised the face. It was Arkadios, the Greek tutor who had so rudely run out of his home when he'd asked him to translate the document he'd found in Publius's room. For a moment the Greek stared at him. Then abruptly the face vanished and the shutter slammed across the window.

139

***

It was dark by the time Marcus returned to his farm. Two heavy looking bags hung on either side of his saddle. Someone had lit four welcoming torches beside the gate. His horse's hooves clattered on the stones and on hearing the noise one of his slaves ran up to grasp the beast by the reins. Marcus wearily swung himself down onto the ground. Then he unfastened the bags and heaved them over his shoulder. Their contents jingled. Another torch had been fixed at the entrance to the farm house and in its flickering light he saw Flavia standing in the doorway her arms folded across her chest. Without a word he pushed past her and into the long room where, with a loud thump, he dumped the two heavy bags onto the oak table. Flavia had followed him inside, her face unhappy and angry.

"Where did you go?" she asked hoarsely.

"I went to see Numa but he was not there. I don't know where he is. They couldn't tell me in Rome either."

Flavia was staring at the two heavy bags on the table. "Why did you go?" she snapped.

Marcus turned to face her placing his body between her and the table. "I went to ask him for ten thousand Denarius so that I can find out who killed my son."

Flavia stared at her husband. "We don't have that kind of money," she snapped. "What is in those bags? What have you done?"

"Numa was not there like I said," Marcus replied, "So I went to the money lenders in the forum and borrowed the ten thousand from them."

Flavia cried out as if she was in pain. "You borrowed the money Marcus? How are we ever going to repay such a sum?"

Then his wife's face darkened and her eyes widened.

"What did you give them as collateral?" she demanded.

"The farm, the slaves, everything that I own," Marcus replied. Flavia looked disbelieving. Then she shook her head. "And Laelia and my son?"

Marcus nodded, "Yes them too, I will sell them as slaves if I have too."

Flavia stared at him. Then she took a step forwards and slapped her husband hard across the face. Marcus did not flinch but when she tried to hit him again he caught her hand.

"Someone murdered my son and I will see justice done whatever it takes," he said grimly, "and if you or anyone else tries to stop me I shall not hesitate to use the full power of my position as head of this family. Is that clear Flavia?"

She seemed to shrink from him. Her eyes were red and tears were coming down her cheeks. Her fingers grasped at her hair.

"You drove Livia away too," she cried, "You made her unhappy and forced her out of our home. She ran away because of you. Could you not see that she wanted you to be her father. Could you not see that she craved your love and acceptance. But instead of a father you acted like her owner. She needed your love and approval but you, you stubborn old man, you couldn't do that could you because she was a slave and it would go against tradition! Well tradition be damned!"

Marcus looked hurt. It showed for just a brief moment. Then he gazed at his wife, his face stern.

"I have said what I have to say," he replied quietly, "and now I ask for your support and loyalty Flavia. Will you give it to me?" Flavia tried to stifle her tears. She looked up at the ceiling. The room descended into silence broken only by her sobs. Then Flavia wiped her face with the back of her hand and looked at her husband.

"You are a most uncompromising man Marcus," she said hoarsely, "but I trusted in you once and I will do so again."

Chapter Nineteen - What ten thousand can buy you

The Subura stank as usual but Marcus hardly noticed. He made his way through the narrow alleys trying to remember how he'd found Mamercus's dwelling. In one hand he grasped the two heavy bags of coin whilst his other hand rested lightly on the pommel of his sword. He looked tense. The Subura was not the place to come to, especially with ten thousand Denarius in his hands and potential thieves around each corner. He would have to find Mamercus's place soon before some of the local scum sensed what he was carrying.

He glanced up at the sky. It was near noon and it was a hot cloudless day. The money lenders in the Forum had welcomed him in surprise. They knew his reputation for he'd been coming to the Forum for many years now but they had not expected him to actually want to do business with them. They had told him this to his face. It was their way of showing their contempt for his new position as a debtor. It had been a humiliating experience having to ask them for a loan. The Argentarii, the money lenders, had nearly to the last man been foreigners, mainly Greeks but there had been Egyptians and Jews amongst them too. He'd swallowed the humiliation but his pride had been soothed when he'd managed to come away with a good interest rate of 1/3 percent a month. The money lenders had warned him that if the full loan was not repaid within a year they would take steps to confiscate his property and haul him in front of a magistrate. He knew what that meant. If he didn't repay the money he and his family would become the slaves of the Argentarii. The thought sent a shiver down his spine. He could not think of a more humiliating fate.

Mamercus seemed to have been expecting him for a troop of filthy children appeared from nowhere and pointed Marcus in the right direction. Six hard looking and powerfully built men were lounging outside the door to Mamercus's Insulae, apartment block. They were armed with swords and knives. Marcus recognised two of them from his previous encounter. None of the men seemed to have a broken nose. Catching sight of Marcus they gestured for him to step inside. Their eyes glided casually over the two leather bags but if they had guessed what the contents were they did not show it. Marcus approached wondering how news of his presence in the neighbourhood had travelled so fast.

"Your sword, give it to me," the thug he'd kneaded in the balls said as he came up to the doorway.

Marcus stared at the man who stared back at him.

"You will get it back," the thug said.

Marcus lifted his gladius from his belt and handed it to the thug and then without a word he ducked and stepped through the doorway into the cool dark hall. The room was exactly as he remembered it. Mamercus was stretched out on his couch eating a fig. His naked pot belly protruded out over his waist. Two naked girls were sitting on the other couch painting their nails. They looked bored. Marcus recognised them from his previous visit.

"Do you never wear any clothes?" he snapped at the girls.

The two girls looked up offended and then across at Mamercus for guidance. The boss of the Subura ignored them. Instead he

144

swung his feet from the couch and stood up running a hand across his fat stomach. He smiled as he noted the two bags in Marcus's hand.

"You are a brave man to come walking into my neighbourhood with such a large amount of money," he grinned.

"I see that you have increased your protection," Marcus said moving towards the couch upon which the two naked girls were sitting. "When I last came here you had only three men outside, now its six. Feeling vulnerable?"

Mamercus's smile faded from his face. "Actually it's eighteen men, six are in the back and you missed the other six guarding the entrance to the alley."

"Get up," Marcus snapped at the two girls. The women's faces coloured in annoyance but again they looked to Mamercus for guidance. The big man gestured for them to get up and as they did, Marcus sat down. The two girls glided over to the other couch with barely concealed irritation.

"Who are you afraid of?" Marcus said looking at Mamercus.

Mamercus stroked his chin, "No one, it's just a precaution. When a man like you brings a lot of money into the neighbourhood it can excite some of my more stupid and volatile subjects."

"It's all there," Marcus said dumping the bags on the ground.

Mamercus snapped his fingers at the two girls. "Count it," he ordered. Then he glanced at Marcus, "You surprise me, you know. I didn't think you would come up with the money."

The girls leaned forward and each snatched up a bag. They undid the leather strings that fastened the bags and then turned them upside down pouring the contents onto the floor. The silver coins tumbled and jingled onto the stone and as they did so the girls gasped in awe. Mamercus licked his lips. Marcus stared impassively at the gleaming pile of coins on the floor.

"Who killed my son?" he said quietly.

Mamercus was still staring at the coins. Then he wrenched his eyes from the floor and looked away.

"The man who murdered your son is known to you, Marcus. You have known him for a very long time. His name is Senator Quintus Valerius Numa."

Marcus was staring intently at Mamercus.

"Numa saved my life at Telamon," Marcus growled, "I think you are mistaken. He would never do such a thing."

Mamercus shook his head and turned to look at Marcus. "No, I am not mistaken. He had your boy killed."

"Why, why would Numa do something like that?" Marcus was on his feet. On the floor the girls looked up in alarm.

Mamercus smiled grimly. "You really don't know your son very well do you? I can see that now. Publius was working for Numa, did you know that?"

"Working for Numa?" Marcus looked confused. "Doing what?"

Mamercus shook his head. "You really surprise me Marcus, your ignorance is so pathetic and yet charming too. You should really have spent more time with your son. Maybe then he would still be alive."

The boss of the Subura grinned again. "Let me explain something," he paused. "Numa is a god damn Carthaginian spy, don't you get it!" he thundered as spit from his mouth spread out across the room.

Marcus took a step back and steadied himself. Mamercus had thrust his jaw forwards in an aggressive posture.

"Your son did some low-level work for Numa," Mamercus growled. "As an actor, the rich and powerful often hired him as entertainment. His job was to report on what he'd heard at the parties, gossip, that kind of thing, nothing more serious than that."

Mamercus paused and his aggressive stance gave way to amusement. "The poor boy thought he was working for us. He thought Numa was hunting spies. He thought he was doing his patriotic duty. He never understood that Numa was the actual spy."

"So why kill him?" Marcus said.

147

Mamercus took a deep breath.

"Publius found something or knew something. I don't know for sure but something upset Numa pretty badly. He was looking for something, claimed your boy had stolen it from his house. Numa was desperate to find it. The two of them had an argument that night at the Consul's home. Numa accused your son of stealing. Whatever your boy took it seemed to have rattled the Senator. Numa was scared."

"Scared?" Marcus inquired sharply.

"I have seen fear in all its forms," Mamercus growled. "Numa was scared. Your boy knew something about him. Whatever it was, it cost him his life. I wish that I knew what it was. That would make an interesting, profitable twist to the story."

Marcus's face was unreadable. Then he spoke slowly and carefully.

"Hiring my son to report on gossip at parties seems a weak reason to employ him. There must have been more?"

Mamercus glanced at Marcus and there was contempt in his voice as he spoke.

"Your son had learned to speak Punic. A useful skill when hunting for Punic spies, don't you think?"

Marcus stood rooted to the floor. His mind was racing. Then at last, after what seemed like an age, he looked up at the fat man sizing him up.

"You say that Numa is a Carthaginian spy and yet you are happy to do nothing about it. We are at war with Carthage. Your failure to report this could be construed as treachery, the penalty for which is death. Tell me, Mamercus what does Numa have on you that prevents you from speaking out?"

The silence in the room seemed to grow poisoned. On the floor the two naked girls rose silently to their feet as if guided by an unseen signal, and left. Only Mamercus and Marcus remained. The boss of the Subura was panting slightly and there was a dangerous gleam in his eyes.

"I think the time has come for you to leave," Mamercus said quietly.

Marcus was silent. Then he allowed himself a little contemptuous smile. With a last glance at the coins on the floor he moved towards the doorway.

"And if I ever see you around this neighbourhood again," Mamercus hissed, "I will kill you and then I will kill your pretty wife too."

Marcus stepped outside without replying.

Chapter Twenty - Old friends

Marcus sat on his horse staring up at the white house on top of the steep hill. It was dusk and a mud-spattered riding cloak was wrapped around his shoulders. On his belt resting against his right leg hung his gladius. Along the old salt road a group of farm hands were returning home from a hard day's work in the fields. They were carrying baskets and pick axes and wore wide brimmed hats against the sun. The labourers were singing. Marcus paid them no attention. He looked reluctant as he sat without moving, gazing up at the villa.

He'd been a young man in the summer of two hundred and twenty-five BC but the memories of that terrible year were still fresh. Gallic raiding parties had crossed the Apennines and had swarmed southwards, burning, killing, raping and looting everything in their path. Not since the terrible days when Brennus had sacked Rome, had the countryside experienced such terror and dread. The Gaul's had outwitted one Roman army and defeated another at Faesulae and once they'd pillaged enough Roman farms and towns and could carry no more loot they had turned northwards back towards their homes. Marcus had been enlisted into the cavalry of the 4th Legion commanded by the Consul Aemilius. The Romans, smarting from their setbacks had been intent on revenge. That had been the overwhelming feeling that summer, revenge, revenge, revenge. Marcus had been ordered north and the Romans had finally caught up with the Gallic raiders now numbering some seventy thousand men, at the coastal town of Telamon along the Via Aurelia. Marcus could still vividly remember the battle. It was something that he would never forget. It had been his first. He'd been twenty-seven years old.

Sandwiched between two consular armies, one attacking from the south and the other from the north, the Gaul's had made a desperate stand, dividing their forces into two fronts. Marcus's eyes flickered restlessly as he remembered it all. The sight of the Gaesatae, the Gallic mercenaries from across the Alps going into battle stark naked, the blaring of the countless Carnyx, the boar headed Gallic battle horns, the line upon line of Celtic chariots, the grim murderous mood amongst his fellow cavalrymen. The Gaul's big, brawny warriors had been taller and bigger than the Romans and they'd look ferocious with their strange alien braided hair and their huge unwieldy weapons. They had fought like demons but in the end the battle had turned into a massacre. The Gaesatae, stark naked had been cut to pieces by volley upon volley of arrows and spears for the Romans had simply not bothered to engage them in close quarter fighting. Forty thousand Gaul's had died that day. Marcus had fought on one of the flanks and it was here, late in the day when it had become clear that the raiders were being slaughtered, that a Gallic warrior would have killed him had Numa' spear not cut him down first. Numa, Marcus thought, had saved his life that day. Numa was the finest friend he'd had.

Everything fitted. He'd thought it through on his way back from the Subura. Every time however when he had tried to look at it from a different angle he had come back to the same conclusion The Punic letter he'd found in Publius' apartment must have been what Numa was looking for and if his son had taught himself to read Punic then Publius would have known what the letter said. Publius had wanted to talk to him about something? The two of them had never talked. Whatever was stated in that letter it must have upset Publius enough to want to come to him. It must have been important enough for his son to want to speak with him. The thought had depressed him and he'd known then that he'd failed Publius as a father. He'd known that he should have done better.

Reluctantly he dug his knees into his horse's flank and steered the beast up the steep path that led to the villa. The gate to the grounds of the house was open and Marcus walked his horse up to the porch. The four stone heads of the Valerius family stared back at him in stony silence, willing him to go back. He slid to the ground, tied the reins around one of the pillars supporting the vestibule and then banged on the door with his fist. After the second knock the door was opened by the bald headed foreman. The man glared at Marcus with barely concealed hostility.

"I told you yesterday," the man growled, "He is not here."

Marcus was about to reply when he was interrupted by a weary voice coming from further inside the house.

"It's alright, let him enter."

Marcus stepped through the door and into the entry hall. Behind him the foreman closed the door and folded his arms across his chest. Marcus noticed that the man was armed. The floor of the hall was decorated with a simple mosaic pattern of a black dog set in an oval white circle. On the three walls around him were more statues and stone heads of long dead members of the Valerius clan. Without taking off his riding cloak he stepped into the atrium. The large open space formed the centre of the villa. The floor had been paved with great white stone slabs and covered with animal skins and at its centre the roof opened out to the sky so that the atrium resembled more a courtyard than a room. Wooden pillars, holding up the roof formed an inner

152

square of silent sentinels, through which, across the open space opposite him, a hearth was burning, the flames licking greedily at the blocks of wood. Numa stood beside it feeding more wood into the fire. In his other hand he held a cup of wine. His back was turned to Marcus. From the bedroom's upstairs Marcus could hear the excited voices and squeals of children playing.

"You shouldn't have come," Numa said staring into the fire.

Marcus glanced around the atrium. The two of them were alone.

"But I suppose I should have known," Numa continued as irritation crept into his voice, "You never give up. You never know when to leave things alone. I knew Mamercus was a greedy man. I knew that he would demand a high price but I didn't think you would pay. You surprise me Marcus, I didn't know that Publius meant so much to you."

Numa turned and faced Marcus. His cheeks were unshaven and he looked tired.

"If only you hadn't gone to the money lenders. If only you hadn't mortgaged your farm and been so stubborn. We were friends, we could have remained friends and all this," he raised his arms, "would never have happened."

"But it has happened," Marcus replied.

Numa nodded and took a sip of wine. "Yes," he muttered.

"Publius was just like you. He had to poke his nose into other affairs. If only he'd done as he was told and been a quiet, sensible boy then I wouldn't have had to kill him."

153

Marcus stirred on his feet.

"You came to my house," he said slowly, "You sat at my table with my wife in the room and you told us that Publius was like a son to you. You told us that if we needed help you would be there to help. How could you sit at my table, in my house and say such things, knowing that you had just killed my boy?"

Numa lifted his chin and eyed Marcus. "I did what was necessary," he declared. "I did what any man would do in order to survive. It was your son or it was me. Publius took something from me, something important, something that could ruin me. He had to die Marcus, I couldn't let him live."

"And yet you are still a ruined man," Marcus said.

Numa took another sip of wine. Then suddenly he laughed as if in relief. "I was ruined years ago. All this," he gestured at the walls around him, "They were going to take it away. I had lost our entire family fortune, everything, down to the last copper coin. They were going to take everything from me. They were going to haul me up before a court and have me stripped of my place in the Senate. I couldn't allow that to happen. Who could ever face one's forefathers and explain the shame that I had brought upon the family. Who could ever stomach such a thing?"

"So you decided to take Carthaginian gold instead."

Numa turned and gave Marcus a sharp look. "I see Mamercus has been talking more than what is good for his health."

"I know what you have become," Marcus said.
154

Numa looked down at the floor. "A man will do strange things when he has to. Maybe it would have been better if I hadn't saved your life at Telamon. Maybe it would have been better for both of us."

But Marcus shook his head. "I am here to seek justice for Publius. You will pay for what you have done and my son will rest in peace."

Numa looked up at Marcus coldly. Then he shook his head. "No, that is not how it will end."

A tense, dangerous silence descended upon the atrium. Even the noise of the children playing upstairs had stopped. Numa gestured towards the way out. "Go now Marcus, leave my house. I will give you this final honour but know this, when you step through that doorway, you are no longer my friend and if I see you again I shall kill you."

Marcus stood without moving, his face unreadable.

"You tried that once before didn't you," he said. "Two men out on the old salt road. Your honour means nothing. I shall walk through that doorway Numa and when I do I suggest you give some serious thought to what honour really means and use your sword to end your own life, for when I leave I intend to bring this whole sorry matter before the Senate."

At the mention of the Senate, Numa's eyes narrowed. He stared at Marcus for an instant trying to read his thoughts.

"You can try," Numa replied contemptuously, "But they will never believe you. The Senate is besieged every day by citizens claiming knowledge of dark plots and Mamercus will not speak up. I have that man so deep in my pocket that he's forgotten what daylight looks like. Now go Marcus before I change my mind."

***

The door slammed shut behind him. Marcus stood still for a moment on the porch. Darkness was creeping up and in the sky the first night stars could be seen. A yellow moon cast its pale light across the dark horizon. A breeze had picked up and he could hear the wind rushing through the trees. A storm would be on its way. The air had been too hot and too stale for too long. He turned and gave the door behind him a final look. Then he stepped forwards, loosened his horses reins leading the beast on foot he strode out the gate and started to descend the steep path. He was half way down the hillside when a dark figure rose up from behind a boulder and stepped boldly into the path. Marcus's horse whinnied in fright. Marcus's gladius glinted in the moonlight as he pulled it free.

"Did you tell him about the letter?" a familiar sounding voice whispered.

Marcus peered into the darkness, his sword poised to strike. Then the figure moved closer and in the pale light he saw that it was Arkadios, the Greek tutor. The man was cloaked entirely in black.

"I did not," Marcus muttered.

"Good, that's good," Arkadios mumbled, "for if you had done so he would have killed you there and then."

"He still intends to do that," Marcus replied.

But Arkadios was not listening. He pulled his hood down from his head. "The letter, have you still got it?"

"Yes, I have it on me. What's this about? Why did you run away from my home?"

Arkadios looked up the hill. "You should take the letter to the Senate and have it read aloud. You should do it immediately. Something terrible is about to occur."

"What, what is about to happen?"

Arkadios dragged his gaze away from the house and stared at Marcus. "Your son stumbled across something he shouldn't have seen. He shouldn't have taken the letter and he shouldn't have read it. He would still be alive if he hadn't. Your son was a fool but what I am going to tell you, I do for him, for I was fond of him."

Marcus did not move as he waited for the Greek to continue.

"My employer is working for the benefit of Carthage," Arkadios hissed. "He has been doing so for three years now. Two weeks ago a man arrived at this house. He was carrying a letter destined for Numa's eyes only. I saw him hand it over. The man was from the north, a Ligurian I think. I thought nothing more of it until I saw the same letter in your house."

"What does it say?" Marcus said gently.

157

Arkadios's eyes widened. "The letter is an instruction. Numa is to prepare for the arrival of twenty-four men from the north. Carthaginians, soldiers specially selected for their bravery and skill. Numa's task is to get them into Rome and hide them in one of his houses within the city. Then when the signal is given, the men are to go to the Senate house in the forum, barricade the doors and kill every single Senator inside. Numa's instructions are to wipe out the Senate, every last man of them."

Marcus's hand tightened its grip around his sword. He stared at the Greek in disbelief but the tutor looked deadly serious.

"The letter says this?" Marcus said.

Arkadios nodded vigorously.

Marcus turned to stare up the steep track. "When is the next session of the Senate scheduled for?" he grunted.

"Numa is going to the house tomorrow," Arkadios whispered.

Chapter Twenty-One - Hannibal is at the gates

Marcus galloped into the courtyard of his farm with a warning cry. Hardly had his horse come to a halt and he was on the ground still shouting. It was night but in the farm house and the two cottages where the slaves lived he could see the flicker and glimmer of lamps. He heard the creak of a door being opened. Flavia met him in the kitchen. She was dressed ready for bed. She looked alarmed and her alarm grew as she caught sight of her husband's face.

"What is it? Is Hannibal coming?" she exclaimed.

Marcus took her by the arm and guided her into the long room. A solitary oil lamp was burning in its stand along the wall. His face was covered in sweat and he looked tired.

"Pack a few clothes and take some food. Get Laelia ready. We are leaving."

Flavia looked up at him without understanding.

"Just do it," he said brusquely.

"Where are we going? I don't understand Marcus?"

"To Rome," he growled. "I am taking you and the Gallic women to the Lady Clodia. She's a vestal virgin. You will stay with her until this is all over. Now get moving."

He didn't wait for her to reply. Instead he stomped back out of the house, crossed the courtyard and banged his fist on the doors of the two slave houses. "Out," he yelled, "I need to speak with you all."

***

The eleven slaves stood in a line in the long room. They looked worried and bewildered. Marcus sat behind the oak dining table. He still wore his dust covered cloak. Flavia stood in the doorway. She'd changed into her travelling clothes and there was a sack on her back. She was holding little Laelia's hand. The girl looked like she had just been woken up. On the table lay eleven letters, each sealed with red wax upon which Marcus had impressed his signet ring. Marcus was staring at the letters. Long ago he'd prepared himself for the day when Hannibal may once again appear before the gates of Rome but he'd never expected to have to put his contingency plan into action for any other reason.

"I must go to Rome," he said carefully, looking up at his slaves, "My wife and I and all you women will leave tonight. We will take the cart and ox. In Rome the women will stay with the lady Clodia. She is a vestal virgin and she will look after you." He glanced at the eldest of his male slaves, the man who had accompanied him into Rome to collect Publius' body. "The men will stay here and guard the farm. In the next few days, strangers may come asking for me. You are not to let them enter my property, is that understood? If they ask you where I have gone you can tell them what you like. If I don't return within a week, then," Marcus gestured at the letters lying on the table, "You are all to be made freedmen. The official documents are all in there. I have already signed them. You can go where you please. That's all."

The slaves glanced at each other in surprise. Marcus rose to his feet, scooped up the letters and placed them back in the metal box in the drawer. Then he locked the box and closed the cupboard.

"Come, we must go," he said.

***

The wind had grown as Marcus had predicted. It surged through the trees and around the cart but there was no sign of rain. The night was well advanced and a bewildering number of stars sparkled and twinkled in the heavens. The cart bumped and swayed along over the rough stony track as the ox plodded on. Marcus had chosen to take the longer route to Rome in case Numa's men were waiting for him along the salt road. It would add another hour to their journey. Flavia held the reins, her head covered in a shawl to keep out the wind. Behind her in the cart, Laelia and the five slave women sat huddled together like swans going to the market. Marcus rode alongside the cart on his horse, his cloak wrapped tightly around him, a solitary torch in his hand to guide them on their way. He'd told Flavia about Numa's betrayal and his words had made her go silent. He glanced at the slave women. They looked tired and worried. They would be worried about being separated from their men folk. His slaves had not given him any cause to distrust them but he'd been shrewd enough to insure himself. With their women in Rome it was much less likely that the men would misbehave or run away.

"Marcus," Flavia said suddenly her voice rising above the wind.

"How did you come to know a vestal virgin?"

161

"It's a long story," he muttered in reply.

His wife glanced at him thoughtfully. Then she switched her attention back to the track and the ox. With her free hand she fumbled for something around her waist. Then she stretched out her hand. She was holding a small leather bag.

"I want you to take this," she said.

He stretched out his hand and took the small pouch and looked at it.

"What is it?"

"It's poison," Flavia replied calmly, "I have prepared it for the person who killed my son. It will cause them to die in horrible agony. I want you to force it down Numa's throat and send him straight to hell."

***

The circular temple of Vesta stood in the very heart of the forum. It was midnight and Rome lay shrouded in darkness but even at this hour the city was noisy. Marcus halted before the steps to the temple and slid to the ground still holding his torch. A group of drunken revellers passed by along the Sacred Way, singing loudly and on the steps to the temple a man was sleeping rough. Marcus glanced at his wife and the wagon but in the shadows it was difficult to see her face. The Vestal Virgins were the female priestesses of Rome, charged since antiquity to serve the Goddess Vesta, the goddess of the hearth and of purity. A Vestal virgin served for a term of thirty years in which time they were forbidden from marrying and having sexual
162

relations, for only through pure service could the city of Rome remain pure and unstained. The penalty for losing their virginity was to be buried alive beneath the cattle market.

Marcus ignored the temple and calling on Flavia to follow he made his way around the back of the building to the house of the Vestals. This building, three storeys high with an inner courtyard was where the six vestals lived. Marcus strode up to the door and banged his fist on the wood. On his third attempt the door was opened by the night watchman, a slave.

"Lady Clodia," Marcus snapped. "It's urgent."

If the slave thought it unusual to have a visitor at this hour he was careful not to show it.

"I shall wake her," he said stiffly.

Clodia was in her late twenties and strikingly beautiful. She arrived clad in the traditional robes of a vestal virgin, a long white Infula made of wool and a Palla draped over her head and left shoulder and fastened with a broach. She looked annoyed at the intrusion but when she caught sight of Marcus her demeanour changed to one of weary reluctance.

"Is Hannibal at the gates?" she inquired tartly.

Marcus dipped his head in a respectful greeting. "I have come to ask for your help," he replied. "It is not safe for my wife and slaves to remain outside Rome. I would like to put them under your protection for a few days until I have sorted matters out."

Clodia turned to look at Flavia and then down at little Laelia who was holding her mother's hand and who looked as if she was sleep walking. Behind Flavia the faces of the slave women flickered in and out of the light.

Flavia was giving the vestal a careful examination "Can I ask you," Flavia said boldly, "how you know my husband?"

Clodia calmly fixed her eyes on Flavia. "I do not consort with men, if that is the meaning of your question my dear," she replied haughtily.

Marcus took a step forwards and gestured at Flavia.

"Lady Clodia, meet my wife Flavia, Flavia meet my sister Clodia."

"Half sister," Clodia snapped.

Flavia raised her eyebrows in surprise, then she half turned towards Marcus but he cut her off before she could open her mouth.

"I told you it's a long story," he growled. Then he looked at Clodia.

"I have urgent business with the Senate. Do you know which magistrates are in the city and where I can find them?"

Clodia was staring at Flavia. "So this is your wife, Marcus," she said as a smile appeared on her face. "It has taken you a long time to introduce us. I wonder why you delayed it for so long?" Flavia's face, cold and tired looking, darkened.

164

Then Clodia sighed. "Your wife and slaves are welcome Marcus. As for the magistrates, Livius had gone north but the other consul, Nero is in the city for a few days to attend to his religious duties."

***

Consul, Gaius Claudius Nero's house was on the Palatine hill, the most posh and desirable neighbourhood in Rome. It was here on the Palatine that Romulus, first king of Rome had founded the city five hundred and fifty years ago and the attraction of living close to such an illustrious place had never faded. Marcus banged his fist on the door of the house, shouting for it to be opened. A moment later a panel in the door slid back and a face peered out.

"What do you want? Don't you know who lives here?" a cranky voice cried out.

"Wake the Consul," Marcus snapped, "I have urgent news."

The face hesitated. Then the panel slid back and with a creak the door was opened. A big well-built man was standing in the doorway holding an oil lamp. Marcus barged past him, through the hall way and into the atrium. Lamps were glowing on all four sides of the large space and from the rooms radiating out from the atrium he could hear movement and muffled, startled voices.

Marcus turned in a full circle, not knowing where to go. The big man with the oil lamp had followed him into the atrium, he looked alarmed. Then from one of the doorways leading off towards the back of the house, four Lictor's emerged, fully dressed.

"What is the meaning of this intrusion?" a voice behind Marcus suddenly cried out, "who are you and what are you doing in my house at this hour!"

Marcus turned to see the red angry face of the Consul glaring at him. Nero was of short stature and a little overweight. His curly hair was cut short and he was clad in his long flowing white night clothes. He looked around forty-five. Behind him in the doorway of a room stood a plump middle-aged woman dressed in similar attire. Marcus dipped his head in respect.

"Forgive my sudden intrusion Sir," Marcus said. "But I bring urgent news."

Nero's face seemed to change in an instant. The anger vanished to be replaced with sudden concern.

"What has Hannibal done now?" Nero exclaimed as his face and body twitched with a violent surge of energy.

Marcus shook his head and from his tunic he retrieved a letter. He held it up for the Consul to see. Nero's eyes seemed to fix onto the parchment like a starving dog that had been presented with a bowl of meat.

"Do you have someone who can read Punic?" Marcus asked.

Nero stared at him. Then his eyes darted restlessly around the room.

"Why what is this about?" he snapped impatiently.

"You need to read this letter Sir," Marcus replied.

"The gardener," the plump woman now interrupted, "he was a prisoner of the Carthaginians in the first war. He can read Punic."

Nero half turned to look at her, squinted and then grunted.

"Fetch the gardener then," he growled.

A few moments later an old man of around sixty was herded into the atrium by two of the Lictor's. He looked confused, worried and stumbled along as if he had just been woken up. Nero pointed at the letter in Marcus's hand.

"Read it out loud," he commanded.

The atrium grew silent as the old gardener took the letter, rubbed his eyes and hesitatingly at first began to translate out loud. When he'd finally finished, a pin dropping onto the floor would have been audible.

"Well fuck me," Nero said at last, staring at Marcus in disbelief.

Chapter Twenty-Two - No surrender

Marcus and Nero stood at the corner of the street on the Caelian hill watching the heavily armed soldiers moving into position. It was just after sunrise. Marcus looked exhausted and there was grey stubble on his chin and cheeks. The soldiers moved down the street in single file, one column keeping close to the houses and the second doing the same on the other side of the road. They tried to move as silently as possible but it was difficult and the rhythmic tramp of sandals and the clanking of weapons on armour and shields could not be stifled. Nero glanced up at Marcus who was nearly a head taller than him.

"You had better be right about this," the Consul muttered, "Or else I am going to look like the arse of the century."

Marcus's face was unreadable and he did not reply. He'd begun to like the Consul. Nero had none of the usual arrogance and superiority that typified the Patrician class and the man's honest, plain speaking had made him approachable and his simple, transparent motives had made him trustable. Nero had at first been unsure of what to do. There were two legions stationed in Rome for the cities defence but Nero had muttered that he didn't have the authority to order them out of their barracks. His authority, he had explained, was limited to the area of operations which the Senate had assigned to him, namely in the south with the armies facing Hannibal. Marcus had convinced him to change his mind. The constitution be damned he'd said. There was no time to follow formal procedures. Whether it was his own exhaustion or the desire to capture Numa, he'd not shied away from boldly urging the Consul to take action and in the end Nero had.

The two legions stationed in Rome were weak formations, filled with raw recruits who were still undergoing training. The men were not expected to fight but the Triarii of the Legion raised in Etruria had been a crack formation whose men had all seen action against Hannibal. Nero had summoned its commander from his bed and given him an hour to get his men ready. The Triarii, seven hundred men strong had immediately sent half their force to the Senate house to protect the Senate for Nero had deemed it too late to cancel that day's meeting. A cavalry force had been dispatched to Numa's country house but they had soon returned reporting that the house was deserted. Marcus had wondered what had happened to Numa's children and their tutor Arkadios but there had been no time to dwell on it. The guards at all Rome's gates had been reinforced and the remaining six Maniples of Triarii, some three hundred and fifty men, had been dispatched to surround Numa's two known town houses, both of which happened to be on the Caelian. Nero and Marcus had chosen to follow the men whose task it was to surround the largest of these houses.

The soldiers led by their Centurion took up positions on each side of a black painted door of a smart two storied town house. Marcus stared at the men as they crouched along the street, gripping their seven-foot-long Hastae, spears whilst their large oval shields rested on the ground. Nero signalled the officer in charge, who nodded that he'd understood. A moment later a soldier rose to his feet and slammed his fist into the wooden door calling for the occupants to open up in the name of the Senate and People of Rome.

"Now we will have the truth," Nero muttered grimly.

Marcus' eyes were fixed on the town house. Then he caught the slight flicker of movement in one of the windows. A moment later a spear plunged through the air and impaled the soldier who had banged on the door. The man collapsed like a rag doll, his shield clattering onto the stones. The spear was followed by a sudden blood curdling yell and then a hail of spears, stones and amphorae was hurled down upon the soldiers in the street. The Centurion in charge of the assault blew his whistle as his men scrambled to raise their shields and protect themselves from the deluge.

"Got him!" Nero cried in triumph, "You were right. Numa is going to pay for this treachery, he is a dead man!"

Marcus did not reply. In the street the Triarii had rushed to form a Testudo formation and now they advanced upon the door hacking and stabbing at it with their weapons but the sturdy wood did not yield. Another blood curdling yell echoed down the street and from one of the windows a man's barefaced arse appeared. It was followed by howls of laughter from within the house. Another of the Triarii slumped down in the street blood running from a wound to his head.

"Arseholes," Nero growled, "don't they realise that they are all dead men."

The Triarii were retreating to shelter dragging three wounded comrades along with them. In the street two men lay without moving.

"The door won't yield," an Optio, a junior officer panted as he came running up the street towards Nero and Marcus. "Were going to need a battering ram to break it down Sir."

170

Nero was staring at the house. "Damned you will," he cried, "Burn them out. Set the whole place on fire, that will drive them out!"

"But the risk to the city, Sir, the fire could easily spread," the commander of the Triarii exclaimed in alarm.

"Do it, I will take responsibility," Nero snapped.

It took another hour before the unit of Cretan archers had been summoned to the street. In the meantime a crowd had gathered at either end and Nero had felt it necessary to deploy some of the Triarii to hold back the curious onlookers. In the town-house itself there had been no movement for some time and Nero looked uncomfortable.

"There is no other way out of that place is there?" he exclaimed turning to look at Marcus.

Marcus shook his head. "There is just the one door," he replied.

"We have men posted in all his neighbour's houses. They will hear it if he tries to break through one of the walls. Numa is trapped."

Nero grunted in satisfaction and nodded at the archers. "Burn it!" he growled.

The Cretans dipped their tar smeared arrows into a burning metal cauldron that had been brought up on a wagon and then taking careful aim, fired. A dense shower of arrows flew through the air, some slamming into the stone walls and tumbling uselessly to the street but others hammered into the door or

171

disappeared through the windows. A roar of fury rose from within the building and a man tried to pull the shutters across the window but he was struck by three arrows and tumbled out of the window and onto the street below. A grim cheer rose from the ranks of the Triarii waiting to storm the house. Soon thick smoke could be seen billowing from the house and rising up into the sky. Then all began to hear the crackle and roar of the flames inside. The smoke grew thicker, pouring out of the windows like a black river. Marcus, Nero, the Triarii and the crowds of onlookers fell silent as all waited for the inevitable. But the door to the house remained firmly shut.

"No one can survive that," Nero exclaimed at last. He signalled the Centurion down in the street and the officer rose to his feet, scuttled across the road and launched his foot against the door. The door resisted for a fraction of a second. Then it swung inwards twisting on one of its hinges and a blast of heat, smoke and fire surged out onto the street. The Centurion screamed as he was scalded but he managed to fling himself sideways and rolled away clutching his face.

"Alright dampen the place down," Nero cried and a long line of men carrying buckets of water, who had been waiting patiently in a side street, started towards the burning house.

***

It took two hours before the fire was finally put out. Numa's house had been reduced to a ruin. The roof had finally collapsed in on itself and the stone walls that remained were blackened and too hot to touch. Inside, the building was a chaos of burnt furniture, collapsed roof beams and debris of all kinds. Only one unconscious survivor was pulled from the rubble. The

172

others, twenty-three blackened corpses were all found in the atrium lying together. It seemed to Marcus that they had chosen to kill themselves rather than surrender. He picked his way through the debris closely followed by the Consul. There was no sign of Numa's body.

"Maybe he wasn't here after all," Nero growled pushing aside a piece of smouldering, blackened wood.

"He had no reason to think his plans were exposed," Marcus replied. "He was supposed to attend the Senate meeting today.

He wasn't at his country villa and the other house was deserted. He must have been here."

Nero beckoned to one of his Lictor's.

"Bring the prisoner round, I want to speak to him."

The prisoner was brought forward and a soldier poured a bucket of cold water over his face. Then the man was hauled up on his feet and two soldiers pinned him against a wall. The young man groaned and opened his eyes. Nero jutted his chin forwards, so that his face was very nearly touching the prisoner's nose.

"Where is your commander, where is the Senator?" Nero growled.

The man looked at the Consul without understanding. Then as his mind seemed to clear he managed a contemptuous little smile.

"Someone go and fetch my fucking gardener," Nero yelled taking a step back.

It was a while before the old man appeared in the company of two Lictor's. He looked slightly amused to be the centre of attention.

Nero was staring at the prisoner. "Translate," he commanded.

"What has happened to the Roman Senator whose house this was?"

The gardener muttered something and the prisoner spat onto the ground and snapped a few words in reply.

"He says he doesn't know what happened to him," the gardener replied.

"Ask him from where he came from?"

The gardener translated and again the prisoner gabbled a reply in his alien tongue.

"From the north Sir, they came to Rome from the north."

Nero grunted and his eyes were fixed on the prisoner's face.

"Ask him about the man who sent him. Ask him about the man called Gisgo who wrote the letter to the Senator?"

At the mention of the name Gisgo, the man's eyes darkened.

"He says Gisgo is the lord of spies and sworn enemy of Rome. He says that Gisgo will soon have your entrails hung up around the city gates of Rome."

The gardener looked nervous.

"Does he indeed," Nero' eyes narrowed. Then snatching the sword from a soldier's belt he took two steps forward and rammed the weapon into the prisoners eye. The metal sank into the skull with a sickening crack and blood sprayed across Nero's fine white toga. Nero turned away and calmly wiped the blood from his face. Behind him the two soldiers allowed the corpse to flop to the ground.

"Sir, Sir over here," a soldier called from within the smouldering ruins of the house. Nero and Marcus picked their way through the debris until they were level with the man who had called out.

"Sir," the soldier said looking down at the floor. Marcus and Nero followed the man's gaze. Half hidden under a pile of fallen masonry lay the bodies of two children and a adult man. Nero bent down and carefully turned the corpse of the man over onto his back. Then the consul sighed in disappointment. Marcus sighed as he recognised Arkadios. The tutor it seemed had died trying to protect Numa's two children.

"He brought his children here," Nero muttered in dismay. "What kind of a father would put his children in the front line?"

"A sick, ruined, twisted man," Marcus muttered.

"Consul, something else, over here," another soldiers cry jerked both Nero and Marcus' attention away from the corpses.

They climbed back through the debris until they came to the furthest corner of the house from the street. A few soldiers were gathered around something on the floor. Nero and Marcus pushed their way to the front. Before them, set in the floor stones was a dark gaping hole just wide enough to allow a man to squeeze through. One of the soldiers idly pushed a stone into the hole with his foot. It took a few seconds before they heard the sharp clattering impact.

"So this is how he got out," Marcus muttered.

"But where can it lead?" Nero frowned.

"I don't know for sure," Marcus was staring down the spider hole, "but my guess is that the tunnel would connect with the Cloaca Maxima. Once he's in the great sewers he could get out into the Tiber."

"If he could get out, why didn't they all get out? Why did he leave his children behind? It doesn't make sense," Nero shook his head.

Marcus shrugged. "Maybe he didn't tell the Carthaginians about the escape tunnel. Maybe he thought his children would slow him down. Who knows?"

Marcus turned to Nero with a sudden urgency as the Consul grunted and began to make his way back to the street.

"Sir, if he manages to get across the Tiber he could take the road to Ostia and try and get aboard a ship from there, or he could go north along the Via Aurelia or south along the Appian Way. We should send patrols out along all those routes right
176

away. The harbour authorities at Ostia need to be warned and any ships in the port searched. You should send a dispatch to all the neighbouring towns reporting what has happened and ask the local authorities to be on the lookout."

Nero laughed. "Numa is not going anywhere. His actions are known to all in the Senate now. He is a ruined man, who can't ever show his face in Rome again. Let the matter rest with that."

The two of them stepped back onto the street. The Triarii had lifted their crowd control and people were milling about trying to get a glimpse of what was going on. Marcus suddenly saw Flavia standing amongst the crowd and shot her a warning look.

"Sir, I think we should hunt him down. It would be unwise to let him escape and flee to our enemies," Marcus said pressing the matter.

Nero stopped and turned to look at Marcus. There was a hint of irritation on his face and in his voice as he spoke.

"You did well to warn me," the Consul said, "The Senate will extend their gratitude to you for what you have done, but the resources of the Republic are not to be used to settle some private score that you say that you have with that man. I can't afford to have all these soldiers combing the countryside for just one fugitive. We are at war. I am returning south to my command, the day after tomorrow. I cannot spare the time or the men. Let Numa run and go into exile forever."

"The gratitude of the Senate," a single shrill voice suddenly cried out. "My husband has gone ten thousand Denarius into debt so that he could save the Senate, and you talk about gratitude. Well you can stuff your gratitude up your fat, corrupt arses, the lot of you!"

Flavia's cheeks were flushed with anger. Her hands were clenched into fists and they shook with emotion as Nero turned to stare at her in surprise.

Chapter Twenty-Three - A father's decision

Marcus was in his field, bent over hacking away at the stubborn tree root with his pickaxe. He should have delegated the work to a slave but Marcus had never been able to sit and watch others do all the hard work on his farm. He was naked from the waist up and on his head he wore a wide brimmed hat. It was near noon and the day's heat was climbing and his body was soaked in sweat. Scattered around the field his slaves were planting that year's crops. It had been two days since Numa had escaped from his burning house. The male slaves had looked relieved when Marcus, Flavia and the women had returned to the farm. Marcus had noticed the change in their attitude, a slight warming of relations between them and he'd put it down to the letters granting them their freedom. It had made him think about the day when he would have to release them.

Flavia had argued with him the whole way back to the farm. He'd scolded her for her plain speaking before the Consul. He'd been angry at her lack of respect for the office that Nero held but he'd been unable to silence her. The Senate were a group of overweening, pompous pricks, Numa was a demon and lady Clodia was a stuck-up bitch! Marcus had endured his wives tongue lashing in stubborn silence for he'd known that once she was in this kind of mood, nothing would shut her up. The worst moment had come when she'd asked him what he was going to do now. He'd told her that he intended to return to his fields and plant his crops. What about Numa, are you just going to let him get away? she'd snapped. Marcus had taken her hand and had gripped it tightly. He had done everything he could he had explained but now he needed to look after what remained of his family. He had to look after the farm and to ensure that his family survived. He was not going to allow Numa to ruin and destroy more than he already had. Favia had refused to speak to him after that conversation and a whole day had passed in complete, sulking silence.

"Master, look, visitors," the Gallic boy who was working close to him said suddenly pointing towards the farm gate.

Marcus grimaced and slowly straightened his back, glancing as he did so at the gate. Then he swore out loud. Waiting patiently along the track were twelve Lictor's standing in two columns of six on each side of the path. At their head stood a short, slightly overweight man and bringing up the rear was a troop of cavalrymen, their armour and weapons glinting in the sunlight. One of them was holding a standard on a thin wooden pole crowned by the silver figure of a wolf. Marcus slammed his axe into the earth, wiped his hands on his legs and started towards the gate.

"Consul," he said dipping his head respectfully as he opened the gate. Nero and his twelve Lictor's marched into the courtyard. Nero was dressed for war and was in full armour and travelling gear. He turned in a full circle examining the farm and then smiled at Marcus.

"Come into my house Sir," Marcus said, "I shall serve you some of my wine."

"Only if it's home grown," Nero replied.

"It is Sir," Marcus gestured towards the doorway of the farm, "I am honoured by your visit."

Nero stepped through the doorway and Marcus hustled him into the long room. Then he took a small amphora down from a shelf and poured the dark red wine into two cups. As he did so Nero glanced around the room.

"A good home Marcus, you have a good home," the Consul said with a nod.

Marcus nodded his appreciation and handed Nero the cup of wine. As he did so Flavia appeared in the kitchen doorway. She folded her arms across her chest. Nero caught sight of her and a faint smile appeared on his face.

"I am on my way south, back to my command," he said turning to Marcus.

"Then you have come the wrong way," Flavia muttered.

"I have come to your farm Marcus," Nero continued ignoring Flavia, "to give you the official gratitude of the Senate. The Republic is grateful for your service."

"Is the Republic grateful too for the sacrifice that we women are making," Flavia snapped. "You take away our sons, our fathers and husbands and forbid us from wearing our jewellery. When can we expect the Oppian law to be repealed?"

For a moment Nero's face coloured in a slight blush but he refused to look at or reply to Flavia. Instead his eyes remained fixed on Marcus.

"I have also come with a proposal of my own. Why don't you come with me? I could use a man like you on my staff. There is
181

something that I like about this Gisgo, the Carthaginian who wrote that letter. Lord of spies, I need a lord of spies Marcus and I can't think of a better man for the position than you. What do you say?"

Slowly Marcus placed his cup back onto the table. "I have served Rome during sixteen campaigning seasons Sir," he replied in a quiet voice, "but my place is here now with my family and my farm. I thank you for your offer but I must refuse."
Nero looked disappointed.

"The thing about war that excites so many men," he said at last, "is not the chance to close with the enemy but the chance that battle provides to a man for self enrichment. You know this Marcus. You know that a soldier can enrich himself with the spoils of war. Come with me to the south, face Hannibal and I will ensure that you will get your share of the spoils, a share that will outstrip anything that you owe to the money lenders. Does that not constitute providing for your family?"

Nero had spoken well and for a moment Marcus hated him for it. He glanced at Flavia.

"Consul," he replied, "If I may have a moment alone with my wife."

Nero glanced at Flavia. Then without another word he walked out of the room.

Once they were alone Marcus turned to his wife. "I can't just leave the farm, I am needed here."

"I will cope, the farm will cope" she said advancing towards him.

Her expression had changed. "The Consul is right, this is our chance to repay the loans. Besides," Flavia said with a faint smile, "You know that you want to go."

Marcus looked at her for a long moment in silence.

"I may not come back," he grunted.

"I know that," Flavia said halting before him. "But it is the right thing to do. We have been here before, haven't we?"

Marcus nodded and then gently he stretched out his hand and ran it affectionately along her cheek.

"True to the end," he said leaning his forehead against hers.

"True to the end," Flavia whispered fiercely.

Chapter Twenty-Four - Mare Nostrum

The prow of the Mars rose and pitched as the galley ploughed through the choppy sea. A strong western wind pushed the vessel along, filling the ship's sails which bulged and strained at their moorings. Gaius stared out across the sea, his hands gripping the boat's side as the vessel groaned, pitched and plunged. The crests of the waves were tipped white and now and then a big wave slammed into the galley sending stinging seawater cascading onto the deck. The captain of the Mars had ordered the oars to be brought inside and they now lay carefully stowed along the sides of the ship. The rowers sat about in small groups, dozing, eating or gambling. In between them the wounded soldiers had tried to find whatever shelter they could from the biting wind and cold seawater.

To port, separated by a length of two cables he could see the Minerva and the Neptune, one following the other, crashing through the waves. In the dusk he could just make out their captains standing beside their masts peering at the gloomy grey horizon. The ships had followed the example of the Mars and had withdrawn their oars. Gaius turned and caught sight of the Isis behind him. The vessel was pitching and rising like the rest and he wondered how his wife and son would be coping. It was their first time on the sea. Then he wrenched forward and was violently sick for the third time that day.

Behind him he heard someone laughing. He wiped his mouth and turned round. Hanno stood by the mast of the ship grinning. With his one hand he was steadying himself against the wooden pole.

"Not used to the sea are you?" he cried cheerfully. "Ah the sea, the sea, the sea," the Carthaginian seemed to grow nostalgic as he turned to look around him. "It is the sea that made Carthage great you know. It is the sea which gave us the greatest empire that the world has known. We should be eternally grateful for what she has done for us."

Gaius spat overboard and then unsteadily made his way onto the middle of the deck and began to check up on his wounded men.

"Ah if only you knew the treasures and knowledge that is contained in the libraries of Carthage," Hanno went on, "You would know the secrets of the world. They have been gathered together over many centuries Gaius. They say that a man can learn enough for a lifetime by spending just one day in Carthage. One of my forefathers was Hanno the navigator, a great man. Have you heard of him Gaius?"

Gaius shook his head. Around him he could hear the wounded muttering. Arrogant prick, shut him up, who is this twat, Carthaginian arse. Gaius smiled to himself. It was true he thought, Hanno was showing off his knowledge and education. He glanced up at the one-armed man but Hanno had not seemed to notice the discord he was creating.

"Hanno the navigator, you have never heard of him, oh dear boy," Hanno continued as his eyes seemed to fix on the horizon.

"Two hundred years ago or so Hanno, my forefather, was ordered to explore the western coast of Africa with a fleet of ships. He sailed through the Pillars of Hercules and then turned south. He was gone for two years. He founded new Punic
185

colonies along the African coast as far south as where the great sand desert gives way to the forests and the skin colour of men changes to black. I haven't got time to tell you about everything he saw and did for he had so many adventures I could write a book about them. No, I won't bore you."

Hanno looked down at Gaius who was examining a head wound.

"But do you know what the greatest secret was that he discovered out there on the ocean," Hanno was pointing with his finger to the west.

"A fucking cork," a soldier cried and his words were followed by a roar of laughter. "Shut up you Punic arse," another voice cried.

Hanno ignored the cries of protest. He fixed his gaze on Gaius who was smiling.

"Hanno was blown off course one day," the Carthaginian continued, his eyes widening. "The storm was terrible and when it was over, Hanno found himself all alone on the ocean, a single ship in the middle of nowhere." The Carthaginian tutor wagged his finger in the air. "My forefather found land out there, far to the west, beyond the ocean, he discovered a whole new continent filled with strange peoples, animals and plants the like of which has never been seen before. I am telling you, there is a new world beyond the western ocean."

"Well why don't you go there and leave us in peace," a rower bellowed and his cry was followed by raucous laughter.

Hanno sniffed in disgust and fell silent.

"Sir, look," one of the sailors suddenly cried out pointing, "the Minerva and the Neptune are changing course. They are heading towards the coast."

All eyes on the Mars swivelled round to stare to port. The two ships that had been sailing parallel to the Mars were indeed changing course and moving away from them towards the distant smudge on the horizon that was land. For a moment no one spoke.

"Fools," the Captain of the Mars exclaimed, "They are heading off too soon."

"Captain," Hanno interrupted, "You know as well as I do that we are running into a storm. Is it not better to head for land now and ride out the storm ashore?"

The captain's eye twitched in annoyance. "Yes in normal circumstances that is the case," he snapped, "but I know these coasts better than any man alive and if they continue on that course they are going to be dashed to pieces on the rocks. We must keep to the open sea for at least another hour."

"The Isis is following them," a voice cried out.

Gaius rose to his feet and grabbed hold of the mast to steady himself. Sure enough the Isis which had been following behind them was veering away after her two sister ships.

"I am not following them," the captain snapped, "not if you want to drown and be smashed to pieces on the shore. They will have to take their chances."

Gaius felt his heart hammering inside his chest as he watched the Isis fade away into the gathering gloom.

"I do hope Sir, that you are right," Hanno said primly, "for I have no desire to be shipwrecked twice in a single month."

***

The storm finally blew itself out just before sunrise the following morning. All that night as the Mars had tried to maintain her course she had been thrown about on the wild, boiling sea, buffeted by huge waves and driven on by a mighty howling wind and lashing rain. Five men had disappeared overboard, their cries lost in the shrieking, howling night. Now as the seas calmed the survivors huddled together around the mast, sodden, pale and exhausted.

Gaius sat on the deck, he was drenched and his head rested wearily against the side of the ship. His eyes were closed. The Mars had done well to survive. Structurally the sturdy little Bireme looked undamaged but her deck was a mess. Several oars had vanished overboard as had most of the men's belongings that had not been fastened down. To the east, a new sun was rising up out of the sea. There was no sign of land anywhere, just an endless expanse of water.

Gaius's eyes opened as someone knelt down beside him and shook him. It was Hanno. The Carthaginian looked exhausted but there was a cheerful grin on his face. He offered Gaius a small cup of water and the young man took it gratefully.

"The gods have smiled on us," Hanno muttered sitting down painfully beside him. Gaius nodded but said nothing. He closed his eyes once more. Would his wife and son have made it to shore before the storm had struck? The uncertainty of not knowing was eating him up and he forced himself to think of something else but there were no other thoughts in his mind.

"They will have made it," Hanno said as if reading his mind. Conspiratorially the Carthaginian leaned towards Gaius and raised his eyebrows. "Personally I think our Captain is an idiot, we could been safe and dry ashore last night. But in my experience all captains are a bunch of stubborn old dogs. This one is no exception."

"Sails to starboard!" a voice suddenly cried out.

Gaius opened his eyes and blinked. Then he scrambled to his feet and stared out across the sea in sudden excitement. Three white sails had appeared on the horizon. The ships were bearing down on them fast.

"Who are they?" the captain shouted.

The galley fell silent as all waited for the man on look out, high up in the mast, to reply. The lookout seemed to be taking his time.

"They are not ours," he cried at last, his voice drooping in disappointment.

A pained expression appeared on Gaius' face and his shoulders drooped. He stared at the three ships as they closed in. The galleys were coming on, spread out in a single line. Now that they were closer he could see that they were Liburnian's, small but fast vessels. Without warning the two flanking ships suddenly changed course and began to envelop the Roman galley, one to the left and one to the right. Gaius noticed the colour drain from the captain's face.

"Ligurian Pirates," the man murmured to himself and a moment later his cry was heard by all onboard. "Pirates, get to the oars! For fuck's sake move!"

For a split second stunned silence ruled aboard but then the rowers rushed and scattered to their positions but the crew and men were in a pitiful state and Gaius knew with a sudden clarity that the galley was doomed. The men were exhausted and in no fit state to fight and the Mars wallowed and rolled helplessly in the waves. There was no way they were going to outrun the swift vessels that were bearing down on them. The captain screamed his orders and had managed to raise the sail when the lead pirate vessel shot passed on the port side, no more than two oars length away. Gaius caught sight of a line of men with bows standing on her deck. He screamed a warning and tackled Hanno to the ground just as a volley of arrows thudded into the Mars. Men screamed as they were hit, others toppled overboard to be swiftly lost beneath the waves.

The captain of the Mars was still yelling orders but no one seemed to be listening to him anymore. Gaius cautiously raised his head and stared over the side of the ship. One of the flanking galleys was approaching the Mars at full speed, her prow cutting towards him as her bank of oars plied the sea in perfect harmony. His eyes widened as he caught a glimpse of the bronze tipped battering ram that was aimed straight into the flank of the Mars.

"They are going to ram us!" he screamed.

The captain whirled round at the sound of Gaius' warning, his mouth opening in silent dismay as he caught sight of the new threat. Then a second volley of arrows hammered into the Mars and the Captain was hit twice and plunged onto the deck. Gaius hugged the deck, trying to keep his body as low as possible. Around him men were screaming and yelling in terror and confusion.

"Overboard," he whispered furiously to Hanno who was lying beside him trying to cover his head with his hands, "we must get overboard before they ram us."

The Carthaginian was whimpering in fright. Gaius took a deep breath, struggled to his feet, grabbed Hanno under his armpits and heaved him up before flinging himself and Hanno over the side of the galley and into the sea. The water was cold and Gaius gasped in shock. He took in a mouthful of green salty water and spluttered and coughed as he surfaced. At his side Hanno was struggling in the sea, his one arm clutching at the sky in terror. Gaius cleared his face and stared around him. The Mars was only a few feet away. Then with a sickening crunch and crack of splintering wood, the Pirate vessel was upon her and the bronze tipped ram drove remorselessly into the side of the wooden boat. The Mars groaned as a huge hole was torn in her side through which sea water began to pour. Onboard the Pirate vessel Gaius caught sight of figures leaping onto the deck of the Mars and the terrified screams of men as the pirates methodically began to knife all onboard. A dying rower tumbled into the sea close to Gaius and the waves pressed the corpse up against the hull of the Mars. Hanno had found his voice and was yelling and screaming. Gaius lifted his arm out of the water and punched the Carthaginian on the head. On receiving his second punch Hanno fell silent, his eyes turning to stare at Gaius in absolute terror.

The two of them floated in the sea, unseen and unnoticed, between the two ships as onboard the Mars the slaughter of wounded Roman soldiers continued. The Mars itself was dying too. The water flooding into her hull was dragging the boat down and pieces of wreckage and flotsam had begun to appear around the doomed galley. A galley bench, wrenched from its joints banged and pushed up against the groaning hull of the ship. Without thinking Gaius raised his arm once more, took a firm hold of Hanno's hair and dragged the Carthaginian onto the half-submerged bench. Hanno grabbed hold of the flotsam and clamped himself to it like a limpid. Then with his remaining strength Gaius kicked against the side of the sinking boat and holding onto the wood with one hand he began to swim away.

He didn't stop swimming until they were a good hundred yards away. Every moment he expected a shout or an arrow or spear to be launched in his direction but none came. Finally, too exhausted to continue, he simply hung onto the half-submerged wood and turned to stare at the battle. The Mars was going down and the sound of battle had ceased. On the deck of the sinking ship he could see the pirates stripping the dead of their valuables. If only one of them looked in their direction. Then it would all be over.

Gaius spluttered as he took in another gulp of sea water and in this very moment, when his life was in the balance, he found himself thinking about his father. Whatever you do in life, the old man had once told him, do it properly. He wanted to laugh. It was an insane thought but his father's voice seemed to come and go inside his head like trumpets that faded and grew and faded again. He knew he could not last for much longer and with a mighty effort he hauled his body half out of the water and onto the bench. His cheeks rested on the wood and a few inches away he saw Hanno staring at him with wide blood shot eyes.

"I can't swim," the Carthaginian whispered.

Chapter Twenty-Five - The ties of guest hospitality

Slowly the blurred shapes and images began to focus and sharpen. Gaius groaned and rolled onto his back. He could hear the roar and crash of waves breaking onto the rocks and the hiss and bubble of the sea as it surged forwards and backwards up the beach. His eyes flickered open as the bright sun warmed his cheeks. Then he sat up and wiped the sand from his face and as he did so the tide, as if in a final attempt, surged forwards encircling him in sea water, trying to drag him back into the sea. He stared at the water as it retreated. His head hurt. Memories were crowding in his mind like patient messengers who'd waited all night to tell him their news. He remembered the cold water, the saltiness of it on his lips, the endless rocking of the waves, the thirst, the terrible thirst. He turned and looked down the beach. Another body lay a few yards away. Gaius blinked and tried to focus. Then at last he saw the faint rise and fall of the man's chest. Hanno had made it too.

Gaius crawled over to Hanno and slapped him roughly on the cheeks. The Carthaginian stirred and muttered words that Gaius couldn't understand. Then he lifted himself up onto his elbow and was violently sick. Gaius sank back into the sand as Hanno continued to bring up a mixture of bile and sea water.

"Where are we?" Hanno muttered at last.

"I have no idea," Gaius replied turning his head to look around.

The small beach they found themselves on was covered in beautiful, pure white sand. Gaius craned his head to look into the sun. The cliffs towered above them and beyond them the steep green mountains seemed to come right up to the edge of the sea. A seagull hung overhead its beady eye watching them.

Hanno ran his hand over his head and sat up. His face looked pale and there was a dark cut on his forehead where the blood had clotted. He was panting lightly as he stared at Gaius and Gaius could see that he too was remembering what had happened to them.

"If I remember correctly," Hanno exclaimed at last, "You have saved my life four times now."

Gaius frowned.

"The first time when you cut off my arm, dear boy. The second time when you saved me from the salt mines, the third-time onboard ship when the pirates shot arrows at us and then a final time when we were in the water."

Hanno's eyes gleamed with a sudden resolve. "Aristide has made her will clear. I shall serve you Gaius until the end of my days."

Gaius looked solemn.

"I shall hold you to our bargain, nothing more," he replied.

But Hanno shook his head.

"No Gaius, I shall serve you and your house until the end of my days. I will not change my mind. Matters are clear to me now. All this, everything that has happened to me, it was meant to happen."
195

Gaius took a deep breath and scrutinised Hanno carefully.

"But tell me one thing," Hanno continued, "why save my worthless soul? Why did you do it?"

Gaius stared at Hanno and then slowly a smile crept onto his face.

"You have a valuable mind," he replied, "the rest of you is worthless but I respect that head of yours. Make sure you don't lose it."

Hanno grinned and plopped back onto the sand, staring up at the sun.

"I think it best if we try and head for Rome," Gaius muttered looking around him. "My wife and son either drowned or they have got through safely. Either way I won't find the answers here. We must be a hundred miles from where we last saw them. If the convoy got through then they will know about it at Ostia."

Hanno nodded, "Good solid Roman reasoning," he replied.

Then his smile faded and he sat up in alarm.

"Look," he cried, pointing, "there on the cliffs."

Gaius scrambled to his feet and stared in the direction that Hanno was pointing. Then he saw them too. High up, along what looked like a path, stood a man and a boy. They were staring down at the beach and the two ship wrecked men.

***

The Ligurian village nestled high up in the mountains on a rough sloping, boulder strewn plateau between two rugged peaks. The two shepherds had agreed to take them to their village. They had seemed friendly enough and had given Gaius and Hanno their water skins. Gaius and Hanno had taken them gratefully and the cold crisp mountain water had soon renewed their strength. The man had said little and the boy had kept staring at them as if he had never seen other people before. Gaius and Hanno paused at the top of the path to catch their breath. Far below them they could see the blue sea stretching to the horizon. The village itself was a collection of rough and simple huts made of stone, wood and animal hides and slightly above the village the mountainside opened up to reveal the dark entrance to a cave.

People were gathering to stare at the strangers as the shepherd conversed in a low voice with an old red bearded man who seemed to be village leader. The old bearded man kept glancing in their direction.

"Who do you think they are? Celts?" Gaius said uneasily.

Hanno was staring at the villagers.

"Ligurian's," he said at last. "They are too small and skinny to be Gaul's."

"Same people as those pirates," Gaius muttered.

Hanno nodded. "The Ligurians are no friends of Rome, Gaius. They are allied to Carthage. You may want to conceal who you really are."

There was no more time for talking. The village leader was striding towards them. He was a tall, sinewy man dressed in a simple white woollen tunic. He looked around sixty and his face was deeply tanned. He stopped before Gaius and Hanno and placed his hands on his hips.

"Who are you?" he said in broken Latin.

"My name is Gaius and this is my servant," Gaius replied gesturing at Hanno.

"The ship that we were travelling on sank. I only ask you for some food and a place to rest. Then we shall be on our way again."

"You are a Roman," there was a sudden gleam in the old man's eyes.

Gaius nodded. "I am a Roman citizen."

At his side Gaius sensed Hanno stir in dismay.

The village leader was studying Gaius with a curious look. Then he turned to his villagers.

"Fetch some food and drink for these men," he yelled. Then he stepped forwards and to Gaius's surprise stretched out his arm.

"Romans are welcome here," the old man muttered. "Do you know a Senator, by chance, in Rome called Quintus Decius Mus? He is our representative in the Senate. He looks after the interests of our tribe. He is a good friend of my people."

Gaius took the man's hand in greeting and shook his head.

"I am sorry, I have not heard of him."

"Never mind," the bearded man replied. "it doesn't matter. You are a lucky man though. Further up the coast the tribes are hostile to Rome, all the way down to the very borders of Etruria. Their young men are leaving their homes to go and join Hasdrubal. But we have friends to our north. The Taurini are hostile to Carthage. They have a deep feud with their neighbours the Insubres. They hate Hannibal for the Insubres were Hannibal's allies and it was Hannibal who besieged and destroyed the Taurini's principal town."

"Hasdrubal," Gaius exclaimed, "has he crossed the Alps?"

The village leader nodded sourly. "He has," he replied turning to give Hanno a careful examination.

Gaius looked thoughtful. "Have any other Roman ships passed this way in the last couple of days? Three ships sailing together perhaps? "

The village leader shrugged. "We have not seen any Roman ships no. But a galley from Rome is expected any day now. When it arrives you and your slave will be able to return to Rome onboard it."

Gaius looked disappointed but he nodded in gratitude nevertheless.

"Tonight," the bearded man suddenly grinned revealing a toothless mouth, "we celebrate the wedding of my granddaughter. I hope that you will join us."

Gaius managed a smile, "An honour Sir," he replied.

***

It was night. The bon fire crackled and roared as its flames leapt up into the cool mountain air. Nearby a whole sheep was roasting on a metal spit. The villagers sat gathered around the fire in a large circle watching the twirling dancer as she whirled and twisted around the fire. Someone was banging on a drum and the villagers were clapping, hooting and singing. The bride and her groom sat together on the other side of the fire. Gaius and Hanno had been given the honour of sitting beside the red bearded village elder and his wife. They were drinking cups of wine from a large earthen amphora. Gaius noticed that Hanno was drinking heavily. The experience at sea must have rattled him more than he cared to admit.

When the dance finished the dancer bowed low to the newly married couple and the village elder rose to his feet. Walking around the fire he began to recite a story about the virtues of marriage, the commitments and duties, the dangers and the morality. Gaius glanced round at the villagers. They had begun to look bored but they remained silent out of respect for their elder. No doubt they had heard the whole tale many times before. Gaius suppressed a smile. He glanced at Hanno but the Carthaginian did not seem to be listening either. He was staring at the village elder's wife, a woman half the age of her husband. There was a sullen look on her face as she stared at her husband.

The village elder's story finished and was followed by some polite clapping. Gaius dipped his cup into the amphorae of wine and was about to bring the cup to his lips when he became conscious that all eyes around the fire were staring at him.

"We don't have any theatres or actors or arena's in our village," the village leader said turning to Gaius with a near apologetic look, "our only form of entertainment are our stories and it is our tradition that strangers, who share our hospitality, leave us with a story of their own, so please..." The village leader opened his arms wide and gestured at the villagers.

Gaius threw the contents of his cup down his throat in one go. Suddenly he was glad that the darkness hid most of his face for no one could see him blush. He hated public speaking.

"Hanno, tell them the story about your grandfather, the navigator," he ordered.

Hanno seemed to be jerked back to reality. Cautiously he glanced sideways at Gaius.

"He was not my grandfather, he lived over two hundred years ago," he muttered. Gaius smiled at the villagers and gestured for Hanno to get on with it.

Hanno rose to his feet and slowly at first, but then gaining in enthusiasm and vigour, he began to recount the tale of Hanno the navigator's adventures on the outer ocean. The faces of the villagers, who had looked bored only a few moments before, became transformed as they listened, and not a sound could be heard apart from Hanno's voice and the steady roar of the fire. Gaius smiled as he saw that his slave was beginning to enjoy himself.

"On his return to Carthage and on hearing his tale of a new continent beyond the western ocean," Hanno cried, "It was decided by the city's elders that an expedition of twenty ships and three thousand colonists should be sent across the ocean with the purpose of colonising these new lands. The leader of the expedition was an admiral Himilco and he and his fleet duly left Carthage that same year."

Hanno paused and turned in a circle to look at the villagers.

"They were never heard of again. No one knows whether they were caught in a storm or if they made it to this new land that my illustrious forefather had named, New Phoenicia. So after two years had passed and still no news of the expeditions fate had been received," Hanno paused for dramatic effect, "the priests of Tanit and Melcart forbade further crossings of the ocean. Hanno the navigators notes and logs were burnt and all mention of New Phoenicia was forbidden, for the priests had become worried that others, foreigners, Greeks and yes Romans may one day follow Hanno the navigators route and seize their colony. So, over time, the crossing of the outer ocean was forgotten and the memory of this new world lost. But there were a few of us who did not forget and who still wonder what happened to Himilco and his three thousand colonists. The truth lies out there, where the sun sets."

Hanno fell silent. Around him the villagers gazed at him in spellbound awe. Then the village elder rose once more to his feet. He turned to look at Gaius with a curious expression.

"A fine story," he muttered, "But you do keep odd company. Your servant is a Carthaginian, his people are at war with you. Do you have no fear that he will one-day knife you in the back and run off with your purse?"

Gaius gestured for Hanno to sit down. Then he looked up at the village elder. He was beginning to feel the effects of the wine.

"Oh I don't fear him, he's 'armless," Gaius chuckled at his own joke.

Around him however the villagers remained silent and so too did their elder. Gaius cleared his throat. "He is sworn to me and not the kind of man who will break his oath," he said hastily.

The village elder muttered something to himself and then glared at Hanno.

"I will accept your word," he said in a louder voice, "but the men of Carthage are not welcome here. Hannibal and now Hasdrubal," he spat the names out as if they were poison, "they come into our land and tempt our young men away from their families and their tribes and then they lead them to their deaths, all for the sake of a little glittering gold. What do we gain from this?"

Gaius nodded. "Well spoken Sir," he replied.

The village elder grumbled. Then he sat down beside his wife and men began to cut up the roasting sheep and serve the meat. Gaius ran his hand over his head. He'd drank too much and suddenly he felt tired. He lifted his head and glanced at the stars wishing suddenly that his wife and son were with him. He would find them. They would be alright. He would do as the village elder had suggested. He would rest here in the village and then when the Roman ship, that the elder had talked about, arrived they would take her back to Rome. At Ostia, someone surely would know what happened to the rest of the convoy.

Something woke Gaius that night. He lay in the simple hut staring up at the dark conical roof. He could hear nothing. He rubbed his eyes wondering what it was that had woken him. Then he glanced across the floor at Hanno, but the spot where the Carthaginian had been sleeping was empty. Gaius sat up in alarm, suddenly fully awake. Where had his slave gone? Rising to his feet he poked his head out of the doorway. The night sky was quiet. The village was fast asleep and the great bonfire had been reduced to a pile of glowing embers. He jerked his head up. A torch was burning inside the cave mouth. He blinked. He was sure that there had been no light there when he'd gone to bed.

Careful to avoid tripping he made his way across the short distance that separated the cave from the village. Far below him he could make out the dark blue of the sea against the blackness of the night. As he approached the cave a figure rushed past him and he froze in shock but the person didn't seem to notice him and he or she was gone within a few moments, swallowed up in the night. Gaius' breath came in shallow gasps. Then he crossed the final few yards to the cave mouth. A single burning torch had been placed in a crack in the rocks. Gaius paused as he heard a grunting noise and then small, panted gasps. He peered around the corner and into the cave. Hanno stood with his back to him, completely naked pumping his pelvis into a naked woman. She stood, legs spread out, half bent over, her hands gripping the cave wall. Hanno's single hand had clamped itself onto the woman's neck as he rhythmically thrust himself inside her. As Gaius watched the woman arched her back and squealed and a moment later Hanno gave a loud grunt of satisfaction and buried his head in the woman's neck. They hung there for a moment. Then Hanno stepped back and the woman turned round and Gaius caught sight of her face. It was the village elder's wife.

She smiled at Hanno and without saying a word began to dress herself. Hanno sat down on a rock, still naked and watched her as she put on her clothes. Then with a farewell smile his eyes followed her as she stepped out of the cave. Gaius flattened himself against the rock face as the woman passed by within a couple of yards but she didn't see him. He waited until she was gone. Then he stepped boldly into the cave. Hanno jumped in shock and emitted a strangled cry as Gaius appeared.

Gaius ran both his hands through his hair as he stared at his servant in dismay. "What have you done, you fool!" he hissed.

"Do you know who that was?"

"His wife," Hanno had managed to recover from his shock.

Gaius raised his hand in exasperation. "Yes his wife. Oh you fool. When the village elder finds out he's going to have us thrown from the cliff top." Gaius pointed his finger accusingly at Hanno, "Of all the women you have to fuck, you have to choose his wife, the wife of our host, the man who has so generously provided us with everything we need. And this is how you honour his hospitality."

"Well he deserved it," Hanno replied with a hurt expression, "He shouldn't have suggested that I was a thief and a murderer."

It was Gaius' turn to emit a strangled cry.

"Besides she was gagging for it," Hanno continued. "I saw it in her eyes when I was telling my story. If he can't keep his wife happy, that's no concern of mine. Anyway he will never find out. She won't tell him."

"You were seen," Gaius hissed. He glanced round. "Someone saw you. I nearly ran into them on the path. Get dressed, I know where they keep their horses, we'll take them. We got to leave now before things get ugly."

Hanno nodded and began to gather his clothes.

"Sorry Gaius," he mumbled as he dressed. "I suppose this means we are not going to Rome onboard that ship after all."

"No," Gaius shook his head in irritation, "Plans have changed."

He closed his eyes as he tried to picture the last map of northern Italy he'd seen. "If the Ligurian's further along the coast are hostile and preparing for war," he said with his eyes still closed, "then we had best avoid them. The Taurini however are no friends of Carthage. The closest Roman colony from here, I reckon, is Placentia. We'll head there first. Then from there onwards to Rome."

"You will find them Gaius," Hanno said trying to sound comforting, as he struggled into his clothes.

Chapter Twenty-Six - The singing wives

Livia stood beside the roasting pig and stared at Getorix. The tavern was slowly coming back to life after her song had silenced the drinkers. Livia felt exhausted. She had never ever done something like that before. She had never dared to sing before anyone but little Laelia. The song had released something, an emotion inside her, a deep sense of satisfaction and trumping her tiredness was a growing sense of excitement.

"Drusilla sends her greetings," she said remembering the Sybil's words. Getorix was a tall powerful looking man with a black beard. He was wearing a green cloak with a white border and he looked around thirty. He stared back at her coolly but at the mention of Drusilla's name his eyes flickered in recognition.

"What do you want?" he said brusquely as Livia approached. The people in the tavern had begun to resume their conversations as the tavern returned to its previous loud, chaotic state.

Livia paused to examine Getorix. Sitting around the druid were half a dozen, tough and hard looking men. They all had dark beards and there was no hiding their hostile, aggressive attitude.

"I was told that you know where I can find Titus?"

"I don't know any Titus, go and look somewhere else. This is no place to be asking questions."

"I think you do know who Titus is," Livia replied lifting her chin stubbornly.

Getorix had already turned his back on her. Now he paused and slowly turned to look at her again and as he did so Livia knew with a sudden insight that this man would never be her friend. There was a hostility, an anger about him that could not be reconciled. Getorix eyes narrowed and Livia suddenly felt scared. Getorix was a violent man, a man who only needed a small provocation to start a fight. He was just like her she thought, violent and aggressive, but he was a grown man, far stronger than she was.

"Are you calling me a liar?" he said in a tone that sent a shiver down her back.

She shook her head and bit her lip. Getorix glared at her. Then he gestured to the men around the table and they rose and began to make their way to the tavern door. Getorix turned to look at Livia.

"Who are you?" he snapped harshly in his guttural Latin.

"I am his sister," she replied mustering up all her remaining courage.

For a moment Getorix looked surprised. Then a faint smile appeared on his face but the smile was cold and contemptuous.

"Like I said, I don't know any Titus. Drusilla made it all up." Then he stepped out of the door and was gone.

Livia's shoulders drooped as the door slammed shut. The encounter with Getorix had scared her. She'd never been afraid of the boys who had taunted Laelia or the farm hands who had leered at her, but this man, he scared her more than any man ever had. She blinked and turned to look at the people in the tavern. Had her whole long journey been for nothing? Had the old Sybil really been talking nonsense?

Livia was suddenly conscious that she was surrounded by four women. They were older than her. They crowded around her staring at her with stern faces and their arms were folded across their chests.

"Gods, girl you do have a voice," one of them, a woman with red hair exclaimed.

"How old are you? Where have you come from?" another with black hair asked.

Livia looked startled. "From Rome," she muttered distracted.

The red head nodded, "That was a pretty brave or desperate thing that you did. I thought you may be looking for money but you don't seem..." Her voice trailed off.

"Girl, do you know what we do?" a blond-haired woman touched Livia's shoulder and Livia turned round. The woman regarded Livia critically.

"Claudia over there," the blonde said pointing at the red head, "has two sons serving with Scipio. Domitia here," she said looking at the black-haired woman, "lost her husband in Sicily and I haven't heard from my own husband in more than a year. He is with the Consul Nero in the south."

Livia smiled politely unsure of what they wanted from her.

"We sing in taverns, " the fourth woman with brown hair said. Then with her hand she reached for her hair and pulled off her wig to reveal her true black hair beneath. "My name is Faustina," she said with a smile. "All of us have men involved in this war. We try and help them by singing. We raise money by singing. The proceeds go to the wounded, the invalids, the cripples, the men that no one wants once their duty to the Republic has been fulfilled. They call us the singing wives."

Livia looked surprised. She glanced at the women as one by one they pulled their wigs from their heads and revealed their true hair. Faustina's words reminded her of Flavia and her children's stories. She had never really thought about the war. It had just always been there, like it was natural.

"Will you join us. We could use a voice like yours?" Claudia said.

Livia smiled sadly.

"Another time perhaps," she replied, "I am looking for my brother, Titus. I thought the druid would know where to find him."

"My son is called Titus. Getorix knows him well," a voice said sharply. Livia spun round and stared at Faustina who had spoken. Then her eyes widened and a tear suddenly appeared in her eye.

211

"I think I am Titus' sister," she whispered.

The colour drained from Faustina's face. "Gods," she exclaimed. "Oh Gods."

***

The four women sat around the wooden table. Faustina's house was a simple two room dwelling made of wood and thatch. A fire was burning in the fireplace and over it a copper pot filled with stew was warming up. On the floor lay a few scattered animal skins and on a shelve, beside the hearth, stood a single clay pot. Apart from that the room was bare and devoid of furniture. Livia sat on the opposite side of the table. She looked anxious as she watched Faustina examining her small phallic charm that had hung around her neck. Then the older woman looked up at Livia and nodded. A tear appeared in both women's eyes.

"It is his," Faustina sniffed, "But I am not your mother, Livia. I am Titus' mother but not yours, do you understand?"

Livia nodded silently. "Tell me about my father, please," she whispered.

Faustina looked down at the phallic charm. Then her hand closed around it and she sniffed again, took a deep breath and blew the air from her cheeks.

"His name was Viridomarus. He was a Celt," she sighed. "He belonged to the Boii. They are a Gallic tribe that live along the northern edges of the Appenines. I am of Etruscan origin myself, Livia, but when the Boii invaded my ancestors land they did not force us Etruscans to leave, they allowed us to stay and our two peoples settled down peacefully and lived together. I

212

met your father at Bona as the Gaul's like to call Felsina and we were married. Titus was born soon afterwards. He is like you, I suppose, half Gaul and half Etruscan but he takes after his father. My husband gave him the same charm as you wear and scratched our initials into it. The V stands for his name and the F stands for myself. He had two such charms made, just two. They were originally intended for him and myself. I gave mine to Titus."

Livia looked down at the table. "They always said I had a Gallic streak in my face," she murmured, "and now I know why."

Faustina was silent for a while. Then she looked up at Livia.

"We were married for three years before he left. It was in the year of the great Gallic uprising, eighteen years ago now. The Boii were restless. They feared a Roman attack and the conquest of their land. So they decided to attack before they were attacked themselves. Your father was tempted by the prospect of all the bounty and loot such an invasion offered. I tried to stop him from joining the war bands but he went anyway. I never saw him again after that. They say forty thousand Gaul's were killed at Telamon. He was probably amongst them."

Livia stared at the table. "What about my mother, do you know who she is?"

Faustina shook her head. "No, I have no idea who she is child. I can only assume that your father raped her during the invasion that summer. She must be Etruscan or Roman but it's impossible to say. Ofcourse my husband may still be alive and living with your mother but I doubt it. He was a warrior. Farming
213

would bore him and there was a restlessness about him. He always yearned for something more, something bigger and better. He was never satisfied with what he had. I don't think he had it in him to stay with one woman for any length of time. I do not hate him for abandoning me but neither do I love him anymore. He made his choice and that is that, child."

Faustina paused to scrutinise Livia. There was a compassion in her voice as she spoke. "Reconcile yourself with the fact that you won't find your mother. None of your father's friends returned from that war. No one knows where he went or what he did but I am glad that your mother gave his charm to you, for that charm has brought you to me and Titus."
Livia nodded and dabbed at her eyes.

"You are welcome to stay here in my house," Faustina continued, "in the summer months I travel with my friends from town to town, we sing, but Titus and I live here in the winter. But if you want to return to Rome I will understand."

The four women around the table were watching her.

Livia shook her head and tried to smile. "I will stay," she replied. "You are my family now. I won't ever leave. I have a future here."

Faustina rose and came round the table and wrapped her arms around Livia and this final act of acceptance seemed too much for Livia and she bowed her head and broke into great sobs, her shoulders heaving, as she let go of all the tension inside her, as she finally let go of everything that had happened to her on the long journey from Rome.

When she had finally composed herself she tried to smile.

"Titus," she inquired, "is he here in Placentia? I would like to meet him."

Faustina had returned to her seat. She sighed. "Titus lives with me. He is a hunter, he should be back shortly."

There was a reluctance in her voice that made Livia frown. Faustina catching her look continued, "Titus takes after his father. He hates Romans, he hates my people too. You will have to get used to his behaviour. It's all the fault of Getorix. The druid has been like a father to Titus since my husband vanished. It is good that Titus has found a male role model but Getorix only fills my boy's head with hatred, bitterness and anger. Titus will do anything and everything Getorix asks of him. You can't criticise Getorix without getting into an argument with Titus. Just a warning," Faustina said with a wry smile.

Livia remembered the look on Getorix's face as he had stared at her in the tavern and the fear those eyes had induced in her. Just then the door to the house opened and a lanky young man of around eighteen entered. He was tall and his long red hair cascaded down onto his shoulders. He was holding two rabbits and strapped across his back was a bow and quiver. He stopped in mid stride as he caught sight of the women sitting around the table. The thin wispy outline of a beard was just visible on his chin.

"Who is this?" he said in guttural Latin, gesturing at Livia with the rabbits.

Faustina rose to her feet. "This is your sister, Titus. She has come to live with us."

215

Chapter Twenty-Seven - The hunter will sing

Throughout that evening Titus said very little but as Faustina and her friends talked, Livia noticed him watching her carefully from a distance. It was still dark outside when she heard him rise from his mattress, the following morning. Quietly he picked up his bow and moved across the room to the door. He was about to close the door behind him when Livia stopped him. Quickly she stepped outside. She was dressed in her new Palla, the hood of which she had pulled over her head to keep out the cold night air.

"Going hunting? Can I come along?" she whispered.

Titus stood rooted to the spot. In the darkness she could not see his face. For a moment he didn't reply.

"I hunt alone," he said at last in his guttural Latin.

Then he started out into the darkness and the speed of his stride caught her by surprise. Livia ran after him.

"What do you want?" he exclaimed angrily turning on her as they neared the settlement gate. "I told you, I hunt alone."

Livia did not reply but when he started out again, she kept pace with him. The gate was closed but the armed colonists on sentry duty recognised Titus and the gate was opened a fraction to let him out.

"Bring us back a rabbit Titus," one of the guards called out.

Then he caught sight of Livia and his boredom was replaced by a dirty smile.

"What have we here?" the guard exclaimed.

"She's my baby sister, it's not what you think," Titus snapped in an annoyed voice.

Then they were through the gate and the darkness swallowed them up. For what seemed like an age Livia stumbled after her brother, struggling to keep up with his furiously fast pace. It was difficult to follow him in the dark and she scraped and scratched herself numerous times on trees, branches and bushes. Both of them were silent. Titus seemed to be able to find his way around in the darkness with the skill of a bat and now and then Livia got the impression that he was showing off. He headed deeper and deeper into the forest with the confident assurance of someone who knew where he was going. Then at last he paused. Dawn was upon them and the light was strong enough for Livia to see him properly at last.

"If I were to run, you would never catch me. You will be lost in the forest. Then what will you do?" Titus cried in irritation.

"First of all," Livia replied catching her breath, "I am not your baby sister. I am sixteen and I walked here all the way from Rome and I survived. You have no idea what I had to do to survive. You are not much older than me. You are not that special."

Titus snorted with derision. "What do you know about me? You know nothing. I don't even know if you are telling the truth. You may have fooled my mother but maybe you are just some poor
217

runaway slave with nowhere else to go. Maybe you are out here to steal from us with your poor sob story. Who are you? What do you really want?

"To get to know my brother," Livia replied standing her ground.

The dark green trees crowded around them. Titus turned to look at her and in the growing light she saw that he looked annoyed.

"You shouldn't have come here," he snapped. "Hasdrubal will begin besieging Placentia within weeks and when he takes the town, the Roman women are going to get raped and murdered. That's what's going to happen to you."

Livia looked away and fiddled nervously with her fingers.

Titus paused. "Sorry," he muttered, "I shouldn't have said that." Livia took the phallic charm from around her neck and stuck out her hand showing her charm to Titus.

"We have the same one, our father gave his to me," she said. "I am his daughter like you are his son, we are of the same blood." Titus peered at the charm and grunted. Then he reached up and took off his charm that hung around his neck. He held it out beside hers. The two were identical in every way. He stared at the two phallic charms in silence. Then his fingers closed over his own and he placed it back around his neck and as he did so Livia noticed that his annoyance with her was fading.

"So what do you feel?" he grunted, "Celtic or Roman?"

Livia looked up. "I am going to buy some land and build a farm," she said. "I am going to raise a family on that farm and one day
218

my children or their children will become Roman citizens. People are going to treat my children with respect. My children are going to stroll through the city with dignity. My children are never going to be slaves."

Titus stared at her as if she was mad. "You sound like my mother," Titus said with sudden scorn. "Well I am a Celt, my father was a warrior of the Boii and I too am a warrior."

"Your mother is a wise lady," Livia retorted.

"My mother is a bitch," Titus said as he started off again along the forest path.

***

Titus was an excellent hunter, Livia could see that. He had a hunters instinct for where his prey was and also a strange respect for the animals that he caught which she rather liked. She spent that morning following him around as he checked up on his traps and nets. In one snare they found a bird, in another a rabbit and the nets on the river bank produced six slippery, fat fish. Titus scooped them up and tossed them into the sack he was carrying where the fish wriggled and twisted until at last they died. It was near noon when he finally finished his inspection and the two of them sat down on some rocks beside the fast-flowing stream. From his belt Titus undid his water skin and took a long drink before finally offering it to Livia.

"So what did you do when you were a slave?" Titus said staring out across the stream and the forest beyond.

"I looked after a little girl, mainly," Livia replied.

"So you have no skill? You have no trade? What will you do to survive?"

Livia shrugged. "No one taught me anything. My duties were to look after the little girl. That's all I did." She paused. "No, that's not right. I can sing, I can make some money from singing, just like your mother."

"I thought you said that you wanted to buy some land and become a farmer. But you know nothing about farming?"

Livia looked across at Titus but he was staring into the forest. She bit her lip. It was true, she hadn't gotten the first clue about farming.

"I can learn," she replied. "Maybe you could help me. Maybe Faustina could help too."

"My mother has no interest in owning a farm," Titus retorted. "All she likes to do is travel and sing. She will never put down roots."

Titus shook his head in annoyance. He paused. Then he glanced down at her.

"Have you ever done it with a man?"

Livia looked away with an embarrassed smile, "No," she replied, "Have you?"

"Not with a man," Titus gave her a disgusted look, "but I have a woman in Sena Gallica. She's older than me. We used to live near the town for many years before we came to this place. I grew up there."

220

"Why do you ask?" Livia said looking down at herself.

"You really don't know much do you," Titus shook his head. "If you are a virgin it will make it easier for you to find a husband. The Romans don't allow slaves to own land. They won't allow you to own anything. If you want to buy that farm only your husband will be able to do it. You need a man, Livia. I can introduce you to some of my friends but none of them want to be farmers."

Livia looked glum. Titus was right she thought. As a runaway slave she would never be allowed to own any property. She had after all stolen herself from her owner. She was a fugitive.

"You could buy the land," she said cautiously. "You could help me build a farm. You and my husband."

Titus snorted scornfully. Then he looked up and allowed the sun to warm his face.

"Can you keep a secret?" he said at last.

She nodded.

"When Hasdrubal arrives I am going to join his army," Titus said. Livia turned to look at him in surprise. "Why, why would you do that? What has this war got to do with us?"

"Everything, it has everything to do with us," Titus snapped.

"Our father died fighting against Rome. Have you forgotten that or have all those years as a slave in Rome turned you into a Roman? Hasdrubal will give us the opportunity to take revenge
221

for Telamon. He will give us the chance to slaughter these Romans once and for all."

The fury in his voice startled her.

"Are those your words or someone else's?" she retorted.

Titus turned to look at her. "What do you mean?" he said sharply.

"Nothing," Livia shook her head and looked away. "I just don't see the point of fighting and dying in someone else's war."

"Ah," Titus said with a dismissive gesture, "you are just a girl. What do you know of such matters anyway."

Livia did not respond at first. She looked deep in thought. Then at last she spoke. "I never knew him, our father, but sometimes when I am angry I sense his presence in me. I sense his warrior blood. I sense his violence. Does that make sense?"

Titus was staring at her in open mouthed surprise. Then quickly he looked away. "Getorix will be able to tell you about such matters," he muttered. "Come, let's go and visit him now. He lives not far from here in the forest."

***

Getorix, the druid's home was a simple round hut that stood alone in the midst of the forest. It had been constructed of wood, stone and thatch with a single entrance covered only by a dirty brown blanket that hung from a roof beam. In the surrounding trees around the hut, animal carcasses hung from branches.

Titus gestured for Livia to stay back as he approached the dwelling calling the druid's name. A moment later the blanket was flung aside and Getorix appeared. He was dressed in the same clothes in which Livia had seen him the day before. He glared at Titus as if the young man had caught him in the middle of something. Then he caught sight of Livia and he stopped.

"Why have you brought her here?" he cried.

Titus swallowed nervously and lowered his eyes. "The girl is my sister. She has come to stay with us. She has come from Rome," he replied beckoning for Livia to approach. "She is my father's daughter, Sir. She claims that she can sense his warrior blood inside her. I was just wondering if you could tell us what it means?"

Getorix turned again to stare at Livia. His eyes narrowed. "Your father's daughter," he repeated to himself. Then he looked at Titus.

"Well what have you brought me?" he said.

In reply Titus lifted the bag that contained the fish off his back and laid it down at Getorix's feet. Then he took a respectful step back.

Getorix opened it up, peered inside and sniffed. Then he looked up and straight at Livia.

"Come here girl," he growled and there was something in his voice that seemed to compel her towards him. She stepped forward and as she did so Getorix fixed his dark eyes upon her.

Livia felt her stomach churn in growing fear as the druid thrust his arm towards her.

"She is scared, Titus, like the rest of her kind," Getorix snarled contemptuously. Livia halted before him and looked up at the druid. There was no light in the man's eyes. The druid's black eyes seemed to be sucking everything they saw into their dark cores as if they were whirlpools from which there was no escape. Then with a speed that she hadn't thought possible, Getorix's hand grabbed her by the throat and he lifted her boldly off her feet. For a fraction of a second his face contorted into something hideous and monstrous. It may have lasted for just a fraction of second but Livia saw him and she wanted to scream in fright but instead something else happened. A terrible all-consuming rage flooded through her, bursting upon her with a violence that she'd felt before, when that boy had started pushing Laelia about on their way home after picking the wild flowers. Her windpipe was being crushed but the rage surged through her giving her strength she had not known she had possessed. Before she could act however, Getorix had released her and she stumbled backwards as she hit the ground. The druid was staring at her in surprise. Then he grunted in disbelief.

"You are right Titus," he said in a changed voice, "the girl has her father's warrior blood inside her. She has the battle madness. She could become a berserker if she was trained for war."

The druid took a step back, his eyes examining Livia with growing interest. "Yes, like your father," he muttered, "a berserker. This is strange indeed. What portent, I wonder have the gods sent us?"

224

Chapter Twenty-Eight - In a father's footsteps

During the following week Livia spent much of her time with Faustina and her friends. They practised singing and Livia had noticed the respect she'd received every time she sang. The women's respect was something she was not used to and her confidence soared. Faustina seemed to have grown fond of her and sometimes Titus too had paused to hang around and now and then she'd caught him smiling at their antics. Livia had enjoyed herself. She like the women's company, she liked the singing and her newly won respect but in the back of her mind she yearned for her true ambition. She yearned for the life that Marcus led. Whenever Titus had been in the house she had caught herself thinking about what he'd said. She would need a man if her dream of a farm and a family were to become a reality. She didn't know where to start looking for a husband. But maybe a husband would come along when she least expected it. She could wait. It wouldn't stop her. Titus was a free born man. Her brother would be able to buy land with the money that she and Faustina would earn from singing. Together they would build the farm. Then she could look for a husband. Then she could start planning the future. That was how it was going to be she had resolved.

Faustina and her friends were preparing to leave the colony. They did it every summer, heading south to the Roman towns in Etruria and Umbria where they would perform their songs, giving some of their proceeds directly to any wounded or invalided soldiers that they came across. In consequence, their reputation had grown and many towns were all but too happy to put them up. This year however Hasdrubal's invasion had added an element of urgency for soon all communications with the

Roman lands to the south would surely be cut and the women would be trapped. A final convoy of ships was leaving within days for the journey down the Po and the relative safety of the Adriatic coast. Faustina had already prepared a place for herself, her friends, Livia and Titus onboard the ships. The colony too was anxious to get all non-essential colonists out of the settlement. They would be sailing as soon as the boats arrived.

Livia stood washing clothes in a barrel of water outside the house. It was late in the afternoon and from inside she could smell the delicious scent of roasting boar and fresh bread. She'd not had the courage to tell Faustina that her son did not intend to come south with them. She had promised Titus, she had promised to keep his decision to go and join the Carthaginian's a secret. Every time he had risen and left the house she had wondered whether it was for the last time. The knowledge of his imminent departure had weighed on her. Without Titus all her plans would come to nothing. She needed Titus. Without Titus she would have no one. She couldn't just let him throw away his life because of a war that had nothing to do with them. As she scrubbed the clothes she suddenly felt a hot flush of anger and determination. He will need you before the year is out, the Sybil's warning rang in her mind.

It was evening when Titus at last returned from his hunt. Slung over his shoulder he was carrying a dead fox and two rabbits. There was a triumphant glint in his eye as he dropped the animals onto the table. Faustina was away and for the moment Livia and Titus were alone in the house. Livia folded her arms across her chest as Titus sat down to skin the animals with his hunting knife.

"I am going with you," Livia announced.

Titus paused and then looked up at her.

"Going with me, where?"

"When you leave here to go and join this war. I am coming with you."

Titus raised his eyebrows. "No, I am going alone," he shook his head and resumed his skinning.

"I am coming with you if you like it or not," the determination in Livia's voice made Titus look up. He looked annoyed.

"No, you are not," he growled. "I don't need my baby sister around me. The Carthaginian camp is no place for someone like you."

Livia looked amused. "I can handle myself," she replied. "Don't think that I can't and I will be coming with you. That's the final word."

Titus laid his hunting knife down on the table and stared at her.

"Women don't order me around," he cried angrily.

Livia slammed her fist into the table so hard that the vibrations made the knife jump up into the air.

"I am coming with you!"

Titus stared at her in amazement. Then he blushed and shrugged and looked away.

"Fine," he growled "But I am not going to look after you all the time. You are going to be on your own."

"Fine," Livia replied. Then she pulled out the other chair and sat down.

"Why?" Titus looked annoyed again, "Why are you so keen to come with me? The Carthaginians are marching to war."

"To save your worthless head," Livia replied looking away.

Titus was quiet for a long time and the two of them sat in brooding silence. Then at last he picked up his knife and began his skinning again.

"Getorix is going too. We are leaving soon," he muttered. "Make sure that you are prepared to leave right away. I can't afford to have you slowing me down."

Livia sighed in disappointment. Getorix. She'd had the insight on the day that the druid had grabbed her by the neck. Getorix's hold over Titus was poisoning her brother's mind. Faustina was right. If only she could break the druid's influence over her brother, she may be able to persuade Titus to change his mind. She may be able to persuade him to come home and forget about the war. But Getorix was not to be underestimated. She was sure that he had sensed her purpose. He was a clever man. That was the reason why he had taken an instant dislike to her. Getorix sensed she would fight him for influence over Titus.

***

It was in the dead of night when Titus' hand shook Livia awake. She rubbed the sleep from her eyes and stared up at him. He was fully dressed and his bow and hunting knife were strapped to his body. Across his back he was carrying a sack. He looked tense.

"It is time," he whispered.

Livia glanced across the room to the sleeping form of Faustina. Then she lifted the blanket from her body and Titus smiled in surprise. Livia was already fully dressed. She only had to put on her sandals and her Palla. The two of them had reached the door when a voice spoke from the darkness.

"I know what you are going to do Titus," Faustina's face remained hidden in the dark but there was a sadness in her voice that nearly made Livia's heart stop. "I can't stop you and I won't try. You have your father's blood and if you must follow in his footsteps, then so be it. But if you can, come back to me alive. There will always be a home for you here."

At her side Livia could sense Titus bursting with tension. Then without a word he opened the door and vanished into the night. Livia lowered her eyes guiltily as she sensed Faustina' presence watching her from the darkness. Then she too stepped through the doorway and disappeared after Titus into the night.

Chapter Twenty-Nine - Roman courage

The narrow forest path twisted through the trees and Gaius and Hanno had to be careful not to be knocked out of the saddle by low hanging branches. They looked tired and hungry. The horses slowly picked their way along the path which seemed to lead ever deeper into the forest. Gaius already hated the trees. They seemed to crowd around him, barring his way at every possible turn, shutting out the daylight and now that they were close to Placentia, every tree seemed an ideal place to shelter an enemy warrior who was just waiting to ambush them. They had entered the forest only yesterday but already it seemed like an eternity.

Up ahead he could suddenly hear running water and through the trees he caught a glimpse of a river and beyond it the forest began to finally open up. Gaius was about to urge his horse forwards at a trot when Hanno, who was riding ahead of him, raised his one arm in sudden warning. The Carthaginian had halted and stood motionless on the path staring at the river through the trees. Cautiously Gaius nudged his horse alongside Hanno.

"What is it?" he whispered.

Hanno held his finger to his mouth and then pointed towards the river. The water was not too wide and it looked fordable. Then Gaius saw four horsemen emerge from the trees on the far bank. The horsemen rode their beasts down to the water's edge and the horses lowered their heads to drink. Gaius could hear his heart thumping in his chest. The horsemen were Numidians.

"Scouts," he mouthed and Hanno nodded.

The two of them sat silently on their horses and instinctively Gaius reached down to stroke his beast and calm the horse. After a few moments one of the Numidian horsemen said something in a language Gaius couldn't understand and the four riders turned away from the river and disappeared southwards into the trees. Gaius and Hanno waited for a while longer until all seemed quiet again.

"They must be Hasdrubal's men," Gaius whispered, "He must be marching on Placentia. This is bad news. We will need to hurry."

Hanno nodded and then urging his horse forwards he made his way through the trees and down the river bank and into the water.

***

The sight of Placentia's walls was a very welcome relief after the days spent in the wilderness and Gaius and Hanno rode the final half mile at a gallop. It was early in the evening but as they approached the western gate of the colony they noticed that the gates were closed and sharpened wooden stakes had been driven at an angle into the ground before the palisade. They pulled up before the defences and Gaius suddenly noticed half a dozen bowmen aiming their weapons at him. He raised his hand in greeting.

"Open the gate. I am a Roman citizen!"

The bowmen did not move and nor did the bows that were aimed at Gaius and Hanno.

"Oh for fuck's sake, open the gate. I am a Roman citizen," Gaius shouted crossly. "Two men are not going to attack the town on their own, now are they?"

The men on the parapets didn't answer. Then slowly with a creaking noise the gate swung open just a fraction and a head poked out.

"What do you want?" a man shouted.

"To be let in you idiot," Hanno roared impatiently.

The man's head vanished and for a moment all was silent. Then the gate swung open and Gaius and Hanno twisted around the wooden stakes and rode on through the gate and into the town. A throng of armed, anxious looking colonists stood waiting for them just inside the walls. They were armed with a variety of weaponry, from swords and spears, to scythes and clubs.

"Sorry," a man muttered taking the reins of Gaius' horse. "We are expecting the Carthaginians and Gaul's to arrive at any moment."

Gaius did not answer him. Instead he slid from his horse and looked around him.

"Where have you come from?" another colonist asked as he stepped forward. "The last ships left here two days ago."

"From the Ligurian coast, across the mountains," Gaius replied without looking at the man. "Who is in charge of this place?"

"That would-be senator Quintus Valerius Numa," another colonist replied. "He showed up here a few days ago. He's taken command of the town. A right prick if you ask me."

Gaius whirled round and stared at the peasant who had spoken out.

"Senator Numa, are you sure?"

The colonist nodded and there was a muttering from the men around him.

"This is good news," Gaius cried with a grin, "I know Senator Numa. He is my father's closest friend. He saved my father's life at Telamon. You are in good hands, gentlemen. Numa knows how to fight."

The colonists muttered amongst themselves. They looked unimpressed.

"If you say so," a voice replied, "but if that is the case then maybe you want to ask him why he wants to open the gates and allow this Carthaginian and Celtic scum to enter our colony."

"Yes," a few voices cried in agreement. "If you know the senator then speak with him. We want to fight. We are not going to let these invaders take our land. This is our land. The treachery of these Punic swine is well known. We can't trust them to keep their word. It is better to fight."

Gaius looked surprised. He glanced at Hanno who was watching the scene impassively.

"We are on our way to Rome," Gaius said, "We were hoping to obtain supplies and maybe transport south. Our horses are worn out."

"Forget it," another colonist raised his club in the air. "The mountains south of here are crawling with hostile tribesmen. No Roman will get through. The only route out is along the river and that will be cut soon if not already."

Gaius looked frustrated. He turned to stare at the colonists and they stared back at him with the sullen, grim determination of men prepared to defend their hard-won frontier.

"I will speak with Numa," he said at last.

***

The office of land registry, the building where Placentia's official founding charter and the colonists land registration documents and title deeds were kept and disbursed, had, through the town's lack of a more important and prestigious building, been turned into the colony's command post. A colonist armed only with a spear was lounging outside on sentry duty.

Gaius stepped through the doorway, opening and extending both his arms in a gesture of greeting as he saw the figure of Senator Quintus Valerius Numa sitting in a chair drinking wine. Gaius was grinning.

"Senator Numa," he cried, "It is most fortunate to find you here. You remember me don't you. I am Gaius, Marcus' youngest son?"

Numa choked on his wine as he caught sight of Gaius. His face was covered in a grey beard that looked several weeks old. The colour drained from his cheeks and he coughed and spluttered as he jumped to his feet.

"I am sorry, I didn't mean to startle you so rudely," Gaius said respectfully. "But you do remember me don't you Senator?"

Numa was staring at Gaius as if the young man was an idiot. His face had turned very pale and one of his hands was trembling. Then quickly he looked away.

"Yes I remember you Gaius," Numa murmured.

"How is my father? Well I hope, and my mother Flavia, have you any news from them?" Gaius said embracing Numa.

Numa refused to look the young man in the eye. "They are well," he murmured again. "They were well the last time that I saw them."

Gaius smiled and took a step back. Then he smiled again.

"That's good news," he nodded. "And what about Publius, my brother. Still an actor? Still gay as a pony?"

Numa looked up at the ceiling with a pained expression as if someone was torturing him.

"He is well too," Numa nodded in a voice that was nearly a whisper.

"Good, this is good news. I haven't seen them in over two years," Gaius said turning to Hanno, "They will be worried about what has happened to me."

Hanno nodded politely but did not reply. His eyes were fixed on Numa. An awkward silence descended on the office.

"We are heading to Rome," Gaius said at last, "My ship was attacked by pirates and we thought it best to journey here. The Taurini were friendly. They gave us food and kept us on the right path." Gaius smiled again but the atmosphere in the office seemed to be weighing against his light heartedness.

"You won't be getting to Rome anytime soon," a new voice said suddenly. Gaius turned round to see a tall man with a wrinkled weather beaten face. The man was dressed in a standard white woollen army tunic over which he was wearing a fine mail shirt made up of thousands of tiny, interlocking rings of iron. On his head he was wearing a round, bronze helmet with a raised central knob. He looked around fifty.

"All routes out of here are blocked. The colony is cut off. You will have to stay with us and ride out the storm, or die in it," the man added.

"Who are you Sir?" Gaius said feeling a slight frustration with the man's words.

"My name is Varro," the man replied. "I am Placentia's sole surviving land commissioner and until the Senator's arrival here, I was in charge of the colony. "

It was the Roman custom, Gaius knew, that when a new colony was founded, three land commissioners would be sent out to organise the administration and distribution of the colonies new land to its Roman colonists.

"What happened to your colleagues?" Gaius asked.

In response, Varro drew his hand across his neck. "These are difficult times," he added, "difficult times."

Gaius turned back to look at Numa. The Senator seemed to have regained his composure for some colour had returned to his cheeks. Gaius looked puzzled.

"The colonists are saying that when Hasdrubal's army arrives, you want to open the gates and surrender the town. Is this true?"

Numa cleared his throat and glanced carefully at Gaius. "I thought it best," he muttered. "We can't hold the colony against a determined attack and if we surrender now, the Carthaginians will spare the town and its people. I am just trying to save these people's lives, Gaius."

Gaius glanced at Varro. It was clear from his face that the land commissioner did not agree but Varro maintained a respectful silence.

"But, is it not, the duty and purpose of a Roman colony," Gaius said with a frown, staring at Numa, "to hold a conquered people in check? It is a colonies duty to hold this land for Rome. The colonists are all volunteers. They know what is expected from them and they are willing to fight. If Placentia were to surrender, the colony would break its solemn vow to the Senate and People of Rome. I for one would not like to show my face in Rome with such a reputation."

"Duty, reputation," Numa murmured to himself.

"Senator," Varro said quietly, "I agree. The colonists are willing to fight. On Hasdrubal's approach, we should close our gates and refuse him entry. We should show him some Roman courage."

Numa was staring at the floor and Gaius was suddenly shocked by how feeble his father's old friend had become. The Senator looked like a broken and tired old man. The fight had completely gone out of him. Numa was nothing like the man he'd once known. The Senator's former, blustering, confident and self-assured self-had utterly vanished. What had happened?

Numa gestured to Gaius with his hand.

"Fine, if that is what you want, if that is what the colony demands then let it be so. I am going to place you Gaius in charge of the town's defences. Maybe you can do a better job than I have done."

"Sir, I am the colonies land commissioner. The command of the colony should be mine," Varro interjected.

But Numa shook his head.

"No," he replied with sudden viciousness. "I want the glory of Placentia's heroic defence to be his responsibility," he said pointing at Gaius.

Chapter Thirty - We fight

As Gaius strode purposefully down Placentia's main street Hanno cleared his throat.

"You know the Senator, this Numa?" Hanno asked.

Gaius nodded. "He is my father's friend. I have known him all my life."

"I don't like him," Hanno replied sharply. "There is something odd about him. What Senator gives away his authority so easily and casually and did you see how his hand trembled. It was as if he was afraid of you."

Gaius frowned, "Yes he is a changed man, you are right. I don't remember him having been so feeble. He never used to have a beard either. Anyway," Gaius sighed, "it looks like we are going to have stay here for the time being. I have work to do."

Hanno was staring at the colonies wooden palisade, "We could just take our chances Gaius," he said. "We could take a couple of fresh horses and make a dash across the mountains. If we ran into Celts, we could say we were Hasdrubal's men. Many Roman deserters have joined the Punic armies. What do you say? Better than being trapped here like a rat in a sinking ship."

But Gaius shook his head. His eyes glinted with sudden purpose.

"Numa has asked me to defend the town," he replied solemnly. "Ofcourse I would like to be heading to Rome, Hanno. But when

240

a Roman Senator, a family friend asks me to fulfil such an important task, I will not refuse. It is my duty to obey and defend this colony. It is every Roman's duty to heed his nations call. Varro is right. It's time to show some Roman courage."

Gaius did not see the faint smile that crept onto Hanno's face.

"The honour of being placed in command has gone to your head," Hanno replied good naturedly. "But you are a young man and young men are easily swayed by such things."

Gaius smiled as his servant's rebuke.

"Well it is your fault then. If you hadn't been caught fucking the village elder's wife, we would have been in Rome by now and that's the last I want to hear about the matter."

Hanno dipped his head respectfully but the smile remained on his face.

Gaius climbed one of the ladders that led up onto the parapet of the wooden walls. The armed colonists on duty glanced at him curiously. He strode up and down the walk way staring out across the field of broken tree stumps and the Po to the north. Gaius had never held command. He'd only ever been a simple soldier in the Hastati. Now because of a Senator's words, he commanded the fate of an entire colony. He blushed as he suddenly became aware of the heavy weight of responsibility. How had his Centurion commanded the Maniple? How had Scipio managed his army? He hadn't got a clue he realised. Varro was climbing up the ladder towards him. He approached Gaius with a stern look.

"I have served for thirteen campaigning seasons, son," Varro growled. "I was with Marcellus when he recaptured Syracuse and I took part in the siege of Capua. Why don't you hand the command over to me. We both know that it should be mine, whatever the Senator says."

"You heard Numa, he has put me in charge. I can handle it," Gaius retorted. Varro folded his arms across his chest and stared at the younger man.

"Do the right thing, give me the command. This is my colony. You don't live here."

Gaius turned to look out across the ramparts. He was silent for a moment. "Alright, " he said at last, "I will compromise with you Varro. We shall share command. You can be responsible for the southern and eastern sections of the wall. I will take the men on the north and west side. Agreed?"

Varro looked surprised. He studied Gaius for a moment. Then he nodded. "It is agreed," he replied.

"How many colonists are there in the town?" Gaius asked.

Varro moved up to stand beside him. The two of stared at the distant river. "We were six thousand, eleven years ago," Varro sighed. "But many have died or left since then. At the last census there were two thousand eight hundred and fourteen Roman citizens, eight hundred and twenty three wives, hundred and sixty three children and about a thousand allied Gaul's. Nearly all the outlying farms have been abandoned and we are completely reliant on supplies brought by river. Four hundred citizens together with wives and children left on the last transport out of here a few days ago."

"What about the Gaul's, are they trustworthy?"

Varro shrugged, "They are a mixed group. Most have stayed because we allowed them to keep their land. There are some fugitives and others are here just for the wine and the money they can make from us. I suppose that they are fighting for their land and future just like we are but I have divided them up and spread them around the perimeter. That way it should lessen the chances that they will desert or rebel."
Gaius nodded in appreciation.

"Apart from supplies, what other weaknesses do we have," he said lowering his voice.

Varro nodded at the north gate. "That's your weakest point," he said. "The wood is rotting and weak. A battering ram would only need a few blows to break through. Whatever happens, don't let them get close." Varro's face had grown sombre. "And ofcourse if Hasdrubal brings artillery with him, then it will all be over very quickly."

***

The Gaul's attacked Placentia the following morning. Gaius was resting inside the colonies command post when he heard the warning cries. A moment later the shrill clanging of an alarm bell rang out across town. He rushed down the main street towards the northern wall. Ladders had been placed at intervals along the walls and armed colonists were already clambering up them onto the ramparts. The men already there, clustered together in
243

small groups as if the presence of their comrades gave them courage. All around Gaius, men were rushing to their positions. The alarm bell was still clanging away. Then a moment later the deep throated blare of a Carnyx, the boar headed Celtic war trumpet replied. It was followed by half a dozen more. In the watch tower that had signalled the alarm, it's occupants were hastily preparing the northern wall's solitary Scorpion. The Scorpion was a crossbow like machine, standing on a tripod. It which could hurl an iron tipped bolt across a hundred yards with terrible accuracy. It was designed not to break up an enemy attack but as an anti personnel weapon, a sniper's weapon.

Gaius caught his first glimpse of the Gaul's as he scrambled onto the parapet. He gasped in dismay at the sight. Swarming towards the town's northern wall was a thick tide of screaming, baying warriors. There had to be thousands of them. Some were clad in mail armour, others were stark naked but most just wore their colourful Gallic trousers, animal skin leggings and simple brown leather body armour. They surged across the open tree trunk studded field, brandishing their oval shields and long swords. As the first attackers came within range, Gaius heard the taught twang of the bowmen firing their arrows. The arrows could not fail to miss a target but the screaming human tide did not even seem to notice.

The foremost warriors poured through the lines of sharpened wooden stakes and into the ditch below the wooden palisade. A few unlucky Gaul's were impaled on the stakes by the sheer pressure of bodies from behind them. Their sickening cries were quickly lost in the tumult. Gaius ran down the parapet. He was still clad in his white woollen army tunic and was wearing no armour. His only weapon was his short Spanish sword that hung from his belt. The colonists had formed a thin line along the

244

rampart. Here and there a man picked out a target and flung his spear down at the Gaul's in the ditch six yards below. The Gaul's were filling up the ditch, slipping and sliding in the mud, trying to hack away at the thick wooden tree trunks that barred their advance. Their ferocious, blood curdling snarling, as if they were wild beasts, was terrifying.

Gaius stared wide eyed at the scene. His heart was thumping wildly in his chest. Not since the attack on New Carthage had he been this frightened and during that assault the Romans had outnumbered the Punic defenders by twenty-five to one. The Carthaginians and Iberians had, for the most part, looked similar to the Romans. The Gaul's however, with their large powerful frames, wild long hair and savage appearance, were a truly terrifying sight and if the colonists had had somewhere to flee to, Gaius knew that they would have run.

The Celtic assault had slowed and looked like it had run out of steam after the first wild charge. The thousands of warriors pressed up against their comrades, trying to get at the wall. Then Gaius noticed the assault ladders. Parties of Gaul's were moving forward holding the ladders above their heads.

"Prepare for ladder assault," he yelled repeating the words he'd heard his Centurion use at New Carthage.

None of the colonists replied, nor was he sure that they had heard him. Gaius suddenly wondered what had happened to Hanno. But there was no time to dwell on his slave's whereabouts. The Gallic ladders were approaching the wall.

"They are too short!" a shrill Roman voice suddenly cried. "They are too short!"

245

The cry was taken up by more and more defenders along the wall and suddenly Gaius could hear the Romans hooting with savage laughter. He stared, rooted to the ground, as one of the ladders was pushed up against the wall and sure enough the ladder did not reach all the way to the top of the palisade. Gaius raised his sword in fierce elation and relief. In the ditch below the Gaul's milled around in confusion. Their attempts to hack their way through the wall had come to nothing and suddenly they began to feel the barrage of spears and arrows from above.

Then with the speed that took all the defenders by surprise, the Gallic warriors turned and began fleeing towards the river. It was so sudden that Gaius did not fully understand what was going on. The Gallic retreat gained momentum as the flood of warriors, surged up out of the ditch and through the line of wooden stakes. Encouraged by the retreat the defenders harried them with every missile that they possessed until only the dead and dying remained on the battlefield.

***

The second assault came within hours. Gaius was standing in the watch tower that overlooked the northern gate when he saw the enemy emerging from the trees. The Gaul's advanced at a walk, in a broad line but they seemed to be in no hurry. Just out of range they halted.

"What are they doing?" one of the two colonists who was manning the watchtower hissed.

"They are waiting," the other colonist said coming to stand beside his colleague.

"For what?" the first man replied.

Then Gaius saw it. Bearing down on the northern gate was a tight knot of men. They were pushing a battering ram towards the gate. The ram rolled along slowly on four solid wooden wheels its huge bronze tipped, oak beam pointing ominously at the Roman defenders. The Gaul's had protected their flanks and heads with large oval shields similar to those used by the Romans. They were advancing in Testudo formation.

Gaius and the two men in the tower stared with growing horror as the ram jolted and swayed towards them. From the wall's the colonists began to fire arrows, as the ram came within range, but the missiles slammed harmlessly into the shields and the wooden carriage and the ram kept on coming. Then from behind the shelter of their shields, eight Gaul's suddenly leapt clear. They had bows in their hand. A moment later Gaius heard the whizz and thwack of an arrow as it buried itself into the chest of one of the men beside him. Another hummed as it struck the wooden parapet. The second colonist staggered back clutching at his throat, gurgling as an arrow punched into his neck. He crashed into the railing behind him and toppled over the side.

Gaius flung himself flat as two more arrows whizzed over his head and lodged themselves in the towers roof. Then as fast as they had appeared the Gallic bowmen rushed back behind the cover of their comrades shields. The remaining colonist lay on the floor groaning softly. Seeing that the bowmen were back under cover Gaius jumped to his feet and grabbed hold of the Scorpion. The weapon was loaded and he swivelled it round and aimed at the ram. Just then a Gallic-bowmen sprang clear and without thinking Gaius fired. The bolt hit the warrior square in the chest and sent him staggering backwards until he

247

collapsed onto his back. Gaius scrambled to reload. A volley of arrows thudded into the watch tower but their aim was not as good as the first attack. Gaius raised his head. The ram was nearly at the gate. The Roman defenders were throwing everything they had at the Testudo but the Gaul's stubbornly refused to give up.

Gaius depressed the Scorpion and fired straight into the wall of shields. The bolt smacked into a shield but did not pierce it. In growing desperation Gaius snatched another bolt and loaded it into the weapon. Then as he peered down at the ram he caught sight of a man running along the ramparts of the wall. It was Varro. He was shouting orders at the defenders. The ram had reached the gate and the great oak beam swung back and then with a sickening boom it smashed into the gate. The wooden gate groaned under the impact but it held. Gaius stared down at the scene, unable to move as a growing sense of despair took hold. The Celts were going to break into the town after all.

From the ramparts a dozen defenders simultaneously heaved buckets of fine white sand down onto the attackers below. The sand rattled and tumbled onto the shields and down through the cracks between them. Within a few moments a second load of buckets was emptying more sand onto the Celts before the gate. Then a third wave of buckets appeared. The impact was immediate, unexpected and devastating. From below their shields Gaius suddenly heard the Gaul's shrieking in pain and terror. A moment later the Testudo formation exploded as the Gaul's dropped their shields and weapons, turned and ran, clawing at their own bodies.

Within a second, from further along the wall, a dozen or so burning arrows arched gracefully into the air and hurtled down, thudding and smacking into the abandoned battering ram. Three Gallic warriors lay on the ground, writhing in agony. They were trying to rip their clothes and armour from their bodies. One of the fleeing Celts was hit by a burning arrow that sent him spinning and tumbling to the ground. He lay still as the flames began to devour his body. From the walls Gaius suddenly heard men cheering. Before the gate the battering ram had begun to burn.

***

"The northern wall was your responsibility," Varro said glaring angrily at Gaius. "If I hadn't arrived the Gaul's would have broken into the colony. They would have killed everyone and it would have been your fault. Damn it Gaius, you nearly lost the town."

The two of them stood on the ramparts of the wall. Dusk was approaching but the Gaul's had made no further attempts to attack the town. Gaius looked embarrassed. Then he turned to look at Varro.

"You are right," he replied, "Your action saved us all. I am grateful."

Varro muttered something to himself and then glanced out across the wall. "Well you are a young man, you have got a lot to learn."

"What did you throw at them?" Gaius asked unable to contain his curiosity any longer.

"Hot sand," Varro replied, "It gets everywhere and into everything. No armour or clothing can protect you. The hot sand burns, it leaves terrible burns on the skin. It's a very effective weapon. I saw the Greeks and Carthaginians use it at Syracuse."

"Sir, look!" one of the colonists cried.

The men on the wall turned to look in the direction in which the man was pointing. At the edge of the forest to the west, horsemen had appeared. The riders began to spread out as they slowly enveloped the colony.

"Numidians," Varro said grimly, "So Hasdrubal has finally arrived."

Gaius' eye was drawn to a small cluster of riders who sat motionless at the edge of the forest. The men were staring across at the town. In their midst sat a man dressed in the finest looking armour Gaius has ever seen. On his head he was wearing a Thracian helmet. To Gaius it seemed the man was staring straight at him.

"Hasdrubal, there he is," Gaius said pointing.

***

It was dark when Gaius slumped down on a mattress inside an abandoned house. He was exhausted and the near disaster at the northern gate had rattled him. Hanno sat at the table, slicing an apple into small pieces. A solitary oil lamp burned beside him.

"Where were you today?" Gaius said unable to sleep.

Hanno had been silent ever since he'd returned to the house.
"I was entertaining a young lady," he said with a thoughtful look,
"a lady who had a rather interesting story to tell."

Gaius turned over onto his side and glanced at his slave. "You
mean to say that you were fucking, whilst the town was being
attacked?"

"I can't help it that women feel attracted to me," Hanno smiled
shyly. He glanced down at his crotch. "They can't believe my
size," he added.

Gaius ran his hands down his face. He was in no mood for
crude jokes.

"So what interesting things did this young woman have to tell
you?"

Hanno laid down his knife. "Well," he sighed, "the man who
slept with her a few hours before me, was Senator Quintus
Valerius Numa. The Senator told her that he'd given the
command of the town's defences to you because, " Hanno
paused, "he expects you to fail."

"What?" Gaius sat up.

Hanno nodded. "Strange isn't it. I told you there was something
odd about him." Then Hanno turned to look at Gaius and his
face looked concerned.

"And there is something else that bothers me Gaius. The Gaul's twice concentrated their assault against the northern gate. They made no effort to attack the other walls. How did they know that the north gate was our weakest point?"

Chapter Thirty-One - The Six Messengers

Hasdrubal sat on his horse staring at the Roman colony. It was getting dark but he could still make out the men on her ramparts. They were staring back at him and for a moment, just for a moment he had to admit to himself that he was impressed by the valiant defence he'd witnessed.

Then he turned to look down at the Gallic king who stood beside him.

"Why did your men attack without my orders," he snapped irritably. "I instructed you to surround the town, not to attack it. You were supposed to wait until my army arrived."

The Gallic king, a giant of a man shrugged. "The town looked like it could be taken," he replied in broken Punic.

"Well a fine mess you have made of it," Hasdrubal said turning to look at the smouldering ruin of the battering ram that now blocked the entrance to one of the gates.

Hasdrubal was silent for a moment as he studied the town's walls.

"When can I expect the artillery to arrive?" he said glancing round at the general who commanded his engineers. The officer, a Libyan from Utica sat on his horse staring with tight disapproval at the dead and broken bodies of the failed assault, that littered the ground before them.

"They have had some difficulty crossing the river Sir," he replied smoothly in perfect Punic, "but the main assault engines and catapults will be here by sunrise."

"Good, excellent," Hasdrubal growled, "When they arrive get them into position immediately and let the Romans see them. It may persuade them to surrender."

"Sir," the engineer officer dipped his head in acknowledgement. "In the meantime we will besiege them. Nothing comes out, nothing goes in." Hasdrubal glanced round at the riders clustered behind him searching for a face. "Gisgo, get over here now," he cried.

For a moment nothing happened. Then from the trees a solitary rider appeared and trotted towards Hasdrubal. The man on the horse was wrapped in a brown blanket. He refused to look at Hasdrubal as he approached and Hasdrubal suddenly relished the humiliation that his lord of spies was experiencing. Yes it felt good to see the great, arrogant Gisgo so humbled.

"Whatever happened to your man inside the town?" Hasdrubal snapped, repressing the urge to laugh out loud at the bedraggled state of his spy master. "Was he not supposed to hand the colony over to us on a plate? You assured me Placentia would open its gates to us, but they look pretty closed to me!"

Gisgo raised his chin and stared at the Roman walls in silent bitterness. He looked tired and harassed.

"I do not know what has happened to him," Gisgo muttered. "I can only assume that something or someone has thwarted our plan. My man would not betray us. His love of our Gold is too strong. I will see what I can find out."

"Yes do that," Hasdrubal replied scornfully, "But maybe you should choose your agents with better care next time. Your man has failed us twice now and cost the lives of twenty-four excellent soldiers. If he fails again, I will see to it that you are charged for neglect of your duty. You will hang on a cross, Gisgo. Is that clear?"

"Hannibal will never allow that," Gisgo retorted.

"My brother will not lift a finger to save you when he finally hears about your incompetence," Hasdrubal roared. "Now get to work before I have you crucified here and now!"

Gisgo looked startled and for a single moment, he looked scared. Then he swung his horse round and vanished back into the trees. Hasdrubal watched him go with cruel delight. There had been a time when as a young man, Hasdrubal knew, he would never have spoken to his officers like that. But that was before he'd held high command and seen the bitter rivalry, the petty personal squabbles, dislikes and arguments that had split the Carthaginian generals and the war effort in Spain. Three Carthaginian generals had led armies in Spain and none of them had wanted to co-ordinate their campaigns with the other. Their lack of unity had led directly to the fall of New Carthage and had so disgusted Hasdrubal that he had finally resolved to leave the mess that the Spanish war was becoming, and go and join his brother in Italy.

He gestured to his bodyguards and then turned his horse around. The riders followed silently as he trotted into the woods.
255

Hasdrubal rode amongst the trees and through the lines of Iberian and African infantry that were settling down in small groups around cooking fires. Placentia would fall within a day once his artillery got to work. He wasn't worried. It would be better if the town surrendered though he thought. He was far from home and even light casualties amongst his best troops, the Iberians, Africans and Numidian's could not be made good. He needed to conserve them at all costs, until the decisive battle.

As he arrived back at the camp where his men were still erecting his tent and the baggage train was still arriving he slid to the ground and handed the horses' reins to a slave. Another slave handed him some food and he spooned the hot soup into his mouth, glancing as he did so, up at the sky where the first stars were becoming visible. A sudden melancholy seemed to come to him. That morning, six riders, four Gaul's and two Iberians had ridden off southwards, carrying letters intended for Hannibal's eyes only. The letters contained coded instructions to his brother on the planned rendezvous with him and his army. Now as he ate his soup Hasdrubal wondered what Hannibal was doing. It would be a truly joyous occasion when the two of them met again. Eleven years was a long time. So much had happened. They would feast. They would drink and they would hunt in the forest like they had once done. They would remember how they had once been. Two sons of the Thunderbolt, as the Romans had called Hamilcar. Two sons marked for greatness, two sons trained for war and battle and afraid of nothing apart from that the sky may one day fall down on their heads.

Hasdrubal smiled to himself. He could already picture the Roman panic at having to confront two sons of Hamilcar, together at the same time, within seventy-five miles of Rome. With the union between the two armies complete, the day would soon come, the day his father had dreamed of, the day when a Carthaginian army would once and for all destroy the usurping power of Rome. It was for that day that both he and Hannibal and Mago too had spent their entire lives preparing.

Chapter Thirty-Two - Deliverance

Hasdrubal woke with a cry. Outside it was still night. His guards though were alert and at the sound of his startled cry they rushed into the tent, weapons drawn.

"It's alright, I am alright," Hasdrubal grumbled irritably, gesturing for them to leave.

Alone again he stared up at the dark roof of the tent. He didn't feel tired anymore. The dream had been startling. Hasdrubal never dreamt. But today he had. He had seen his father Hamilcar. His father had been standing, motionless, in the middle of a river. The water had come up to his waist and Hamilcar had been looking directly at Hasdrubal. Then his father had raised his arm and beckoned for him to come and join him. Hasdrubal's eyes widened as they remembered that slow calling motion of his father's hand. What did this mean? Was this a warning?

Hasdrubal suddenly felt his heart thumping in his chest as he thought again about the day on which his father had been killed. He and Hannibal had managed to escape the Iberian ambush but only because his father had led the attackers in the opposite direction. Hamilcar had not even had time to say anything to the brothers before he had made his decision. He had not had a chance to say farewell. He'd been wrenched from them with the suddenness of a lighting strike and after evading the Iberians for long enough to ensure his son's escape, Hamilcar had finally been cornered. But he'd not allowed himself to be taken. Instead he had plunged into the river Jucar and drowned. He'd chosen death before dishonour. He served us with a final example

Hannibal had said afterwards. We shall meet him again in the next world where we will relive what has been before, Mago had said. Hasdrubal closed his eyes. Something felt wrong. Something felt terribly wrong.

Unable to sleep he got up and strapped on his belt and weapons. Then he flung a cloak over his shoulders and stomped out of the tent. His guards followed behind as he strode moodily through the trees. The Carthaginian and Gallic soldiers were for the most part asleep, curled up around their cooking fires but here and there a few were awake. The men were in good spirits and greeted their general with enthusiasm but Hasdrubal hardly noticed them. He could not shake off the sudden premonition of impending disaster. At last, at the edge of the trees he halted. A few hundred paces away, lit by the pale moon light, he could just make out the wooden walls of Placentia. His sharp eyes cast around in the darkness until he saw them. Positioned in a semi-circle around the northern and western walls were the black hulking shapes of his artillery, catapults and bolt throwers. The siege engines sat like great silent black beasts, in the night, waiting to pounce and tear their prey to pieces. Hasdrubal grunted in approval. He'd given the Romans a day to think about their position but so far they had refused to open their gates and the siege had continued. But when morning came he would order his big black beasts into action. Hasdrubal was confident the machines would crush the enemy within a single hour.

He placed his hands on his hips and thought again about the strange dream. His father's body had never been found. Hamilcar had managed to leave nothing behind apart from his name and his legend. Hasdrubal, despite his mood, allowed himself a quick smile. Hamilcar had died like he had lived. The old man had put himself in an unassailable position for eternity.

Suddenly Hasdrubal heard cries of alarm. He turned in the direction of the noise. Then with a whooshing sound, flames leapt up into the night sky. More cries of alarm followed some of which were cut short. A man screamed. Then he saw more flames shooting up into the air.

"What's going on?" Hasdrubal bellowed.

No one answered. Then closer by there was another explosion of flames and then another. Hasdrubal whirled round, shouting but no one seemed to know what was happening. Hasdrubal drew his sword as around him the forest erupted with more explosion of flames, cries and shouting. Then silhouetted against the fire he caught sight of one of his siege engines. It was on fire. The colour drained from Hasdrubal's cheeks. He was being attacked. The enemy had sallied out of the colony and were attacking his artillery.

"Sound the general alarm, they are attacking the catapults!" he roared. But already he knew that it was too late. The forest was littered with raging fires. The darkness hid the enemy assault and Hasdrubal roared in frustration. His guards were spread out in a circle around him, weapons drawn.

Then from the darkness a young officer came running. He gasped as he caught sight of Hasdrubal and for a moment he was bent double, panting for breath.

"The enemy have attacked the siege catapults. They are on fire Sir," he panted. "The Romans came out of nowhere and killed the sentries. They took us by surprise. We can't see them. They are like ghosts. They are throwing fire pots onto the engines and setting them alight."

Hasdrubal stared at the officer as if the man had personally offended him.

"Have the officer whose responsibility it was to guard the artillery, executed," he snarled. "Do what you can to save the remaining catapults."

***

When dawn finally came the extent of the disaster became apparent to all. Littered along the edge of the forest, the smouldering remains of the Carthaginian artillery and siege engines were a testament to the determination of the Roman attack. Not a single catapult or bolt thrower had survived. The speed and precision of the Roman attack appalled Hasdrubal as he rode along the line inspecting the damage. It would take weeks to construct new machines, weeks in which a Consular army would have time to come to the colonies aid. He sat on his horse staring at the ruined machines in disgust. All the effort he'd spent building these machines. What an utter waste of time. He could have been in Umbria by now. He turned and stared at Placentia's walls. The defenders were visible on the ramparts. Oh how they would be laughing at him. The thought brought on a surge of rage. The destruction of his artillery was not the only blow he had suffered that morning. His officers had reported that two thousand Gaul's had slipped away from his army after the attack. Clearly some of his allies didn't think he was going to win.

Hasdrubal turned and rode back towards his tent. He was wasting his time trying to take this colony. It was insignificant anyway. No, he thought making up his mind at last, it was time to head south and rendezvous with Hannibal. The decisive moment for both Carthage and Rome lay in that meeting. He slid from his horse and a slave took the reins.

"Have the generals come to my tent immediately," Hasdrubal snapped at one of his aides, "were leaving this cursed place."

***

Hadrubal was in his tent studying a map when one of his guards entered. The man saluted smartly.

"The men who you asked for general, they are here."

Hasdrubal looked up and nodded. "Good, let them in," he replied. He turned his attention back to the map of Italy. When he looked up again, two men were standing before him. They looked like Celts. The older man was wearing a green cloak with a white border. He looked around thirty. The younger man, a youth of around eighteen was staring at him in naked awe. The boy had long red hair that fell down to his shoulders.

"Good, good," Hasdrubal said taking his time to size the men up. "My officers tell me that you two know the land around Ariminum and Sena Gallica?"

"I am a druid of the Boii," the older man replied with a fierce glint in his eyes. "Rome is my enemy and I will fight her wherever I find her."

"I don't need more soldiers," Hasdrubal interrupted, "I need guides. My army needs men to act as guides. I am not familiar with these lands through which I must pass. Now do you know this area around Sena Gallica or not?"

"Titus knows the land very well," the druid replied. "He grew up along the banks of the Metaurus as did I."

Hasdrubal grunted and examined the two men once more.

"And you are willing to enter my service?" he asked.

"We are willing and we will not disappoint you Sir," the boy said with a fanatic glint in his eyes.

Chapter Thirty-Three - Lord of spies

Marcus sat in his chair trying to suppress the urgent desire to laugh. It was mid-morning and already he could sense that it was going to be a hot day. Outside the army tent in which he found himself he could hear the shouts and cries of the soldiers as they worked to improve the camp's defences. Not that any improvements were necessary Marcus thought. Nero, the Consul had already chosen an excellent defensive position for his forty thousand strong army, but it helped to keep the men busy and prevent them from getting restless and bored.

He forced himself to concentrate on the man who was talking to him. The man, an astronomer, was explaining how he had deduced Hannibal's next move from the way in which the stars were arranged. When the astronomer at last finished speaking, Marcus rose to his feet, nodded solemnly, turned round, so that no one could see his face and rolled his eyes in despair. He'd been in the Consul's camp for just over a week and already he was bored senseless. Nero had been as good as his word. Marcus had become his lord of spies, as the Consul liked to call the newly created post. Marcus's job was intelligence. I need a man with a farmer's instinct and common sense, the Consul had said. Nero had given him the task of finding out what Hannibal would do next. To help him, Nero had gathered together a priest, a lawyer, a mathematician, an astronomer and a linguist. The men, Nero had explained would be at Marcus' beck and call. They were experts in their respective fields. The Consul had however forgotten to mention that none of them had served in the army or had ever done intelligence work before. It seemed to Marcus, that the men he now commanded were simply Nero's friends and acquaintances who needed to be given a job. If the Consul thought such a learned but strange bunch of men were going to guess what Hannibal did next then he was badly deluded. The astronomer had been bad enough but before him the priest had said he knew what Hannibal would do from studying the entrails of a slaughtered chicken.

The mathematician was up next with his report but Marcus raised his hand.

"Enough for this morning. I will speak with you about it tonight."

Without another word he strode from the tent and into the brilliant sunshine of a June morning. He had to get away, just for a few hours at least. If he stayed any longer with those men and their crazy theories, he would go mad. He glanced towards the camp gate and noticed that a mixed group of cavalry, skirmishers and water carriers were about to go out on patrol. The unarmed water carriers were carrying empty leather bags and water skins. They had gathered around a pack of mules. The pack animals had more empty water skins tied to their backs. Without waiting, Marcus undid his horses' reins and leading the beast on foot he strode towards the patrol. Their commander a young Patrician with sharp intelligent eyes examined him warily.

"Mind if I ride with you?" Marcus asked.

"We're going foraging," the young Decurion said. Marcus could see that the young man was struggling to place him in the structure and hierarchy of the army.

"I am on the Consul's staff," he replied. "If you can spare the time I would like to have a closer look at Hannibal's army."

"We'll see," the young Decurion muttered blushing slightly, "My orders are to avoid contact with the enemy."

"Let's hope for your sake then that the enemy doesn't find us," Marcus replied.

For a moment the Decurion looked uncomfortable. Then he turned to his men and gave the order to start moving. The riders, skirmishers, water carriers and their mules started to file out of the camp gate and then turned south down the steep mountain path. A mile away the walls of Canusium glinted and reflected the sunlight. Marcus nudged his horse forward until he rode beside the young officer.

"Were you at Cannae?" the young Patrician asked glancing to the east. Marcus followed his gaze. Nero had been shadowing Hannibal's army for weeks and the strategic movements and counter moves of both armies had brought them close to the old battleground of Cannae, where nine years ago, Hannibal had won his great victory.

"If I had been at Cannae," Marcus said gently, "I wouldn't be here now. I would be dead or serving my disgrace in Sicily."

The patrol entered a small wood and a short while later they emerged onto the crest of a ridge. In the valley below a river wound its way through the hills towards the distant sea. They turned east and began to descend the ridge towards the wide-open plains that they could see in the distance. Marcus turned to stare across the river valley but he couldn't see any movement. Hannibal's camp he knew, was just beyond the crests of the hills, two miles away.

Marcus turned to look north with a grim face. There was nothing more he could do for Publius. His quest for justice had gone as far as it was going to go. Maybe Numa had taken his advice and had ended his own life. Maybe even now he was crossing the sea to the mythical land of the Britons, fleeing to the very edge of the world. Marcus shook his head. He would never likely find out what had happened to Numa, nor would he waste any more time on him. Flavia may have difficulty letting go but there were solid practical reasons why they should move on. They had to get on with living their lives and he needed to look after his farm. His thoughts turned to Livia and the grim determination on his face deepened. Flavia's accusation had touched a raw nerve but the girl was gone, she wasn't coming back, whatever Flavia may secretly hope for. He would buy his wife a new slave girl to replace Livia and if Gaius too had been killed, he would adopt a new son. Someone would have to take over the running of the farm once he grew too old.

The path was descending steeply. Around them the jagged, dry and dusty rocks were interspersed with a few stunted trees and dense tangled undergrowth. Marcus felt the sun's heat on his neck and shoulders. Up ahead, the cavalry who formed the vanguard suddenly peeled off and began picking their way down the slope towards the river. The column of skirmishers and water carriers guiding their mules followed. Marcus nudged his horse to one side to let the men and animals pass. Logistics was not an exciting part of a general's job but it was the most crucial. Once, years ago he'd heard the Consul Aemilius remark that a general always faced four enemies when on campaign. There was the enemy general and then there was thirst, starvation and the weather. The Consul was right Marcus thought. Without supplies an army would wither without a single battle having to be fought.

He looked up at the hills above the river on the opposite bank, but he could see no movement. He grunted and then slowly urged his horse down to the river bank. The water carriers had already reached the river and were wading into the stream, filling their leather bags and skins with water. The skirmishers had fanned out in a protective screen and the cavalry troop together with the young officer in command sat on their horses, at the water's edge, allowing their animals to drink. One or two of the men had dismounted and were scooping water into their helmets and raising them to their mouths. Marcus was about to allow his horse to drink when there was a cry of alarm from the skirmisher picket to his right. Startled, all eyes turned in that direction. The two skirmishers were edging backwards. Their throwing spears were raised, pointing up river. Then Marcus caught sight of movement amongst the trees on the opposite bank. A moment later a group of Numidian horsemen burst from the wood and trotted up to the river bank. They halted as they caught sight of the Romans.

At his side Marcus sensed the young officer was about to open his mouth. Instinctively he reached out and gripped the man's arm.

"Wait, let's wait and see what happens," Marcus snapped.

The Numidians were eyeing the Romans warily. Then they urged their horses forwards and plunged into the shallow river. At his side Marcus heard the Roman cavalrymen unsheathing their swords. Some of the water carriers scrambled back up the bank in panic. But the Numidians did not go far. They halted a few steps into the river and sat on their horses staring at the Romans. Then behind them Marcus caught sight of another group of men, equipped with the same leather bags and water skins as the Romans.

"They are foraging for water too," Marcus spoke rapidly. "They haven't come to fight. Order the water carriers to finish their task and let's get out of here. But do it slowly, show the enemy that we are not afraid. They will think we have larger numbers than we actually do."

The young officer did not argue. The Romans and Numidians stared at each other in silence from across the river as the water carriers hastily continued with their work, casting nervous glances up stream. On the Carthaginian side of the river their men, after a moment's hesitation began to do the same. Then when the last bag and skin had been filled and loaded onto the mules, the young officer ordered the retreat and the Romans began to withdraw back up the hill. On the opposite bank the Carthaginians watched them go. Then they too turned their horses round and vanished back the way they had come.

"We had better return to the camp by a different path," Marcus said as the patrol made it back up to the top of the ridge.

"Why? It's the shortest and fastest way back to the camp?" the officer replied.

"You don't know the Punic mind," Marcus said grimly. "They are masters of the ambush. Those cavalrymen will know our strength and composition by now. They will also know what path we likely came down. It's how they fight. They lure you into a sense of security and then attack where you don't expect it. I was there at Trebbia with the Consul Scipio when I saw

Hannibal trick and ambush an entire army. Let's not make the same mistake, take a different path back."

The officer looked at Marcus in annoyance but Marcus shook his head. "Remember your orders," he said, "you are to avoid contact with the enemy."

The Patrician sighed and shot Marcus a disapproving look.

"Fine," he snapped, "We will return the long way then."

***

The patrol had been walking for over an hour when one of the cavalrymen came riding back up the path towards Marcus and the young officer. His face was flushed. He pulled up beside them.

"Six riders approaching along the path, I think they are Carthaginians Sir."

"Have they seen you?" the young officer exclaimed.

The rider shook his head. "I don't think so. Their horses look worn out."

The officer glanced at Marcus, "What do you say, should we take them or is this another of your Carthaginian ambushes?"

Marcus was staring at the rider. Then he scratched his neck.

"Take them prisoner. I will interrogate them," he replied.

The officer nodded to the rider, "Make sure that you cut off their line of retreat and don't let them see you. Let them come up the path." The rider turned and rode back down the path. Then quickly the skirmishers were ordered to spread out on either side of the track. Marcus, the officer and a couple of cavalrymen remained standing blocking the trail. Behind them the water carriers gratefully lowered their burdens to the ground. The train of mules stood still in dumb silence.

It was not long before the six riders appeared, plodding slowly up the path. They looked weary and their clothes were caked in dust. As the lead horsemen caught sight of the Romans blocking the path his horse reared up on two legs nearly throwing him to the ground. Then the skirmishers jumped up from their hiding places and advanced on the riders from both sides, their throwing spears raised and pointed at the strangers. The young officer urged his horse forward and raised his sword.

"Get down from your horses now. Get down on the ground!" he shouted.

The riders looked startled and surprised. Then the last man turned and with a hoarse yell urged his horse down the slope. He had managed a few paces before he and his horse were struck by four Javelins that brought man and beast crashing to the ground. A moment later the Roman cavalry came thundering up the track.

"I said get down on the ground!"

The lead rider stared around him in confusion. Then seeing that escape was hopeless, he muttered something to his fellow riders in a language that Marcus could not understand. Then
271

slowly he dismounted. The others did the same and as they did so the skirmishers rushed forwards and brutally kicked the men onto their knees. Marcus watched impassively as the men's hands were bound behind their backs. Finally he had some prisoners that he could interrogate. Now at last he could start doing some proper intelligence work.

His eye was suddenly drawn to a leather dispatch case hanging from one of the horses saddles. He frowned. That was odd. He dismounted and strode towards the riders horses, noticing as he did, that all of them were carrying the same dispatch cases. His curiosity grew. This was very odd indeed. With his Pugio, dagger he cut the leather straps that tied the case to the saddle and as he did so, from the corner of his eye, he noticed one of the prisoners glaring at him. From the case, Marcus pulled a tightly rolled scroll that was fastened by a wax seal. His eyes widened with growing excitement.

"What is this?" he held up the scroll and turned to look at the prisoners who were kneeling in a line on the ground.
None of the men replied but as they saw the scroll in his hand, their faces darkened with growing rage and despair.

"Who sent you? Where are you going?" Marcus shouted.

Still the prisoners remained silent.

"Him," Marcus said pointing a finger randomly at one of the men, "if they don't want to talk, then kill him."

Two of the skirmishers grabbed the prisoner by his hair and began to drag him away. Then one of the riders spoke in broken Latin.

272

"Hasdrubal sent us. We were on our way to find his brother Hannibal."

Chapter Thirty-Four - A bold and resolute move

"Sir, wake up, Sir," a hand shook Marcus awake. He stirred and blinked at the man who stood over him. It was the lawyer. The man looked excited. In one hand he was holding an oil lamp. Beyond him through the tent opening, Marcus could see that it was still night.

"We have cracked the code," the lawyer said triumphantly.

Marcus rose to his feet without a word. He had been sleeping in his clothes. He flung his cloak around his shoulders and turned to the lawyer with an appreciative nod. "Good well done, well done," he murmured.

Then he was striding towards the tent where his men had been working. The lawyer followed close behind. The camp was peaceful and quiet and in the dark sky the serene moon bathed the night in its pale light. Marcus' mind however was racing and despite his calm demeanour he was struggling to contain his excitement. To intercept a dispatch between Hannibal and his brother was unheard of. If they could read what one brothers was saying, it could change the outcome of the war. Capturing those six riders had been a remarkable piece of luck for which the Republic would, no doubt, forever be grateful.

He had brought the prisoners back to the Consul's camp. The dispatch cases had all contained the same letter. It had been written in Punic but it had been in code. Marcus had immediately instructed his men to get to work deciphering it whist he had concentrated on interrogating the prisoners. The riders, three Gaul's and two Iberians had however been a disappointment. They had known nothing apart from the name of the man whom had given them the letters and the person whom they were supposed to deliver them to. They had told him that they had left Placentia and had been hoping to find Hannibal near Tarentum but that they had lost their way. Seeing that nothing more could be gained from interrogation, Marcus had ordered the men locked up and placed in solitary confinement. Part of the advantage he now had over Hannibal was that the Carthaginian general did not know his brother's messengers had been intercepted. Nor did Hasdrubal.

Marcus flung aside the tent flap and stepped inside. His men were hunched over a table in the middle of the space talking amongst themselves. They straightened up and fell silent as he entered.

"You have broken the code?" Marcus said with a faint smile.

The men nodded. They looked bleary eyed and exhausted but triumphant. Finally, Marcus thought, feeling a sudden warmth for his learned colleagues, they had had a chance to prove their worth and what a contribution they had made. He would ask Nero to have them rewarded.

"What does the letter say?" Marcus said as they made space for him at the table.

All of them were staring down at the captured parchment that lay before them. Beside it was another parchment on which someone had written a translation with words crossed out here and there.

The linguist cleared his throat and picked up the translation.

"Well," he said, "the letter is written by Hasdrubal himself, we are sure of this. It is indeed addressed to his brother Hannibal. There is a lot about how good it will be to see him again. A few details about his journey through Gaul and across the Alps. Then here is the important part, I shall read it aloud, Sir."

"My men and I are in good shape and will soon take Placentia. I have with me many of our old comrades. I have brought the remaining elephants and the beasts have survived the mountains well. I also have in my possession a great horde of gold and silver which I am bringing to you. The Gaul's are proving ready and enthusiastic allies and many have come to serve me. Their faith in our cause is no doubt bolstered by memories of your passing and the great disasters that you have inflicted on the Romans. Long may it remain so. I must now tell you, brother where I wish us to meet. My opinion is that the eastern route into the heart of Italy will be best and I therefore intend to advance on Ariminum and from there take the Flaminian road to Narnia in southern Umbria. I shall wait for your arrival at Narnia. Do not let the Romans delay you or wear yourself out in minor skirmishes. I intend to reach my destination no later than the end of June."

The linguist paused and Marcus was suddenly aware that all of them were staring at him, waiting for him to speak. As the silence in the tent lengthened it seemed to grow pregnant with excitement. Marcus was staring at the letter, his mind racing, his heart thumping in his chest.

"None of you are to leave this camp," he said at last, looking up.

"None of you are permitted to speak to anyone about what we have just read, on pain of death. Is that clear?"

The men around the table nodded solemnly. Marcus took the letter and the translation and carefully rolled them up. Then he glanced around the table and a smile appeared on his face.

"Well done gentlemen, well done indeed."

***

It was nearly dawn. Marcus stood in the centre of Nero's tent as the Consul sat on his bed reading the translation of the captured letter. When he was finished Nero, rubbed the sleep from his eyes and looked up at Marcus, pondering what he had just read.

"It could be a ruse, a Carthaginian trick to deceive us?" Nero asked.

Marcus looked thoughtful. Then he shook his head.

"I think the letters are genuine. One of the riders died trying to escape, he must really have wanted to avoid being caught and of course we would never have run into them if we hadn't taken a different path back to the camp. Besides if it were a ruse why write the letters in code. It has taken us four days to break the damn thing. I think we can trust that the letters are authentic, Sir."

Nero nodded and bit his fist as he pondered the matter.

"Consul," Marcus said formally, "If I may make a suggestion?"

Nero gestured for him to continue.

"If Hasdrubal is marching south and intends to meet his brother at Narnia it is vital that he is stopped before the two of them can join forces."

"I am aware of that," Nero growled irritably, "But it's Livius's task to stop Hasdrubal. My orders from the Senate are to watch Hannibal."

Marcus nodded respectfully, "But suppose, " he continued, "now that we know where and how Hasdrubal intends to advance, he is suddenly faced by not one Consular army, but by two. Our forces would outnumber him. We would have an excellent chance of defeating him."

Nero was staring at Marcus as if he had gone stark raving mad.

"What are you saying? That I should take my army north and join forces with that arrogant arse Livius? It cannot be done Marcus, the Senate has ordered me to operate against Hannibal, I cannot abandon those orders and besides, do you think that Hannibal will just sit here quietly and watch us depart without doing anything about it. It's lunacy."

But Marcus shook his head. "No Sir," he said firmly, "It is not lunacy, its brilliant."

Nero was watching him carefully. There was a tension in the Consul's eyes and Marcus was suddenly aware of how important for him personally the following words were going to be.

"You do not need to take your entire army north," Marcus said quietly, "Leave the bulk of the men here under your second in
278

command. Let them continue to shadow Hannibal. Issue strict orders that the enemy should not be engaged. Then with a select corps of men, say your best Legion and some cavalry we head north. We march fast and light, we send scouts up ahead warning the villages and towns on our route to come down to the road side and provide us with all the food and water that the men need. Then we rendezvous with Livius. Hasdrubal will not be expecting to fight against two Consular armies. We will annihilate him."

Nero was staring at Marcus, his left eye twitching with nervous energy. But Marcus could see that the Consul was beginning to like the idea.

"How long would it take?" Nero muttered more to himself than to Marcus, "March to Ariminum, fight the decisive battle and then march back to Canusium?"

"We would be gone for at least a month," Marcus replied. "It will take us ten to fourteen days to march the two hundred and fifty miles from here to Livius's camp. I don't think you can expect more from the men, even your best."

Nero nodded.

"I can handle the Senate," the Consul said gruffly rising to his feet. "These are extraordinary times and sometimes protocol must be abandoned. But," he raised his finger in the air in warning, "What about Hannibal? If he gets any indication that I have taken my best men and gone north he could fall on the remainder of my command and obliterate them. He could march on Rome, the road would be wide open. It's a risk, Marcus, a terrible risk. You are proposing that I abandon my command,

279

take away my best men, and hope that Hannibal doesn't find out, for a whole month!"

Marcus nodded solemnly, "Risks must be taken in war time Sir."

The Consul shot him a withering look and Marcus knew he was pushing it.

"Regards Hannibal," Marcus said quietly raising his fingers to stroke his chin. "I suggest that we deceive him to our real intentions. I have a plan."

Nero was instantly alert, his eyes and ears seemed to prick up like a hungry wolf. He gestured for Marcus to continue.

"You are right," Marcus said slowly, "We cannot underestimate Hannibal. He has proved that time and time again." Marcus paused. "Hannibal must be aware that his brother has crossed the Alps and is intent on joining him. He must be waiting for news about where Hasdrubal intends to meet him. He will be anxious for any news from the north. So I propose that we give him this letter," Marcus gestured at the captured parchment, "except that the letter that Hannibal receives will be a forgery. My men will copy the original letter exactly as it is now except we will make a few changes here and there." Marcus paused again. "For instance we will explain that Hasdrubal is besieging Placentia. Hannibal too, if I remember correctly, tried to take Placentia and failed. He will know how long that siege took. Then here where it says the month upon which Hasdrubal hopes to arrive at Narnia, we will change this from June to August. That should give you just enough time to race north, defeat Hasdrubal and return to your command." Marcus paused for a third time, "With luck our forged letter will keep Hannibal in the south until mid July or so. It's not a huge amount of time but it will be enough, Sir."

Nero looked out of breath. His face had grown flushed with sudden excitement. He bit his fist once more as the tick in his left eye twittered like mad.

"It will take a brave man to deliver that letter to Hannibal," he muttered.

Marcus shifted on his feet. "Actually, "he replied, "the man who will deliver the letter will not know anything about it. He will be dead."

Nero looked up puzzled.

"When we captured them, one of the messengers was killed trying to escape. But he is still going to deliver his message," Marcus said grimly. "I shall arrange to have his corpse and that of his horse planted at night beside the river. The Carthaginians come down to the river to collect their water. We will arrange it so that they will find the corpse and they will find the letter in its original case. We will make it look like the man was attacked by bandits."

Nero's ears burned and he fidgeted with his hands.

"Gods Marcus," he murmured at last, "I am glad that you are on our side."

Chapter Thirty-Five - Livia's ambition

The Carthaginian army camp was like nothing Livia had ever experienced before. She followed Titus as they emerged from the forest and strode towards the line of sharpened wooden stakes that had been driven into the ground at an angle. The stakes appeared to be the only defensive fortifications. There was no wall or ditch to protect the camp like the one she had seen at Placentia and the few guards at the main entrance did not challenge them as they approached. The men looked relaxed and confident. One of the guards, a deeply tanned young man smiled at her as she and Titus passed on into the camp.

"I am going to find an officer," Titus said looking around him. "Stay here."

Livia made no reply and she watched Titus wander off towards a cluster of tents in the centre of the camp. In front of the tents, a line of battle standards had been thrust into the ground. As he finally disappeared from view she turned to look around her. Row upon row of white tents stretched to the edge of the rectangular camp. There were soldiers everywhere. Some were sitting around cooking fires, eating, sleeping, washing themselves and cleaning their weapons whilst others were moving about talking and laughing, training and practising with their weapons. As Livia looked on in astonishment, a formation of men dressed in simple white woollen tunics and no armour passed by. In their hands they held slings and across their backs each man carried a leather satchel. She stepped out of the way to let them pass. Then from behind her she heard a sudden trumpeting roar that froze the blood in her veins. She turned and took a few steps forward in order to see around one of the tents. And there, standing in a circle were the greatest, strangest beasts she had ever seen. The great animals, with their huge ears and white tusks, rose above the men who were tending to them. Livia stared at the elephants, unable to look away. She couldn't believe that animals could be so huge.

Suddenly she was surrounded by a small group of men. She blinked in surprise. The sight of the great grey animals had so utterly caught her attention that she hadn't noticed them approaching. The men, unshaven and rough looking grinned and said something to her in a language she couldn't understand. She shook her head to indicate that she didn't know what they were saying. Then from behind her someone suddenly grabbed her arm and spun her round. There was a dim look on the man's face. He smiled as he lazily pulled her towards him and Livia suddenly smelt wine on his breath. Without thinking she raised her hand and raked her nails across the man's face with such force that he loosened his grip with a howl of pain. The next few moments seemed to blur into a mess of confused action.

Livia was aware of angry cries and shouts that she could not understand. Then the circle around her descended into chaos. One of the men tumbled to the ground as if someone had pushed him. Two others jumped back in alarm as a woman with long blond hair and wearing leather armour burst into their midst. The woman was shouting in another language that Livia could not understand. She heard the metallic ring of a sword being unsheathed. One of her assailants took a step towards the fierce woman who had come to her rescue and raised his weapon. Then the man's head jerked back and he cried out as someone behind him grabbed him by his hair. A knife appeared,
283

hovering over the man's exposed neck, and after a pause the man dropped his weapon onto the ground.

Livia stared in surprise as she saw that the person who had jerked the man's head back was another woman. Then she noticed five more women wearing leather armour and holding daggers. They were glaring at her assailants, their hands resting on the pommel's of their swords. The man who had been pushed to the ground slowly got up and looked around him in embarrassment. At his side his friends muttered angrily as they stared at the women who had come to Livia's rescue. Then abruptly they turned away. The man whose face Livia had raked stumbled after them pressing his hand to his face as he tried to stem the bleeding. The woman with the long flowing blond hair approached Livia with a fierce, unfriendly look. She said something to her but Livia could not understand the language. The blonde frowned when she did not reply and then turned to another, smaller woman with black hair and an olive coloured complexion.

"Which camp are you in?" the woman said in thickly accented, broken Latin.

Livia shook her head, "I don't know, my brother and I have just arrived. He has gone to speak with an officer. Who were those men?"

"They were Iberians, they are from the Iberian camp," the dark-haired woman replied slowly. "They think that woman exist only for their pleasure. Stay away from then in future, you hear. They are dangerous men."

"Thank you," Livia nodded her appreciation and her gesture was understood by all the women without the need for a translation, for their aggressive, unfriendly faces softened.

The black-haired woman nodded and turned away but Livia caught her by the arm. There was an intense curiosity in her voice as she spoke.

"I have never seen women wearing armour and carrying weapons. Do you fight, do you really fight in battle, like a man?" The woman nodded, "We are warriors. There are only eight of us here but amongst our people women have the right to fight if they want to."

"What camp are you in?" Livia asked.

"Our people are the Boii and this is our land," the woman replied.

***

When Titus returned he looked in a good mood. "They have put me in the Gallic camp," he exclaimed happily, "I will be receiving the same pay and conditions as all the other Gallic tribes. The Carthaginian officers have divided the army up into camps. Each nation's contingent has its own pay and conditions. The Gaul's they say are amongst the best paid."

"If you can manage to survive until pay day," Livia replied but her brother didn't seem to notice the sarcasm in her voice.

"Come, " Titus said beckoning for Livia to follow him, "Let's go and find them."

285

The two of them made their way deeper into the camp. They passed a long line of siege engines and catapults and then a troop of Numidian horsemen.

"Getorix is here too," Titus said as they continued on.

"I don't like him," Livia replied. "He scares me to death."

Titus smiled good naturedly, "Don't be scared of Getorix," he replied. "He is not really a druid, you know. He only spent two years as an apprentice to a real druid before giving it up. But he likes to tell people he is a druid."

"But you are scared of him," Livia replied raising her chin.

Titus shook his head but did not reply.

Livia closed the gap between them. "Titus," she said struggling to keep up with his fast pace, "What are we doing here? This isn't your war. You can make a living out of hunting. Together we can buy a plot of land. We could build a farm. You can find a wife and I a husband. We can start our own families. That's what's really important. Not this war. This war will give us nothing. Let's just go home."

Titus's pace did not slacken.

"We have talked about this already," he snapped, his voice growing annoyed. "If you don't like what I am doing then leave, go back to Placentia. I am going to fight against the Romans just like my father once did."

Livia did not reply but the stubborn expression on her face remained. She had seen Marcus leave his farm six times when she was growing up. On all six occasions he had been gone for nearly all the summer and most of the autumn too. His military service had been hard on Flavia and all the family and the farm but Livia had understood why it was necessary. Someone needed to go out and defend the land from those who wanted to take it away and give it to others. Marcus had only been doing his duty and Livia liked that. She liked a man who took his duties seriously. But what Titus was doing could not be called duty. There was nothing noble about what Titus was doing. He was a pawn in someone else's war. He was not defending his own land. He was about to throw away his life for nothing.

"Why do you hate the Romans so much. You are half Roman yourself. Are you really going to make war on your mother's people?" Livia said with a sudden upsurge of energy.

Titus glanced at her taken aback by the emotion in her voice.

"Why do you care so much about what I do or don't do?" he retorted.

Livia bit her lip. "You know why I care," she replied fiercely, "because you are the only family that I have got and I don't want to lose my stupid, pig headed brother."

Chapter Thirty-Six - The guides

The Carthaginian camp had moved three times in the past five days. Livia sat in the tent that she had been sharing with eight other women, camp followers like herself. She was mending some clothes with a thread and a bone needle. At the other end of the tent two women were preparing a stew over a small fire. It was noon. Livia looked tired and there were dark patches under her eyes. She had hardly seen Titus in five days. Once the Carthaginian army had started to move south she had been stuck in the rear with the baggage train and the rest of the camp followers. The women who had followed their men were not listed on the army muster rolls and so had been forced to scavenge for their own food but for most of the time the soldiers had shared their rations with their families. Titus too had brought her some bread and stew and she had supplemented this by bartering food in exchange for mending clothes. Some things had not changed she thought wryly. She had spent seven years of her life mending Laelia's clothes.

On the third day the army had finally arrived before the walls of Placentia and the siege of the colony had begun. Livia had wondered whether Faustina had made it out or whether she was trapped inside the town. The news of the two failed Gallic assaults on the settlement had soon spread amongst the camp followers and many anxious women were seen searching for loved ones amongst the weary and dispirited warriors who returned. Titus however had been held back in the reserve, ready to storm into the town once the defences were breached. Then just that morning everyone had been woken up by the sound of sudden fighting from the siege lines that surrounded the colony. The rumour had gone round that the siege engines and catapults had been destroyed by a surprise Roman attack. Livia had believed it. She had seen the burning fires with her own eyes.

Now as she expertly finished patching a woman's cloak she thought again about the strange Celtic women warriors whom she had met. She realised that she knew hardly anything about her father's people. If she was half Celtic it was important to know the customs and traditions of her father's people. Many of the Gallic women only spoke their own language though and when Livia talked to them in Latin she was often greeted with hostility and suspicion. But the information she had gleaned intrigued her. The Gaul's were a far more egalitarian society than the Romans. A woman could become leader of her tribe. Women had acted as ambassadors on diplomatic journeys. They had prevented war between neighbouring tribes. They were allowed to fight if they chose to and most pleasing of all, Livia had learnt that a Celtic woman had the right to divorce her husband if he proved impotent, too fat or if he was in love with another woman or man. She smiled as she thought about what Marcus would make of that. One of the Gallic women had even claimed that it was the very freedom that Gallic women enjoyed which had turned their men into such fierce warriors.

"Out!" a voice snarled suddenly.

Startled Livia looked up and her cheeks paled. Getorix was standing in the tent's entrance. Without a word the two women who had been tending their cooking pot got up and left the tent. Livia was left alone. She rose to her feet and folded her arms across her chest.

Getorix took a step inside the tent and the flap closed behind him. He stooped and sniffed the contents of the pot. Then he looked up at Livia and she felt the familiar dread in her stomach, that his eyes seemed to invoke.

"What do you want?" her voice was barely louder than a whisper.

Getorix took another step towards her and instinctively Livia took a step back. He smiled as he caught the fear in her eyes.

"I hear," he said quietly, "that you have been trying to fill my boy's head with all kinds of nonsense about leaving and returning to that bitch of a mother of his. I have come to tell you that Titus doesn't want to hear such idle women's talk any longer. Do you understand what I am saying?"

"He's not your boy," Livia replied as she squeezed her hands into fists. "He is my brother, he does not belong to you and nor do I. Leave us alone."

Getorix raised his eyebrows. "Leave you alone," he repeated.

"Maybe," he said. "But if you speak to Titus again about wanting him to leave, I am going to come here and cut up that pretty little face of yours. Is that clear?"

Livia felt a sudden stirring inside her.

"With what," she said with sudden contempt, "You are not even a proper druid. I think you only know how to frighten women and children. You aren't half the man that my brother is."

Getorix's face seemed to turn purple and with a violent lunge he smashed his foot into the cooking pot sending the clay pot flying against the side of the tent and its contents splattering onto the ground. Then he was coming at her, his fists raised ready to strike. But before he could reach her, a loud voice outside that sounded like it was rapidly coming closer was calling out his name.

"Getorix, Getorix!"

Then the entrance flap was thrown open and Titus rushed into the tent. As he heard his name being called out Getorix had lowered his fists. His face was just inches away from Livia, so close that she could suddenly smell the wine on his breath. He turned and seeing that it was Titus, he glared.

"Well what is it?" he growled.

Titus had stopped in his tracks. He was staring at the broken pot and the spilt food that lay strewn across the ground. Then he looked up.

"The captain is asking for us," he replied. "We are to report to Hasdrubal's tent immediately. The general himself wants to speak with us personally. The captain mentioned something about becoming guides. We're leaving Placentia. The army is about to march. They say we're heading for Ariminum. We're going home."

Getorix turned his back on Titus and pointed his finger at Livia in silent warning. Then he whirled round and was striding from the tent. Titus however hesitated. He glanced again at the ruined meal and then up at Livia and as their eyes connected Livia thought she saw a sudden guilt on her brother's face.

Chapter Thirty-Seven - The heroes of the day

Beyond the walls of Placentia the fires burned lighting up the night sky with a sinister hellish glow. Gaius and his men came storming back though gate and into the colony. They were jubilant. With the gates securely closed behind them Gaius raised his arm and roared in triumph. Around him the colonists who had formed the raiding party raised their weapons in the air and yelled and shouted. Men turned to hug each other in delight, others bounced off each other's chests with raw energy at their stunningly successful raid. The guards who had remained on the walls stared down at the raiders, grinning from ear to ear. Even Varro, standing beside the watch tower near the northern gate could not help nodding in respect as he caught sight of Gaius. The raiders milled around hooting and celebrating as Gaius climbed up onto the parapet to survey the damage they had inflicted.

"Excellent work," Varro said slapping Gaius on the back. "I didn't think your idea would work. I thought you were leading those men to their doom, but you have proved me wrong. You are learning young man," Varro added with a twinkle in his eye.

"I hope that we got them all," Gaius grinned as he wiped the sweat from his brow. "I suppose we will find out in the morning."

Varro nodded and turned to stare again at the burning Carthaginian artillery. "That will teach them not to be so stupid," he stifled a laugh. Then he turned to Gaius and gestured towards the darkened colony and the loud, ecstatic men below the walls. "Open a couple of barrels of wine and make sure your men have a few drinks. They deserve it."

Gaius gave the ruined Carthaginian artillery a final glance. Then he turned, grinned at Varro and without another word scrambled down the ladder.

***

It was the middle of the night but no one cared. Gaius and the two hundred or so men who had taken part in the raid were crammed into Placentia's Roman tavern. The two barrels of wine that Varro had talked about had turned into eleven and most of the men were completely drunk. Gaius and Hanno sat at the table closest to the hearth in which a log fire had been lit. The men in the tavern had broken out into a rousing patriotic song and the noise must have been audible in the Carthaginian camp. As they sang a young man jumped up onto the table sending cups of wine flying in every direction. The singers broke into great roars of laughter as the young man attempted a dance only to miss his footing and go crashing head first into his comrades, sending them all sprawling.

Gaius chuckled, raised his cup to his lips and then placed it down on the table without drinking. Across the tavern, with his back to the wall, sat the figure of Quintus Valerius Numa. The Senator looked stone cold sober and he was staring at Gaius in a calm, neutral expression that suddenly made Gaius' hairs stand up on his neck.

"Oh you have noticed him have you?" Hanno said in a mocking voice. "He has been staring at you like that all evening."

"You should have a drink," Gaius said. "I thought you liked wine?"

"I do, but not tonight," Hanno replied and there was a tightness in his voice that unsettled Gaius.

He turned to look at the Senator and then raised his cup in salute but across the rowdy tavern Numa made no effort to return the compliment and his gaze didn't waver for a moment.

"What's the matter with him?" Gaius growled. "If the prick doesn't want to be sociable then what is he doing here?"

Hanno too was staring at the Senator.

"It looks to me," the Carthaginian said raising his eyebrows, "that your good friend, the Senator, would like to kill you."

Gaius choked on his wine and burst into a giggle. "Hanno," he said when he'd recovered, shaking his head, "Your talents are wasted as a tutor. You should be up on the stage like my brother Publius. You should be a comedian. Where do you get that ridiculous idea from?"

"I don't know," Hanno looked glum. Then he turned to Gaius with a grim smile and raised his still full cup of wine. "Here is to the heroes of the day."

***

The morning came too soon for Gaius. Wearily he raised his head from the table and held it in his hands, resting his elbows on the table. He had not left the tavern and as he looked around he could see that most of his raiders had followed his example and had fallen asleep where they had been drinking. The colonists snoring filled the room. Gaius glanced at Hanno. The
295

Carthaginian had not left his side. He was still sat on the bench with his head resting against the wall and his eyes closed. Gaius sighed and turned to look to the place where Numa had been sitting but there was no sign of the Senator. He had gone.

Gaius stumbled out of the tavern and into the bright sunlight. Shielding his eyes with his hand he strode towards the walls. The sentries on duty paid him no attention as he clambered up onto the ramparts.

"What news?" he asked one of the men as he came and stood beside him.

In response the sentry pointed to the east. "They are preparing to leave," the man replied. Gaius squinted into the sun and sure enough in the distance he could see groups of infantry and cavalry marching away. Catching sight of Varro standing in the watch tower he made his way along the walls and up to the top of the watch tower. Varro too was watching the enemy movements.

"Do you think it could be a trick?" Gaius muttered staring at the retreating enemy.

Varro looked undecided. "Maybe," he replied, "I don't know. It does very much look like Hasdrubal is leaving though. They are breaking up their camp."

Gaius nodded without saying anything.

"We had some Carthaginian deserters come in this morning," Varro exclaimed suddenly. "Gaul's, they told us that there is a Roman supply convoy of fourteen river barges waiting down

296

river, a day's sailing from us. The deserters say that the boats are waiting until Hasdrubal has gone. It's good news."

"Good news, indeed," Gaius nodded, "When they arrive I will finally be able to be on my way to Rome. I have a pregnant wife and a son waiting for me at Ostia."

Varro glanced cautiously at Gaius.

"I thought you said that you were attacked by Pirates?"

Gaius bit his lip, "We were," he said staring at the distant horizon, "But my wife and son were on another ship. They will have made it to Ostia. They will be there waiting for me."

Varro was silent. Then he patted Gaius on his back, turned and strode away along the parapet.

***

It was just after sunrise two days later when a Roman patrol reported seeing ships coming up the Po. By noon the Roman supply convoy had docked beside the small river bank harbour and a long line of men were hauling the boats supplies into the colony. The colonists were jubilant. Hasdrubal and his army had gone. Placentia had survived her siege in heroic fashion.

Gaius and Hanno were on board one of the river barges negotiating their passage down the Po and onwards to Ariminum when Hanno suddenly touched Gaius' arm. Gaius looked up and saw Numa approaching the boat. The Senator was dressed in travelling clothes and in his hand he held a walking stick.

"I am coming with you," Numa said as he stepped on board the boat.

"Senator, we are glad to have you as company," Gaius nodded respectfully but Numa did not return the compliment. Instead he pressed a small bag of coins into the captain's hand, "Let's be on our way as fast as you can. I want to be in Ariminum within four days."

"Four days," the boat's captain looked dubious, "I am not sure we will be able to go that fast Sir. My men are tired. They have spent fourteen days pulling the boats up river. They need a rest."

"Four days, captain," Numa snapped, "We leave as soon as you have finished unloading."

"But what about the other ships?" the captain protested. "They haven't been unloaded yet?"

"Then we shall sail alone," the Senator replied picking his way to the rear of the craft.

Gaius and Hanno exchanged glances. The boat's captain stared down at the bag of coins in his hand. Then he closed his fingers around the money and shrugged.

"Tell the men that they will not be sleeping in Placentia tonight," he shouted to one of his sailors who was supervising the unloading. "Tell them to get back to the boat at once. We're going back down the river."

Chapter Thirty-Eight – The night watchman

As the river barge pushed away from the bank Gaius saw Varro standing on the wooden harbour jetty. He looked sombre, as if he was sad to see them go. Gaius raised his arm in farewell and on land, Varro did the same. Gaius grinned and gave Placentia a final glance. It was strange, he thought, but in the few days that he had been here, he had begun to like the new town, so boldly planted in the midst of enemies. Then he lowered his arm and turned to look downstream. The Po was a mighty river. The water was wide and placid. It was the largest river he had ever seen. The land along her banks was flat, green and heavily wooded. A lush land, Celtic land, Flavia his mother had called it, when she had taught him and Publius about the geography of Italy. Gaius reached out with his hand to steady himself on the boats single mast, as he thought about his mother and Publius. His mother had not been the best of teachers and Publius and he, as children, had often made fun of her lessons behind her back, but now as a young man he was glad for the gifts his mother had equipped him with. He was glad she had taken the time to teach him for there were so many ignorant, stupid men in the world. He thought of Livia and little Laelia. Laelia would be seven years old now. Yes, it would be good to see them all when he returned to Rome.

He grinned but his happiness was mixed with sudden anxiety. His family would no doubt want to hear about his time in Spain. The slaves would prepare a feast and his father would pour some of his finest and oldest wine. He would spend a whole day filling them in. Then he would take Publius and Livia and the three of them would go into Rome for a well-deserved drink, maybe a few drinks. He would make the usual derogatory comments about his brother's sexual inclination and Publius would pretend to be offended. Then the two of them would tease Livia, proposing suitable boys for her to marry. Then when the three of them had had a good laugh he would tell them about his pregnant wife and his son. He would bring them to the farm the next day and present them formally to his family. It would be good to be home. It had been too long.

His thoughts were interrupted by the bad-tempered muttering of the men around him. The eight men who had pulled the boat up stream for fourteen days and who now acted as rowers were not happy and they didn't care who heard it. Which idiot ordered us to go back so soon? Look at my blisters, Placentia's whores will miss us, four days! You got to be joking, thorny pricks!

"Enough," the boat's captain cried sternly, "You will all receive a bonus when we put in at Ariminum. The whores in that town are better anyway."

But the bad-tempered muttering would not go away.

Gaius turned to look towards the rear of the barge. Numa had found himself a comfortable place from which he could watch the whole deck. Now he sat cross legged on the deck, his back resting against a barrel, his eyes fixed on Gaius. Gaius blinked at the intensity of the Senator's gaze. What was the matter with that man? In his belt Gaius noticed that the Senator was carrying a Pugio, an army dagger which he had not seen him carrying before.

Gaius was aware that Hanno had come to stand by his side. The one-armed man too was staring at Numa.

"Want me and some of the boys to tip him overboard during the night?" Hanno said quietly. "The rowers don't give a toss about their bonus. They are exhausted. I am sure that they will gladly help."

Gaius glanced at Hanno but the Carthaginian looked serious.

"For fuck's sake," Gaius whispered, "The man is my father's best friend. He has known me nearly all my life and you want to murder him? What's the matter with you Hanno?"

"Just an instinct," Hanno replied grimly, "I don't like the way he stares at you. There is something not right with that man. I can feel it. Stay away from him Gaius. He does not wish you well."

Gaius shook his head in dismay. He glanced again across the boat at Numa. Then without another word he began to pick his way towards the Senator. Hanno hissed in warning but Gaius ignored him.

"Senator," Gaius said with a polite smile as he paused before Numa, "a fine day for a river journey but I was just wondering why the haste, why do you need to be in Ariminum in four days?"

"That's my business," Numa responded sharply. He lifted his head to look at Gaius with a strange intensity and Gaius was suddenly aware of bitterness in the Senator's demeanour, a terrible, festering, all-consuming bitterness.

Gaius hesitated. "What brought you to Placentia in the first place? Are you not needed in Rome?"

301

"Questions," Numa replied, "always more questions, why are you asking me these things? What does it matter now?"

Gaius frowned with sudden irritation, "I was just trying to speak with you Sir, as someone who has known you all his life. You are my father's best friend are you not?"

"Your father disappoints me," Numa replied coldly, "My children disappoint me. Everyone has disappointed me."

Gaius shook his head. "I don't understand. How has my father disappointed you?"

Slowly Numa rose to his feet and as he did so Gaius felt a sudden tremor of unease. He took a step back. Numa was staring at Hanno who stood by the boats mast. Numa's lips curled in contempt.

"Tell your slave to stop looking at me like he does? I don't like the look of his face," Numa snarled spitting into the river.

Gaius nearly blurted out that Hanno felt the same about him but he checked himself just in time.

"His name is Hanno," Gaius replied angrily, "and he has my permission to look at anyone he likes in any way he likes."

***

The following morning Gaius noticed that Hanno looked more tired than usual. But when he had inquired about it Hanno had muttered an inaudible reply and Gaius had not pressed the matter. There had not been much to do on board the boat and

302

everyone would have been bored out of their minds if it wasn't for the constant threat of being attacked by Gallic tribesmen. But they saw very few people that day. The rowers had finally given up their bad-tempered muttering and steered the boat in sullen silence. The boat's captain had kept on going down the river during the night, something that was not usually done but the lure of a bonus payment if he reached Ariminum in four days had worked its magic on the master. Numa had hardly moved from the position he'd chosen at the rear and throughout the day Gaius felt the man's eyes upon him, boring into him with their festering bitterness. They had not spoken again since that first conversation. Hanno was right, Gaius had concluded, there was something wrong with his father's friend but he would be damned if he was going to ask the Senator what it was. He had more important matters to think about.

On the third day out from Placentia, Hanno had begun to look positively exhausted. His eyes kept closing and opening and he seemed to exist in a daze. His usual cheerful talkative nature had vanished. Gaius shook his head in puzzlement but left his slave alone. The landscape along the river had begun to change as they approached the delta where the Po flowed into the Adriatic Sea. As the solitary boat drifted along on its journey, the Po began to split into different channels. The high-pitched squawks of sea gulls circling high in the sky greeted them. On the river bank the forest began to give way to flat wetlands and marshes, sand dunes and salt pans. The delta was beautiful and rich in game and as they approached the sea the rowers seemed to relax. They were nearing Roman territory.

Something woke Gaius in the middle of that night. He blinked and stared up at the stars above him, unsure of where he was for a moment. Then he felt the pitch and roll of the boat and the
303

gentle slap of the waves against her side. A cool, salty tasting breeze was blowing and the captain had raised the sail. They must have reached the sea at last. He sat up and stared around the deck. The bodies of the rowers lay curled up asleep beside their oars but at the front of the boat, in the pale moon light he could just make out the figure of the ship's captain staring out into the night. A sudden movement beside Gaius startled him.

"Sorry," Hanno muttered. The one-armed Carthaginian sat cross legged on the ground, a blanket draped around his shoulders. In his hand Gaius saw that he was holding a knife. Hanno was staring towards the rear of the boat where Gaius could just make out a curled figure covered in a blanket.

"What are you doing?" Gaius whispered.

"Guarding you," Hanno muttered, "against him."

Gaius turned and looked again in the direction in which Hanno was staring. Then it all began to make sense and he closed his eyes in silent understanding.

"How long have you been doing this?" he whispered.

"Three nights and three days," Hanno grunted.

Chapter Thirty-Nine – Northern terminus

The town of Ariminum came into view late that afternoon. The boat's captain cried out in delight and turned triumphantly to look at Numa.

"Not many will be able to boast a faster time than ours," the captain chuckled.

Gaius peered towards the shoreline. The sea was calm and the northern wind had provided the rowers with a welcome respite. On the shore he could make out a long sandy beach. Tiny figures were playing in the surf. As they approached the harbour entrance two Roman warships came out to intercept them. The captain, seeing them, ordered the sail to be lowered and the river barge bobbed aimlessly up and down as the warships approached, one to either side, their long ponderous oars moving slowly and in perfect harmony. At the prows of the galleys, bronze tipped battering rams poked their heads through the gentle swell. On the deck of the ships Gaius could see a party of archers and slingers staring back at them. The captain raised his hand in greeting as the nearest Roman ship came alongside and from the Roman vessel her captain returned the greeting.

"Weren't expecting to see you so soon? Did you manage to get through to Placentia?" the captain on the warship shouted across the water.

"We did," the captain of the river craft shouted back, "Placentia is no longer under siege. Hasdrubal has marched away. The last I heard he was heading this way. I reckon he will be at the gates of Ariminum within a week. You boys are going to see some action."

The captain on the warship looked sceptical. "Not unless Hasdrubal has hauled ships across the Alps as well," he shouted back. "But yes you are right, that is what I have heard too."

"What news have you?" the master cried as the two ships wallowed in the sea.

"The Consul Livius has arrived with his army," the captain of the warship shouted. They are camped just south of here along the Flaminian Way and the Praetor Porcius has marched north to try and slow Hasdrubal's advance. But it's good news about Placentia. We're bursting with refugees. They will be glad to hear that news. You had better come into the harbour and tell them yourself."

"What news from Ostia?" Gaius shouted suddenly. It was more in hope than from any realistic expectation. "Have you been to Ostia recently, captain? Any news of a convoy of ships inbound from Tarraco?"

The captain on the warship turned to peer at Gaius. He was silent for a moment.

"I haven't been to Ostia in a year," he cried back, "but I will tell you something else. One of the captains who came into the port a few hours ago is saying that the other Consul, Nero, is marching north along the coast with all possible speed. He is coming to join Livius and unite their forces."

Gaius's shoulder sagged in disappointment at the news but from the corner of his eye he noticed that Numa had suddenly risen to his feet. The Senator was staring at the warship with sudden, intense interest.

Gaius had never been to Ariminum. The city had been built at the mouth of the Ariminus River from whence it had taken its name. The town had been constructed in the familiar rectangular shape of a Roman army camp and the stone walls of the colony looked solid and imposing as they came right down to the water's edge. Gaius could see that the town was larger and more established than Placentia. It has been a Latin colony for over fifty years, and the colonists enjoy Latin rights his mother had once told him. In other words, Roman law allowed the colonists of Ariminum to marry, do business and own land within their community and interact with other Latin towns but forbade them from voting in the Roman consular elections. Ariminum was the most northerly town of Italy proper. It was where Italy started. It was the gateway to Gallia Cisalpina and the northern terminus of the great Via Flamina, the road that led south to Rome. A strategic town and from the huge grain silo's that he could see inside the city, an important logistics base. Gaius faintly remembered hearing it said that one day a new road would be built which would connect Ariminum with Placentia but the war had put paid to that idea. The war had put an end to many things he thought.

The ship's captain guided his vessel expertly through the narrow harbour entrance that had been built at the river mouth. Ships of all sizes rode at anchor within the protective embrace of the two straight harbour breakwaters. The moles were about six yards wide and had been built of great mounds of jagged rocks that had been tumbled into the sea. Running along the landward side of the mole was a solid stone harbour wall. The moles and the harbour wall were interrupted by a single sluice gate that faced the river and another that faced seawards. The two gates were opened periodically to allow the flow of river water to prevent the harbour from silting up. Inside the harbour the wooden jetties running alongside the water's edge were a hive of activity with the loading and unloading of supplies. As they approached, Gaius could see that a large group of people, mainly women and children had gathered along the jetties. They were staring anxiously at the river craft. Further up the shoreline, on the path leading from the river to the city gates a column of people were moving into the city. The men, women and children were carrying their possessions on their backs or pushing them along on carts. They looked wretched and exhausted. Behind them herds of sheep, cows and oxen were being driven towards the city gates.

"Refugees," the ship's captain muttered.

As they came alongside the wooden pier the crowd on the jetty cried out. "What news from Placentia? Is the town safe? Are they still besieged?" The anxiety in the women's voices was unmistakable and urgent.

"The siege is lifted, Placentia is safe," the boat's captain cried raising his arms and from the shore a huge cry of joy and relief rose up. Then as the boat moored the crowd swarmed aboard, mobbing the captain for more news. The ship's captain struggled to maintain his footing as women tugged at his clothes, bombarding him with questions, but despite the ruckus there was a wide grin on the captain's face.

"Looks like he's enjoying himself," Hanno muttered sarcastically as he and Gaius looked on, "Look at him, you would think that he alone had been responsible for the defence of the colony."

Gaius smiled and bent down to gather up his belongings.

"Where's the Senator?" Hanno said suddenly.

Gaius straightened up and looked around the boat. The crowd were still mobbing the captain but there was no sign of Numa. He had vanished.

"He must have slipped ashore amongst the crowd. Let him go Hanno."

Hanno, dark patches under his eyes muttered something in his own language. Then he followed Gaius and jumped onto the jetty.

Ariminum's forum was crowded and Gaius and Hanno had to physically struggle through the multitude as they made their way to the horse dealers stall. Gaius stared around him. Fear gripped the town. Fear bordering on panic. It was everywhere. He saw it in the people's eyes, he saw it in the aggressive soldiers; he saw it in the closed shutters of the houses and in the urgent, harsh haggling between the merchants and customers. The news of Hasdrubal's advance must be sweeping across the whole of Italy he thought. In every Roman, Latin and allied town and village the news must be having the same effect. The very name of Hannibal's brother seemed to be a weapon. The Roman people were being tested like never before. This was not only a war between armies, Gaius realised as he looked about him. It was a battle of nerves between whole nations, a war of stamina, of morale and of willingness to keep on fighting when there was no end in sight. If Rome were to endure and emerge victorious, its victory would not only have been won by her armies, it would have been won by the steadfastness of her people and the strength of kinship that now bound Roman, Latin, Etruscan, Umbrian, Samnite and Campanian together into a great and unbreakable alliance.

The horse dealer was a dark-haired man of around forty who seemed to be suffering from rickets. He nodded curtly at Gaius and Hanno as they eased up to the front of his stall. From around his neck Gaius produced a small bag of coins, showed it to the horse dealer and then placed the bag on the table but kept his hand over it.

"We want to buy two horses, how much?" Gaius asked.

The horse dealer glanced at the money and then scratched his chin. "The army has taken my entire stock," he replied. "All I have got left are two lame beasts. Where are you heading?"

"To Rome," Gaius replied.

The horse dealer looked doubtful, "I suppose they will manage that as long as you don't ride them too hard." He glanced again at the money, "I will give you an honest price, gentlemen. The horses are in the cattle market. Meet me there in an hour and you can see them for yourself. You can pay me then."

"An honest horse dealer," Hanno remarked, "Now there is something I have not seen before."

The horse dealer ignored Hanno. He gestured at Gaius, "You look like an honest man Sir," he said. "If you are travelling to Rome would you be able to deliver a letter for me to my brother? He's a doctor serving with the Consul Livius. The army is camped a day's walk from here along the Flaminian road. I will make it worth your time."

"I hope you do," Hanno muttered.

Gaius nodded in reply and as he did so the horse dealer suddenly leaned forward conspiratorially.

"I am not really supposed to tell you this," he muttered, "but I can't see how they can keep it a secret. The messengers are telling everyone. All the towns and villages know about it."

"Heard what?" Gaius frowned.

"The Consul Nero, he's marching north with his army. They say he's going to join forces with the Consul Livius."

***

Gaius was glad to leave the press of the forum behind him. He found a side street and darted into it closely followed by Hanno. There were fewer people here but as they strode down the street towards the industrial quarter of the town, Gaius turned warily to look behind him. It was probably nothing but he had the strangest feeling that they were being followed. He saw nothing unusual though. People were going about their daily business and no one seemed to give them a second look. He glanced at Hanno but the Carthaginian hadn't seemed to notice his concern. Hanno looked utterly exhausted and Gaius suddenly felt guilty. He should have realised sooner what Hanno had been up on the boat. He should have ordered him to sleep. Now Hanno looked like he was sleep walking.

The horse dealer had told them that the cattle market was at the far end of the industrial quarter. As they strode along the street Gaius could suddenly hear the dull metallic hammering of blacksmiths at work in their workshops and armouries. Black smoke billowed up from the chimneys and the air had become heavy with the smell of burning charcoal. A boy passed by pushing a cart laden with wooden Hasta spear shafts that had not yet had their metal points fitted.

Gaius and Hanno turned into an alley. There were not many people about in this quarter of town. They were half way down the narrow alley when Gaius felt, rather than heard, someone rapidly approaching from behind. He turned to look behind him. Numa loomed up before him, his face hideously contorted, his hand raised high in the air holding a dagger. Gaius had no time to shout or move. The knife was plunging down towards him and as it did Numa's mouth opened with a howling, shrieking roar of rage. Then a body thrust itself between Gaius and the knife. Hanno took the full force of the blow. The dagger went straight into his chest. The Carthaginian staggered under the impact stumbling back into Gaius. A large red stain rapidly appeared on his tunic. Hanno stared down at the knife and his hands closed round it. Then he gasped, staggered back again the alley wall and slowly slumped to the ground. Gaius stared in horror at Numa. The attack had been so swift and violent. He wanted to run but instead without thinking he pulled his sword from his belt. Numa was still shrieking as he advanced towards Gaius. Spit flew from his mouth as he flung aside his cloak and wrenched a sword from his belt. Gaius stumbled back down the

312

alley. Then he steadied himself. The two of them stared at each other and Gaius could hear himself panting. Fear tightened and knotted in his stomach. Numa was not yet an old man. The meek man he'd known in Placentia had been replaced by the fighter Gaius had always known him to be. Numa was fit and he was in good shape. Beside the wall, Hanno's head had slumped to one side. He was not moving.

"Why?" Gaius screamed.

Numa was slowly coming towards him with his sword raised but he looked wary. Saliva dribbled from the corners of his mouth. His eyes were fixed on Gaius with an unshakable, murderous determination.

"If I am not allowed to have anything, then neither is he," Numa hissed. "He took everything from me, so now I am going to take everything from him."

"Who, who are you talking about?" Gaius shouted taking a step backwards. The murderous determination in Numa's eyes terrified him. How could this man hate him so much? What had he done?

"Your father. Marcus!" Numa roared.

A man turned into the alley, stopped as he caught sight of the standoff between the two-armed men, then abruptly turned on his heels and fled.

Gaius' mind was racing. He had no idea what Numa was talking about.

"You were his friend?" Gaius said shaking his head as he took another step back.

Contempt crept into Numa's eyes and his lips curled. He took a step forwards, his eyes darting to and fro, looking for an opening in which to strike.

"Just like your brother," Numa sneered, "So innocent and honest. I am a traitor Gaius. I have sold myself to Rome's enemies. Why can't you see what I have done and what I have become?"

Gaius felt his heart pounding in his chest.

"You are a spy, you are working for Carthage," he murmured.

"Yes, yes," Numa roared raising his sword suddenly and violently, "for three years I have been fucking Rome and no one ever knew about it. Those conceited idiots, those arrogant men in the Senate, who think that they can rule the world. None of them could ever dream that there was a traitor amongst them. How could they? Their class after all belongs to the purest blood of Rome."

"You are mad, you have gone mad," Gaius muttered.

"No," Numa hissed, "No, I came back for you. I was on my way to warn Hasdrubal that the second Consul is coming north but I couldn't leave, could I. Not without killing you. Hasdrubal will pay handsomely for my information. But I came back for you, Gaius. I want your father to feel the pain that I have had to endure."

Gaius glanced at Hanno. The Carthaginian had collapsed onto his side but his eyes were still open and as Gaius looked at him, Hanno blinked.

"You shouldn't have come back for me," Gaius replied, "That was a mistake. You should have run back to your master. You have served him badly."

Numa scoffed in contempt. "When I am finished with you, Marcus will have lost both his sons. He will have nothing left to live for."

Gaius stopped moving backwards and a quiet calm seemed to come to him. "My brother is dead?"

Numa took another step forward, his eyes were darting; his body straining for the right moment in which to attack. "I gutted him like a pig," he hissed, "and now I am going to do the same to you."

Gaius felt a warm rush break over him like a wave. With a howl he flung himself forwards. Numa snarled like a dog and stabbed at him with his sword but at the last moment Gaius twisted sideways and the sword jabbed into thin air. The Senator took the full force of his charge and Gaius smashed into him and the two of them tumbled to the ground in a frenzied tangle of arms and legs. Someone was screaming like a wounded boar and Gaius suddenly realised that it was himself. He dropped his sword and his fingers closed around the Senator's neck. He squeezed. Numa spluttered and tried to raise his arm to stab Gaius but he was pinned down. The spluttering turned to a wheeze and his face began to turn blue. Then Gaius released his grip, grabbed the man's face with both hands and smashed
315

Numa's head into the paving stones. The frenzied attack continued until Numa was no longer moving and the back of his skull had become a fractured mess of slimy, bloody brain pulp.

Gaius staggered to his feet. His hands and tunic were covered in blood and Numa's brains. His chest heaved. He kicked Numa's sword from the man's lifeless hand and the weapon went clattering down the alley. Then, unable to control himself, he launched himself at the corpse, kicking and kicking at Numa's body with all his might. A whimper from down the alley stopped him. Hanno had stretched out his arm towards him. The Carthaginian lay on his side in a large pool of blood. He was trying to speak.

Gaius stepped over the corpse and knelt down beside his friend. Hanno's face had turned very pale and there was a thin stream of blood running down from his mouth. Gaius raised Hanno's head and cradled it in both arms. The Carthaginian opened his eyes and stared at Gaius. Then his face creased into a faint smile.

"I am proud to have known you," Hanno whispered so faintly that Gaius had to bend his ear to Hanno's mouth. "Burn my body, scatter my ashes at sea."

Gaius felt tears running down his face. He nodded that he had understood. Hanno was looking up at him, the faint smile still in place. "I suppose," he whispered, "that I now will never see Himilco's colony in the new world. I did so want to see that place."

Then he closed his eyes and his head rolled to one side.

Chapter Forty - To Rome! To Rome!

Hasdrubal rode on down the track with an aggressive look on his face. His bodyguards followed closely behind. One of his guards, Bostar, was carrying Hasdrubal's battle standard and the general himself was clad for battle in his magnificent armour. It was just after sunrise but already the Carthaginian army was on the move. In front of him groups of Iberian, Ligurian and Libyan heavy infantry were advancing in a long column. The sound of their tramping feet and the jingle and rattle of their weapons was a reassuring noise. The Iberians were amongst the finest heavy infantry in the west Hasdrubal thought and he knew he could rely on them for anything. The Iberians were far from home in a strange foreign land. His Iberians would not run. They would stand and fight for there was nowhere to run too. When the decisive battle came, it would be the Iberians who would drive the Roman infantry from the field. Further ahead, out of sight, he knew would be his fifteen elephants. The beasts may not be numerous but their appearance would put the fear of the gods into the Romans and handled well they would create chaos in the enemy ranks. Hasdrubal allowed himself a brief satisfied smile. The elephants were his terror weapons.

To his left partly shrouded in the early morning fog was another column of Numidian and Iberian cavalry. The Numidian's from the dusty dry wastes of Mauretania and North Africa rode their small shaggy horses as if they had been born on a horse. The finest cavalry in Africa, by far, a captured Roman commander had once told Hasdrubal. The Numidians rode without saddles and protective armour, relying on their speed and mobility to harass the enemy with volleys of spears. It had been the

Numidian cavalry who had allowed Hannibal to envelop and utterly crush the Romans at Cannae but now as he examined his men Hasdrubal wished that he had more of these superb riders, for their numbers were small and they had suffered in the crossing of the Alps.

To his right was a third column of men, plodding through the mist. The warriors looked like ghosts as they vanished and reappeared out of the fog. Hasdrubal's lip curled in contempt. The Gaul's may make up half his army but they had disappointed him so far with their laziness and lack of discipline. Eight thousand more had slipped away from his army since they had started out from Placentia some twelve days ago and their steady desertions had begun to seriously concern Hasdrubal. He had around thirty-five thousand men, enough to face a full Consular army but if the Gaul's continued to desert then the balance would change. He was not concerned by their individual fighting ability for the Gaul was a fine, powerful warrior, but as a unit and group they were nearly impossible to control or move about on the battlefield in any tactically meaningful way. All they seemed to want to do was fight and steal. And then there was the problem of drunkenness. The Gaul's had not once missed a single opportunity to get hopelessly drunk on captured Roman wine.

Hasdrubal turned grimly to look behind him. Strung out as far as he could see was the main baggage train guarded by a strong rearguard of Iberian Cavalry and light infantry skirmishers. In between the carts laden with provisions of all kinds shuffled groups of chained Roman prisoners. The Romans looked miserable, exhausted and starving but Hasdrubal took no joy from seeing his enemy in such a state. The prisoners reminded him of the difficulties he'd begun to experience. Porcius, the

318

Roman Praetor who commanded an army of two Legions had been harassing his advance for the past three days now. The Romans had begun to attack Carthaginian foraging parties. They had left small rear guards to defend river crossings and as they had retreated, they had destroyed bridges, farms and anything that could prove useful to Hasdrubal. The further he had advanced the more scorched the land had become until it had began to feel as if he was marching into a desert. The harassment had not been unexpected but it still disconcerted Hasdrubal because the Romans were destroying their own land. They were not going to give in without a fierce and hard-fought battle. Well the sooner the better he thought grimly.

Two riders suddenly burst from the fog to his right and seeing Hasdrubal they turned and guided their horses towards him. Hasdrubal raised his chin.

"Well, what news?" he demanded.

The two scouts took a moment to catch their breath. "Our advance guard are about three miles from Ariminum, general," one of them replied. "The Consul Livius's army looks like it has joined forces with the Praetor Porcius. They are falling back down the Flaminian road."

"Good," Hasdrubal grumbled, "that means that they fear us. How far before we reach the Metaurus River?"

"The Gallic guides say that the river is about forty miles away," the scout replied. "But they warn that she will be in flood at this time of the year. The river may be difficult to cross Sir."

"Well we will deal with that when we get there," Hasdrubal growled. He lifted his chin once more in an aggressive posture. "What is the state of affairs at Ariminum? Is the town burning?" The scout shook his head. "They have closed their gates on us.

The city itself looks peaceful and quiet. There is no smoke or fire, General."

Hasdrubal looked disappointed as he dismissed his men. The two scouts turned and rode back up the column vanishing into the mist. Hasdrubal tightened his grip on his horses reins. Soon he knew the Romans would turn and make a stand and challenge him to battle. When that day came he would have to make a decision about what to do with the hundreds of Roman prisoners that he'd taken during the skirmishes with Porcius' troops. Some of his officers had argued that the Romans should be executed at once for they were a burden on the army. But Hasdrubal had resisted the temptation up to now. Tradition dictated that he ransom the prisoners for he was always in need of money to pay his mercenaries. Then again, how likely was it that he would get the time to arrange a ransom? He bit his lip with sudden indecision as around him his army advanced through the mist.

It is imperative that I should not be distracted by what the Consul Livius wants me to do. I am marching to join Hannibal. The decisive battle is not here in the north. It will come with Hannibal at my side in front of the gates of Rome. If Livius makes a stand I will somehow have to try and slip past the Romans and make it to Narnia without being blocked or engaged. I must avoid battle at all costs until the union with Hannibal has been made.

Hasdrubal blinked as he realised that he had been daydreaming. He glanced around to see if anyone had noticed. But no one was looking at him. Then behind him he suddenly heard the clattering of hooves and a moment later a party of six riders appeared escorting a solitary man on horseback. The man had a hood draped over his head that concealed his face but Hasdrubal knew who he was. Hasdrubal's face grew cold and ruthless. He glanced silently at the riders for an explanation as they rode up to his side.

"He was trying to sneak out of the camp," the leader of the riders exclaimed, "So we caught him and brought him here," the man shrugged.

Hasdrubal stared at the hooded figure.

"Well is this true Gisgo? Were you trying to desert?"

The hooded man raised his head but made no reply. His hands had been bound behind his back.

Hasdrubal regarded his lord of spies with growing contempt. Since the failure to capture Placentia he'd become suspicious of Gisgo and had entrusted six men to keep an eye on him. Hasdrubal had no desire to share the same fate as his father's son in law who had been murdered by a close friend. Carthaginian politics had always been deceitful and violent and the sad truth was that he could not always trust a compatriot to be on the same side. Hasdrubal understood Carthaginian politics all too well. That personal rivalry and the fractious politics that had so far stained the Carthaginian war effort had been at its worst in Spain where the Romans really should have been driven out a long time ago if it hadn't been for the petty rivalries and jealousies of the Carthaginian Senate and her generals. Only the Barca family and her three sons had followed a consistent war strategy. Carthage should have been thankful to the Barcids for what they had achieved but Hasdrubal knew the old mother city was not. The merchant princes who ruled Carthage were more concerned with profit and how the war was damaging their trade. They did not grasp the fact that if Rome were victorious, Carthage was doomed.

"You assured me that your agent would set fire to Ariminum," Hasdrubal hissed, "You told me that he would burn the Roman supply depots and armouries. Yet my scouts tell me the town looks peaceful and untouched. This is another failure."

The figure beneath the hood still did not reply. Hasdrubal glared at Gisgo.

"You have failed me for the final time," he cried angrily. Hasdrubal turned and nodded to the riders. "Crucify him," he barked.

"No!" Gisgo screamed suddenly, "No, you cannot do that!"

The riders turned and began to pull Gisgo with them. The lord of spies twisted his head and flung his hood from his head as he stared at Hasdrubal with wild eyed hatred.

"You will follow me, son of Hamilcar!" he roared. "You will dine with me and the gods of the underworld before the month is done. I shall be waiting for you. You shall never be rid of me!"

Then still staring wildly at Hasdrubal, Gisgo seemed to bite down into something and swallow. A moment later his eyes closed, white froth appeared in the corner of his mouth, his body went into an uncontrollable spasm, then limp and slowly he toppled from his horse onto the ground.

"Poison, Sir," one of the riders said as the men clustered around the corpse. "He's dead, general," another rider exclaimed looking up at Hasdrubal.

Chapter Forty-One - A brother's faith

The town of Fanum shimmered in the morning sunlight. From his vantage point Hasdrubal could see the small settlement, less than two miles away. Beyond it into the rising sun lay the blue sparkling sea. Hasdrubal's keen eye moved on picking out every aspect of the countryside in which he now found himself. To the south just out sight over a ridge, but no more than a mile away, was the Metaurus River and the coast road that led to Apulia. The long mournful blast of a Gallic Carnyx wrenched him back and he turned to look at his troops as they filed out of their camp and began to form up in their battle formations. Across the fields, some five hundred yards away in the direction of Fanum, he could see the Roman Legions forming up in their own battle line. The officers around Hasdrubal stirred excitedly as they peered at the Roman formations. This was the second time in two days that the Roman and Carthaginian armies had drawn up for battle, only for nothing to happen.

"They are forming their usual triplex acies," one of the officers exclaimed shielding his eyes against the sun. "Cavalry on the flanks, as usual Sir. Skirmishers out front." Hasdrubal grunted as he turned, distracted to stare at the Romans. His mind was torn with indecision. For two whole nights and three days his army had been camped to the west of the Consul Livius and his subordinate, the Praetor Porcius. The Romans were blocking the coast route southwards and both armies had established their camps north of the Metaurus. Hasdrubal had no intention of taking the coast route. He turned to look inland. The Flaminian Way to his rear, up the valley of the Metaurus was open. Why had he not already disappeared up the valley and southwards following the road to Narnia? That was what his mind was telling him to do but the approach of the Romans had ignited a subtle yearning, a yearning that seemed to whisper sweetly in his ear. If he were, alone, here at Fanum, to defeat Livius the Consul, his glory as a general would become legendary. It would rival the glory that Hannibal his brother had already achieved. And there was another thing which he couldn't ignore. The very closeness of the Roman Consular army meant that any refusal to offer battle could be seen as a weakness by the Romans but also by his own men.

"Their army looks like it has grown in numbers during the night," one of his officers exclaimed suddenly, looking puzzled.

Hasdrubal blinked in alarm and focussed his attention on the Roman Maniples that were forming up in their usual triplex acies. The front line would be comprised of the Hastati, the second line by the Principes and the third reserve line by the Triarii. The Roman infantry formations looked like the squares of an extended chess board. Then he too noticed that the size of the forces opposing him had swollen. He took a step back in surprise. Yes there amongst the enemy he could see blackened faces and shields, covered in dust and grime. Those men and shields had not been there yesterday.

Sir, look," another of his officers exclaimed pointing a finger at the Roman cavalry who were forming up on the flanks. "Their horse is much increased in numbers. They didn't have that many riders yesterday, I am sure. Look the horses are lean from exertion."

Hasdrubal stood rooted to the ground as a terrifying thought occurred to him. Last night as he sat in his camp tent he had heard two trumpet blasts coming from the Roman camp, five hundred yards away. He'd thought nothing of it but now the meaning was becoming clear with terrifying clarity. The Roman tradition was to greet a Consul into the camp with a single trumpet. Two trumpet blasts could only mean one thing. Nero, the second Consul must have arrived with his army during the night.

Hasdrubal was suddenly conscious that his officers were staring at him.

"Gentlemen," he said quietly trying to keep his voice steady, "It seems that we are now facing the armies of two Consuls, not just one. The Romans have been reinforced during the night."

"Then they will significantly outnumber us Sir. We will have to retreat. We cannot hope to beat two combined Consular armies," one of the officers exclaimed.

Hasdrubal rounded on the officer furiously, "Retreat," he cried, "we shall do no such thing. Have you forgotten that my brother is waiting for us at Narnia. I have not come all this way from Spain to retreat now that we are so close."

"Then what Sir, what are your orders?" another officer asked.

A pained expression appeared on Hasdrubal's face. He closed his eyes and then opened them again. What did this mean? What message was hidden in the arrival and appearance of the second Consul? Nero, his spies had told him had been ordered south to watch Hannibal in Brutium. But if Nero was here with his army did that mean that Hannibal had been defeated and slain? Hasdrubal was conscious that his officers were waiting for his answer. He turned his back on them and stared up the

326

Metaurus valley. He was conscious that the decision he now had to take would in all likelihood decide the outcome of the war. He would have liked to have had more time but he didn't have that luxury. He had to decide now, right here before the Romans forced him into battle.

Hasdrubal grunted as his mind raced. He would keep his faith with Hannibal. Nero would not have defeated his brother. No one could defeat Hannibal. His brother was invincible. But how then could he explain the presence of the second Consul. Nero could not just have abandoned his command without some form of precaution or...Hasdrubal's eyes widened, ...or Roman trickery. Yes that was what must have happened. Somehow the Romans had learned by what route he intended to advance. His face darkened. Maybe they had intercepted his messengers or maybe Gisgo had indeed betrayed him. The Romans must then somehow have managed to trick Hannibal into remaining a passive spectator. Hasdrubal turned to stare at the Flaminian road as it disappeared up the valley of the Metaurus. His decision had been made. He would keep faith with Hannibal. He would send out new messengers to his brother urging him to advance on Narnia with all possible haste.

"Recall the men into the camp," he snapped as he turned to face his officers. "We will remain there till nightfall. Then when its dark we will quietly leave camp and head up the valley. That will give us a whole night's head start. With a little luck it should put enough distance between us and the Romans to stop them from catching us. Gentlemen, we are going on to Narnia as planned."

Chapter Forty-Two - March of the seven thousand

It was dark. Marcus stood wearily on the north bank of the Metaurus. His feet were aching, he was exhausted and he hadn't washed in nearly ten days but there was a satisfied look on his face as he watched the column of Roman infantry crossing the river. The men too were in high spirits and if it had been daylight he would have been able to see their dust and grime smeared faces and weapons. The Metaurus was in flood and the winter rains and snow had broadened and deepened the river and in places the water had become a raging torrent. In the pale moonlight Marcus could make out the steep, rocky river banks. For the Roman infantry, the ford however was easy to cross for the Consul Livius's engineers had built a boat bridge across it.

They had been marching for ten days nonstop Marcus thought but now at last the little army of seven thousand had reached its destination. Nero had planned it so, that their arrival in Livius' camp would happen during the hours of darkness, so that the Carthaginians wouldn't be alerted to their arrival. Nero's ability to organise things had impressed Marcus. The short, slightly overweight Consul had acted quickly and decisively after Marcus had explained his deception plan. He had got together six thousand of his finest infantry, giving preference to experience over youth, and a thousand cavalry and had ordered them to prepare for immediate service. He had spread the rumour around the camp that he intended to make a sudden raid into Lucania. Then leaving his second in command in charge with strict instructions to avoid a confrontation with Hannibal he had marched away. As soon as he had gone far enough to feel safe from any pursuit he had halted and had addressed his little army in stirring terms. He Nero, he had declared, was leading them to join the other Consul so that they would win unfading glory that would forever be remembered by the Republic and the Roman people. They, Nero had declared, were marching north in order to defeat Hasdrubal and remove the menace that he represented to Rome, to their homes and to their families. A few days of strenuous marching followed by one great and brave effort on the battlefield would win them this glory and this prize. Nero's speech had been well received by the soldiers and they had set out for the north with such speed and stamina that Marcus had thought impossible.

But they had done it. Nero's brave little army of seven thousand had covered two hundred and fifty miles in ten days. It was a magnificent feat and the soldiers knew it.

At last Marcus stirred from his place by the river bank and turned to walk the final mile of his journey. At the Roman camp which was only five hundred yards from the Carthaginian camp, Livius' soldiers lined both sides of the path. The men were handing out food and cups of wine and patting Nero's men on the back in a silent but ecstatic welcome. As Marcus wandered into the camp with a piece of bread and a cup of wine in his hands he heard two distinct trumpet blasts. Fools, he closed his eyes in dismay, what fool had done that? Were they to give away their arrival to the enemy after all?

The Roman camp looked like any other Roman marching camp Marcus had been in. The outer perimeter was defended by a ditch and a wooden palisade and within the camp itself a single street divided the camp into two halves. Row upon row of white tents stretched away into the darkness. The Tribunes were busy at the camp entrance ordering Nero's men left or right as they arrived. It looked to Marcus as if the newcomers were being billeted in the same tents as the Consul Livius' men. As he watched the hushed work of the Tribunes he felt a sudden soaring pride to be a Roman. Here then, with the union of the Consuls, was proof of how well and efficient the Republic could operate in an hour of dire crisis. Here then was final proof that Roman, Etruscan, Umbrian, Samnite and Campanian were slowly being welded into one people. Not so long ago, Marcus knew, many of these soldiers who now patted each other on the back, would have been enemies.

Marcus didn't know where he should go. In the dark he hung around the camp entrance, too tired and elated to think about tomorrow. What a journey they had just endured. What a march? What a welcome? What a cause? The men, they all sensed it. They sensed that what they had achieved in the past ten days was going to change something. Something deserved to change. At last he was approached by a young Tribune. The man eyed him with a puzzled expression as if he couldn't quite place Marcus's rank and position within the army.

"The officers are being billeted in the Consul's own tents," the Tribune said at last playing it safe.

Marcus nodded his thanks and started out in the direction that the Tribune had told him to go.

***

It was late in the evening when Marcus was woken from his short sleep and ordered to come to the Consul's tent. He had not bothered to take off his mail armour. There had been no point. Guards ringed the large tent in which the Consul Livius had his quarters. Marcus stepped inside following behind a Tribune who was wearing an Attic helmet. The tent was large and well lit. Torches burned along the sides at short intervals and beside each stood a slave, so motionless that they looked like statues. Marcus immediately recognised the figure of Consul Nero. Nero stood beside a large oval table that had been placed in the centre of the tent. Around him clustered his principal officers. On the opposite side of the table stood a group of Livius' officers. They nodded in polite greeting as Marcus entered. Of the Consul Livius and his Praetor Porcius, there was however no sign. Nero caught Marcus's eye and gave him an encouraging nod. Marcus glanced around him. He had not noticed it before but there was a definite tension inside the tent.

Then he heard the guards at the entrance stiffen in salute and a moment later the tent opening was flung aside and Livius strode into the tent followed by the Praetor Porcius and a number of other senior officers. Marcus's eyes followed the Consul as he strode around the table and as he did so he remembered the last time he had met the man in Rome. Livius' officers saluted their Consul and moved to surround him as Livius placed both his hands on the table, his eyes staring at the ground. Then Livius looked up and gazed directly at Nero and to Marcus, standing at the back of the crowded tent, it seemed as if the tension within the tent rose by two notches. All the officers were staring in silent anticipation at the two Consuls, waiting to see how they would react to each other. The two men looked like an odd couple, the tall, sober and stern looking aristocratic Livius and the short, slightly overweight and hyperactive figure of Nero. The tent fell silent. Then Livius moved around the table and to everyone's surprise embraced his shorter colleague. The tent erupted with fierce cries of elation and the stamping of feet
331

as the Consuls grinned at each other. Their rivalry in public life was well known but tonight, on this day, they were united with just one purpose in mind. Marcus suddenly heard himself cheering too. The cries went on until Livius raised his hand.

"Gentlemen," Livius said glancing at Nero, "I cannot express the warmth and gratitude that I, my officers and my army feel in seeing my colleague and his men here today. Your march from Canusium shall be honoured by all of us, it will be honoured by the Roman people. I thank you for coming."

Nero dipped his head in acknowledgement.

"Gentlemen, tomorrow our combined armies are going to defeat Hasdrubal. We are going to wipe his stain from the map of Italy," Livius exclaimed.

The tent erupted in more cries and stamping of feet. Livius gestured towards the table and the assembled officers crowded in closer. Nero moved around the table until he was standing beside Livius. Marcus smiled in appreciation. The wily old Nero was showing his unity with Livius. He was showing that he could equal Livius's statesmanship.

"Tomorrow," Livius was saying, "we must confront the Carthaginian. It is imperative that we force Hasdrubal into a battle as soon as possible. My colleague Nero cannot remain here in the north for an extended period. It is imperative that Hasdrubal is not allowed to escape without being forced to give battle. We must destroy him and his army as soon as we can."

Livius looked around at the assembled officers. No one spoke.

"My colleague and I have agreed that I shall have over all command of the three armies that are here today," Livius went on. "Tomorrow when we form up for battle, we shall do so in three columns. I with my army shall command on the left, Porcius will take the centre and the Consul Nero will take the right flank with the men he has brought with him. "

The officers around the table nodded in silent acknowledgement.

"Gentlemen," Livius said staring up at the faces of the officers as they crowded around the table, "I do not need to remind you of what is at stake tomorrow. Everything is at stake tomorrow. This war has dragged on for eleven years now. I do not expect it to end soon but tomorrow will see its most decisive battle. Tomorrow gentlemen, we will either be victorious or else the Republic will fall. There is no one else but us. There is no one else but us who will defend Rome. Tell your men, tell them that the eyes of the Roman people are fixed on us here. Tell them that the time has come to prove themselves worthy of their mighty ancestors. Tell them that the day has arrived upon which Rome will be judged by the gods. It is our honour gentlemen, it falls to us, to honour the worthy cause of our ancestors. Let us not disappoint them tomorrow."

Livius's words were greeted by a storm of cheering and foot stamping. The noise went on and on until at last Livius raised his hand once more.

"Gentlemen, tomorrow we shall do our duty or die doing that duty."

The assembled officers seemed to break up into individual groups and Marcus drifted across to the officers around Nero. The Consul looked flushed but as he caught Marcus' eye he reached out an arm and pulled Marcus towards him. Nero glanced at his senior officers who clustered around him.

"Tomorrow we will take the right flank. Triple acies formation as usual," he snapped. "Our cavalry will protect our flank. Make sure that your men have heard the Consul Livius' words."

The officers nodded in agreement. Then Nero turned to look at Marcus. "Tomorrow Marcus," Nero exclaimed with a faint smile,

"You will command my Triarii. You know that I left their commander behind at Canusium. Well I did that on purpose. I want you to take over command of my two thousand Triarii. They are my most experienced men. If the battle goes against us then it will be your responsibility to save us."

Marcus nodded and glanced at the other officers trying in vain to hide the sudden blush on his face.

"Do you think that you can handle that?" Nero said with a grin. Marcus nodded and saluted. "I can Sir," he replied.

Chapter Forty-Three - Brother and Sister

Livia was tired of walking. She had been walking for over two weeks now. Every morning had followed the same routine. She had risen before sunrise from around the camp fire that she shared with some of the other women camp followers and had prepared a simple porridge meal for herself and Titus. She was managing to survive by bartering, mending clothes and the occasional singing in the evening for the food that she needed. Then as the army had started out once more on its march south she had bid her brother farewell, slung her belongings onto her back and joined the long baggage train. She wouldn't see Titus until he returned to find her at nightfall when the army halted and built a camp. His role as one of Hasdrubal's guides meant that he was always at the front of the army. He would come looking for her hungry, tired but always with a smile on his face. Livia had begun to look forwards to seeing that smile but the way in which he expected her to feed him and look after him irked her.

"I am not your wife or your mother," she had remonstrated with him, "I am your sister, Titus."

He had taken her remarks in his stride and given her a playful push.

It was noon and the sun was making her sweat. Around her the Carthaginian supply wagons and carts rumbled and jolted along the rough country track. The tramp of the soldiers boots up ahead seemed to reverberate through the very earth but she couldn't see them for the dust clouds billowed high into the air. Livia glanced around her trying to pick out the faces of those women who had been friendly to her but it was impossible to find them amongst the mass of people. The camp followers around Livia streamed forwards in a great disorganised mass. Some, and they were mainly women, strode along carrying infants in their arms. Others plodded on with their heavy looking belongings strapped to their back and yet others held on to the carts that were being pulled along by oxen. In some of the wagons she saw wounded and sick men. She would not go near them. Disease could rapidly spread amongst the army, one of the women she had befriended, had warned her.

She took a sip of water from her water skin. Five days ago, when she had gone down to a stream to get some water she had almost been killed. A Roman cavalry patrol had burst into the midst of the foragers sending people running in every direction until the Carthaginian soldiers had driven the Romans off. Livia glanced idly at the chained Roman prisoners who stumbled along beside the baggage train. The men looked in a bad way, thirsty, dirty and starving but the Carthaginian commander in charge of the prisoners had forbidden anyone from giving the prisoners a drink or something to eat. She had seen some of the prisoners collapse along the track, unable to go on. The Carthaginians had been unrelenting and the prisoner who couldn't stagger back to his feet had had his throat cut and his body had been left along the side of the track. Now as she stared at the prisoners, the Romans reminded her of Marcus.

That night after the army had halted and the soldiers had built a camp, Livia confronted Titus. The two of them sat beside the fire eating in silence. The women who shared the fire with them were curled up beside it and had gone to sleep. The fire spat and crackled as Livia spoke.

"Titus, what are we doing here?" Livia said staring into the flames. "You say that you want to fight. Why will you not fight for us, your family?"

Titus finished his meal in silence.

"I hate these Romans," he muttered, "Our father fought them and so shall I."

"Our father is dead," Livia rounded on him angrily, "I am alive, you are alive. Damn it Titus, since when do the dead matter more than the living. It is time you let go of his memory. I have, because you are going to die if you don't. These Carthaginians," she said glancing around her in dismay," they think they are going to win but I know the Romans, they are the most stubborn, ruthless people I know. It is they who are going to win. They are going to cut these Carthaginians to pieces."

"How do you know that? You are just a girl," Titus retorted.

Livia shook her head. "I am right," she said firmly. "The Romans will not rest until every single one of these invaders is dead. They are going to win, Titus and when they do they are going to kill you too."

Titus' face darkened but he made no reply.

"Please Titus, let our father rest in his grave! Let's go before it's too late."

He reacted in the way that she had expected. Titus rose to his feet and stomped off into the darkness without saying another word.

***

The closeness of the Romans, whose camp was only five hundred yards away, had forced the Carthaginians to build a camp with stronger defences than usual. Livia slipped back through the rows of sharpened and angled wooden stakes that pointed outwards. In her hands she was carrying two full water skins. It was getting dark and she'd had to hurry. She clambered down into the defensive ditch and then up the steep earthen bank which the Carthaginian soldiers had thrown up. A couple of sentries, posted on the crest glanced at her with little interest. She was just one of the hundreds of camp followers who were making the short, yet dangerous journey down to the stream.

On the crest of the mound Livia paused, turned and stared at the Roman fortifications which were just visible in the dusk. Once again there had been no battle that day. She had watched with trepidation twice now as the Carthaginian and Roman armies had marched out of their camps and drawn up ready to do battle, only to see nothing happen and the armies eventually retire back into their respective camps. The two armies had been camped on this spot for three whole days and two nights now. The rumour in the camp was that a battle would soon be fought. It was inevitable, the soldiers were saying, as they prepared themselves for what was coming. Titus too had seemed on edge. The closeness of the two armies had heightened the tension and expectation. Livia turned and strode back down into the camp, carrying her heavy water skins. Titus had hardly spoken to her since she had last confronted him. He had made excuses not to be with her in the evening and his absence had hurt and depressed her. But this was not the time to give up and leave without him. She had thought about it of course but knew that she couldn't. She would stay until the battle had been fought and take her chances. Then at least she would have done everything she could.

The cooking fire inside the tent which had been her home for the past three days had gone out. Wearily she dumped the water skins and bent over looking for the flints with which to light it again. As she did so an arm suddenly twisted around her throat and jerked her off her feet. She gasped. She couldn't breathe. The arm was choking her. Someone was trying to strangle her. Frantically, her fingers grasped and flailed as she struggled to free herself but the man's grip was tight and he did not let go. Livia bit down into the man's flesh with all her might and she was rewarded by an outraged bellow of pain. The pressure on her throat relaxed and she tore herself free.

Getorix swung a fist at her, his face grimacing in pain, but he missed. Livia stumbled back in fright, coughing and gulping in air. He advanced towards her. There was nowhere for her to go. She was trapped.

"Bitch, I warned you," Getorix hissed. "I warned you not to speak to my boy like that again. Now I am going to cut your throat."

Livia stared at Getorix with mounting terror. He had unsheathed a knife from his belt. Despite the pain she had inflicted on him he seemed to be enjoying himself. He grinned, "Or maybe I shall rape you first."

A noise at the entrance to the tent made both of them look up.

Titus stood just inside the entrance. He was staring at Getorix.

"What did you just say?" Titus said in a tense voice.

Getorix smiled, shrugged and sheathed his knife. He took a step towards Titus. Then with a speed that took Livia by surprise, Getorix slammed his fist into Titus' stomach. The wind was knocked out of Titus and he doubled up without making a sound. Getorix raised his knee and smashed it into Titus's head sending the young man sprawling backwards onto the ground. Blood was pouring down Titus' face, his eyes were closed and he didn't move.

"Where were we?" Getorix snapped turning back to look at Livia.

Livia stared at Titus' motionless body. Getorix had killed him. Something seemed to snap inside her. Fury came surging down her veins, swamping everything with raw energy and hatred. Hatred for the man who had just killed her brother. With a terrible shrieking cry, Livia launched herself ferociously at Getorix. Getorix hit her square on the face but she felt no pain. She felt only one thing, the urge to kill, to kill and see blood. Her fingers tore into his face, ripping at the skin with strength she had never known before. He screamed in pain. Then her teeth fastened on Getorix's ear and she ripped it from his head. Blood gushed out, splattering her face. His cries of pain turned to terrified shrieks. He tried to stab her with his knife but her hand caught his and she brought up her knee and rammed it into his crotch. Getorix's shrieking was cut off in mid flow as he doubled up in silent agony. The knife tumbled to the ground. Then she was on his back sinking her teeth into his neck. He slowly collapsed to his knees. Blood was pouring from him where Livia had ripped away his skin and flesh. He was moaning quietly in agony. Livia jumped off him and kicked him to the ground. Then
340

picking up his knife she stabbed him in the back. Then again and again in a frenzied attack. Blood splattered her clothing, her arms and her face but she didn't notice. Kill, kill, kill, she felt the blood lust surging through her veins.

"The blood lust," she suddenly heard a voice mutter."

Livia paused and looked down at her hands and the knife. She was covered in blood. Getorix's body was no longer moving or making a noise. She must have stabbed him a dozen times. She blinked as she seemed to come back to reality. Then she looked up. Titus was staring at her, his eyes wide with fear.

"You are berserker," Titus whispered, "That is our father's gift to you."

Livia rose to her feet and dropped the knife and stared down at Getorix's corpse. Titus had spoken the truth. This then was her father's inheritance. This was all he had ever given her. The fury and strength to kill.

"Let's go," Livia said, "Let's go home. Let's buy that farm and start living." There was a determination in her voice that invited no discussion.

Titus was staring at the battered, bleeding corpse. Then he nodded. "I am sorry," he muttered, "I knew he was mistreating you. I should have acted sooner."

"You did what you had to do," Livia snapped. "Now let's go."

The Carthaginian camp was surprisingly full of activity as Livia and Titus stepped out of the tent. The night sky had begun to fill with twinkling stars and Livia was suddenly glad for the darkness hid her blood smeared clothes and face. A few camp followers who had heard the fight stared at her anxiously from around a camp fire but no one intervened as they vanished off into the gathering gloom. But something was not right. The camp should have been settling down for the night. Yet around them soldiers were packing away their belongings and forming up in marching columns. The men were speaking in urgent but hushed voices. By her side Livia could sense that Titus too was puzzled.

"The army looks like it's getting ready to leave," he whispered.

"That is very odd. It's night time, where are they going?"

Livia did not reply. Nothing and nobody was going to stop her now. She was taking her brother from this place.

"Maybe they are planning a night attack on the Roman camp," Titus exclaimed.

"Come," Livia said as they ran up the earthen bank that marked the perimeter of the camp. Soldiers were standing guard on top of the mound. They turned to look at Livia and Titus with suspicion.

"How are we going to get away?" Livia whispered. "You are the guide. You know this land don't you?"

Titus glanced uneasily at the soldiers, "We will have to swim across the Metaurus," he whispered. "They won't dare to come after us but the river is in flood. It will be difficult. Can you swim?"

"What are you doing there?" one of the soldiers cried as he started to walk towards them.

"Run!" Livia whispered and the two of them turned and ran down the earth bank.

"Deserters, spies!" someone shouted. "Stop them!"

Livia clambered out of the ditch and through the lines of sharpened stakes. It was dark and it was difficult to see where she was going. Then she was beyond the camp's defences. At her side a dark figure loomed up. It was Titus. Without thinking Livia grabbed his hand.

"Run," she whispered.

Chapter Forty-Four - The battle of the Metaurus

Hasdrubal was in a foul mood. Everything had gone wrong since his army had marched out of their camp, late last night. Now it was mid-morning and he'd had no sleep all night but tiredness was the least of his worries. The first thing to go wrong on the night march was that his two guides had deserted him. One had been found stabbed seventeen times in a tent and the other guide, the younger one had been seen fleeing from the camp in the company of a young woman. Without his guides Hasdrubal had been unsure of what exact path to take and his army had blundered on through the night. One column had got lost and the other two had continuously come up against the Metaurus river which they hadn't been able to cross due to the river being in flood and also due to the steepness of the river banks. A night march was already a very difficult undertaking but without his guides it had become a nightmare and when dawn had finally come, his men had only come six miles or so from their original camp. Worse, the soldiers were exhausted, frustrated, cold and hungry. They milled about along the banks of the Metaurus in some confusion. Hasdrubal stared at them with mounting frustration. If only he could find a ford by which he could get his all-important baggage train across. Then at least he would have some protection from the Roman armies who would surely be in pursuit by now. He was about to give the order to keep moving up the river valley when a scout came thundering up to him on horseback. The man's face looked flushed.

"Roman cavalry and skirmishers Sir," the scout cried, "They have overtaken us!"

Hasdrubal stared at the scout in silent anger. Then he turned to look in the direction that the rider was pointing.

"What about the Legions? What about the Roman heavy infantry?" he snapped.

"They are not far behind Sir," the scout replied. "They will be here within an hour or two. They are marching fast. They know where we are. They look eager for battle."

Hasdrubal turned away to look at the Metaurus. Then he sighed and his shoulders seemed to sag a little. The night march had been a disaster. He had failed to put any proper distance between himself and the Romans. He looked up and began to study the ground around him. To the south was the Metaurus and to his north he could see a hill with a sharp, very steep rocky cliff face. The hill widened at the top, its crest covered with trees.

"We will make our camp over there," Hasdrubal cried gesturing at the hill. "Get the men building a camp right away. We don't have much time."

Hasdrubal watched as his officers rode away to convey his orders to the troops. He turned again to look at the Metaurus. The course of the river had twisted and bent so many times that he had cursed the water during the night. He glanced up the valley and sighed in regret. If he had managed to stay on the Flaminian Road he would have been alright but the vanguard of his columns had lost contact with the road and had blundered down towards the river. The men had simply followed his advance units. He pulled himself together. What was done, could not be undone. He would build his camp on the hill. The
345

Romans would not dare attack such a strong position. Then tomorrow he would resume his advance down the Flaminian Road. A faint smile appeared on his face as he tried to picture what his brother would look like. It would not be long now before they would re-united.

"General," another of his officers cried as he came riding up. The man looked angry and filled with disgust. "We have been betrayed."

"What?" Hasdrubal's exclaimed, his face darkening.

"It's the Gaul's, Sir. They stumbled onto a Roman wine depot. Many of them are drunk. They are no fit state to fight or build a camp."

Hasdrubal stared at the officer in disbelief. Then he shook his head.

"They are drunk?" he repeated.

The officer nodded and cast an apprehensive glance to the east. Hasdrubal turned to look in the same direction. A bitter taste filled his mouth as he remembered the encounter with the druid and the Gallic war band on the day he had started to descend from the mountains. It was his own fault. He should never have promised the Gaul's the Roman spoils of war. He should have imposed a far stricter discipline on his Gallic allies. Hannibal had done so. His brother had understood their lazy and greedy nature. He should have followed Hannibal's example but he hadn't and now it was too late. As he stared to the east, the direction from which the Romans would come another scout pulled up before him. The man was sweating and panting.

"Sir, the Legions are approaching. They will be here within an hour. I have never seen them advancing with such speed."

Hasdrubal stared at the man in silence. Then he turned to look at the hill that he had selected for his camp. There was no time. The Romans would be upon him before he could start, let alone complete his fortifications. He nodded grimly. So be it then, he would have to fight.

"Order the men to stop work on the camp. Tell them to form up into their battle formations," Hasdrubal cried with a sudden surge of energy. "I want all the Gaul's up on that hill. The steepness of the cliff will protect them from any Roman assault. Get the African and Ligurian infantry to form up over there," he said pointing to the level land below the hill, "They will form the centre of our line. Position the elephants out in front as cover." Hasdrubal turned and pointed at the gently sloping fields that ran down to the edge of the Metaurus. A vineyard was the only obstacle that seemed to break up the flatness of the land.

"Place the Iberians here and our cavalry on their flank," he growled.

"Will they fight Sir?" a young officer at Hasdrubal's side asked.

Hasdrubal nodded without looking at the man. "They will fight and so shall we," he replied grimly. "The time has come to settle the matter."

***

Marcus felt his heart thumping in his chest as he half walked, half ran across the field. The Roman infantry in their neat Maniples were surging across the field behind and ahead of him. The tension on the men's faces was showing but Marcus sensed a different mood too, a mood of grim determination.

"Move, come on, faster, faster," the cries of the Centurions and Tribunes were just about audible over the din of thousands of advancing men. To his left Marcus could see a great cloud of dust where the Roman and allied cavalry were thundering forwards. As Marcus kept pace with his advancing formations a dispatch rider came galloping past heading for the rear.

"What news from the front?" Marcus cried.

"Our cavalry have made contact with the enemy," the rider cried. Then he was gone in a swirl of dust and clumps of mud.

Marcus kept on moving. The Consul's orders were clear. The enemy army should not be allowed to escape. That had been the plan yesterday too. The Romans had marched out of their camp and had drawn themselves up ready to offer battle. It had been the first time that Marcus had had a chance to inspect his men. The thirty Maniples of Triarii whom he now commanded had formed the third line of the Roman army. They were only expected to fight if things went against the Romans. The men, all of them aged in their late thirties and early forties had stood in perfect separate square formations like the squares on a chessboard. Each Maniple was commanded by a Centurion and his Optio, second in command, whose position was at the back of the square formation. The Optio was their mainly to make sure that the men did not flee. The Centurions had stood to the front of their men. As he'd strode up and down the line Marcus had felt the men's eyes on him. The maniples varied in strength between fifty and seventy men, but the men were all veterans with many years of campaigning experience between them.

The Romans were not professional soldiers. This was a citizen army, a militia made up of land owning citizens, most of them small farmers and their sons. The men were responsible for the purchase of their own armour and equipment and as he strode along Marcus had noticed the different individual weapons, shields and armour. But enough of the Roman equipment had been mass produced to give the impression of a standardised and well-equipped force. Marcus had halted before his men as the last Maniple had formed up in the right position.

It was quite something to have nearly two thousand men awaiting his orders. If only Flavia could see him now. Would she believe him when he told her? Marcus had delivered a short stirring speech whose words had been relayed to the men further back by the Centurions and Optio's. When he'd fallen silent, the young Tribune who had been assigned to him had nodded in approval.

"Excellent speech Sir. That will put fire in the men's bellies."

"I do hope so," Marcus had grunted, "For those were the exact and last words of the Consul Regulus before he was killed at Telamon."

The day however had ended with the Carthaginian army retiring back into their camp.

***

"Move, come on, faster," the Centurions were shouting as they practically whipped their men on over the fields. Marcus ran alongside them. The Consul Nero had command of the right flank of the combined Roman armies and that was where Marcus too would be posted. As he ran alongside his troops, Marcus remembered Nero's final instructions.

"If the day goes against us I will trust in you and your men to save us."

The pace of the advance was slowing and the Centurion's cries had started to peter out. Marcus splashed through a shallow brook and his run became a walk. The Maniples ahead of him had halted and had began to spread out in a line, to his left and right. Marcus strode forwards, pushing his way through the ranks until he was standing in front of his men. He gasped at the sight before him. To his left, stretching in a line down towards the Metaurus the entire Roman army of forty-seven thousand men was moving into their positions. Two miles away on the extreme left flank the clouds of dust gave away the position of the Roman and allied cavalry. Across from them, separated by a few hundred yards, across the fields, stood line upon line of African, Ligurian and Iberian swordsmen. But it was not the enemy ranks that caught Marcus' attention. It was the fifteen great grey elephants standing in front of the massed Carthaginian ranks. A murmur swept through the Roman ranks at the sight of the grey beasts. Marcus glanced down at the Hastati and the Principes who formed the Roman first and second lines. How would those young men be coping with the sheer terror that those grey elephants with their deadly white tusks could impose? If the Hastati and the Principes turned and ran then it was very doubtful whether his two thousand Triarii would be able to stem the enemy advance on their own.

From the Carthaginian lines a dozen Carnyx's blasted away. Their mournful, haunting notes echoed off the hills that surrounded the valley. Marcus looked up at the Carthaginian left flank which directly faced Nero's troops. The men facing him were Gaul's and Marcus's heart sank. The Gaul's lined the ridge of a steep hill, so steep it was barely possible to climb, let alone fight ones way up. The Celtic position was impregnable. He turned to his Tribune, his trumpeter and the two runners who clustered around him.

"Let's hope the Consul has his wits about him and doesn't order us up that slope," he grunted.

The four men nodded and Marcus could see the tension on their faces. One of the runners was holding Marcus' oval shield and Hastae, his heavy two-yard-long thrusting spear. The trumpeter was holding his Tuba, the straight, four feet long bronze trumpet, ready to signal the troops. "Don't worry boys," Marcus said trying to sound reassuring, "We are going to be alright."

The blasts of Roman trumpets wrenched Marcus' attention back to the centre and left flank of the Roman line. The Maniples of Porcius' and Livius's Legions and Italian troops had finally gotten into position. The three lines of squares stretched nearly up to the Metaurus. The noise of the Roman trumpets and the Celtic Carnyx faded away and for a short moment the battlefield became eerily calm as men on both sides steadied themselves for what was coming.

Then the stillness was broken by a multitude of Roman trumpets, all playing the same note. Marcus had heard that note only twice before in his life but he knew what it meant. It was the order to advance on the enemy position. He craned his neck towards the Metaurus. The dust clouds seemed to be moving along the river bank. The Roman and Italian cavalry would be charging the enemy horse. Then the Roman infantry on the left and in the centre lifted up their shields, from where they had been resting against their legs, and began to advance. As they did so the Romans began to chant their battle cries and clash their spears into their shields making a terrific noise. Marcus heard the voices of the Hastati as they closed with the enemy.

"Carthage must die, Carthage must die!"

The Roman front line steadily closed the gap. Then as Marcus looked on, a hail of spears were flung at the Carthaginian line and with a loud cry the Hastati, unsheathed their swords and charged at the African and Ligurian infantry in the centre. From the Carthaginian ranks a hail of spears, sling shots and other missiles hammered into the attacking Romans. The elephants bellowed in rage and charged forwards smashing into the Roman line, their tusks wreaking havoc. A man was flung high into the air by one of the enraged beasts and two more elephants were cutting a path through the Maniples as if the Roman infantry were wheat waiting to be harvested. Men shrieked in terror and alarm as the beasts kept on coming, ploughing into the Principes without fear or concern for the thousands of men around them. The din from the screams and shouts of thousands of soldiers, now locked in a desperate, murderous fight, echoed off the distant hills.

Marcus and his Triarii stood motionless as they watched the fighting to their left. The Roman Hastati had reached the Carthaginian front line. The neat manipular formations had fragmented and it was everyman for himself. The Romans came on, surging into the enemy line like the tide washing up a beach.

The Hastati had raised their large oval shields and now, with a dull thud that was audible to Marcus and his troops, they crashed into the Africans and Ligurians, thrusting their metal shield bosses into the enemy's faces whilst their short Spanish swords stabbed and jabbed into every opening that they could find. Men fell to the ground mortally wounded, others slipped on the bodies of the dead and along the line, the desperate fighting seemed to sway backwards and forwards. But the Carthaginians held their ground and the Principes, the Roman second line, began to advance in support of the Hastati. Surrounded by a mob of Roman soldiers, one of the elephants toppled over onto the ground. Then another great beast collapsed, its body pierced by numerous spears. Marcus looked up and tried to see what was happening over on the Roman left but all he could see was clouds of dust beside the river and the same confused infantry fighting as in the centre.

"Sir, look," his Tribune shouted pointing at the Gaul's directly in front of them. Marcus turned. Nero's Hastati and Velites, skirmishers had made a vain attempt to storm the hill but their assault had petered out quickly as the men had found it impossible to climb up the steep slopes. The Hastati and skirmishers were retreating to their starting positions as they came under fire from a hail of missiles and rocks from the Gaul's on the slopes above. Marcus frowned. Couldn't Nero see that it was pointless trying to attack the Punic left wing? What was the Consul trying to do?

A trumpet blast echoed across the battlefield. On the extreme left flank, beside the banks of the Metaurus, the clouds of dust were moving up the river. Marcus stared at the movement with sudden interest.

"Our cavalry must be routing the enemy horse," the Tribune cried excitedly as he too noticed the movement.

Marcus turned to look at the hill in front of them. The Gaul's were laughing at the Romans. They hadn't even bothered to form a proper line. Some of their warriors were sitting down! Marcus felt a surge of rage. Let them laugh. Let them stay out of the battle then. He scratched his cheek and turned to stare again at the Roman left flank. Then he turned sharply to his runner.

"You," Marcus snapped, "Take this message to the Consul Nero. Tell the Consul that I intend to take my Triarii around the back of our army. Tell him that a gap has opened up between the river and the Carthaginian right. Tell the Consul that I intend to strike and envelop the enemy right flank. Ask him for permission to carry out this move, go, now, hurry!"

The runner nodded, turned and sprinted off towards the front of the Roman line. Marcus felt his heart thumping in his chest with sudden anxiety. The move he was proposing was unheard of and utterly unorthodox and if it went wrong and the Gaul's came down from their hill in great strength and crushed the Roman right, then he Marcus would surely be held responsible for losing the most crucial battle of the war. But risks had to be taken. He bit his lip and tried to hide his nerves. The seconds passed by. In the centre, the din of thousands of struggling, fighting and desperate men went on undiminished. The Romans had been fought to a halt and no side seemed to have the advantage.

The runner was sprinting back. Marcus stared at the young man as he approached trying to read his face. The runner was breathing heavily as he came to a stop. He looked up at Marcus and nodded.

"The Consul says, do it," the man gasped.

***

"Let's go, go, go!" Marcus shouted as he started to stride down the front line of his men. A moment later his signaller's trumpet blasted the order for left turn, quick march. The motionless squares of Triarii did not move at first but then the Centurions were repeating the order and the thirty maniples turned as one and began moving around the back of the Roman army towards the Metaurus. Marcus broke into a jog as he strained to move up to the front and seeing their commander break into a run, the Triarii did the same. Marcus had no time to study the battle that was raging on his right. The Triarii of Porcius' and Livius' Legions had already been committed to the battle and few Roman's saw their two thousand countrymen moving across the battlefield behind them. It was about two miles to the river and to Marcus it felt like an age. He jogged on at the head of his men. Despite the roar and din of the fighting he could clearly hear the jangle and rattle of the soldier's equipment. The Triarii were the wealthiest men in the Roman army and they had been able to afford the best equipment. Nearly all of them were clad in chain mail and were holding their large oval shields and heavy thrusting spears.

Marcus's eyes strained. Yes he'd been right, there, between the Metaurus and the Iberians, a gap had opened up in the Carthaginian line. The Roman cavalry had driven the Carthaginian cavalry from the field and had gone off in pursuit of their fleeing enemy. Nothing had filled the gap vacated by the cavalry. Marcus felt a growing sense of elation. Had Hasdrubal not seen the danger? Would the Carthaginian's really allow him to plunge into this gap and attack their infantry from the side and rear? It seemed incredible but as he strained his eyes upon the fighting, it did indeed look as if there was no Punic response. Marcus turned and roared at his troops.

"Move, move, for fuck's sake, faster!"

He came to a panting halt as the first Maniples of Triarii stormed past him down towards the river bank. If the Carthaginians did not close the gap within the next five minutes then they were going to lose the battle. Marcus felt a soaring excitement, that was becoming uncontrollable. There had still been no Carthaginian reaction. Had they not seen his troops moving into position? "Fool's," he muttered to himself, "What fools," he shook his head.

His Tribune and his two runners and signalman caught up with him. All four of them were gasping for breath. Behind Marcus the Triarii were still coming up and forming up into their new positions. The men's faced looked flushed and winded.

"Come on, come on," Marcus growled as he studied the Carthaginian flank which was less than two hundred yards away. Livius's men were locked in a desperate brawl with clusters of Iberians and the Carthaginian's seemed to be winning for the Consul's men were slowly being driven backwards.

"Hasdrubal's best men," Marcus cried pointing at the Iberians. "If they turn and run its all over for the rest of them."

"Sir," the Tribune nodded nervously.

356

Marcus turned and rapidly examined the Triarii behind him. The men were nearly in position.

"Shield, spear," he shouted.

The runner holding his equipment stepped forwards and Marcus grasped the shield in his left hand and the heavy thrusting spear in his right.

"Do your duty for Rome today, boys," he said glancing at his small staff. Then he lifted the shield to his mouth and kissed the wood for good luck, muttering a short prayer as he did so. It had been eleven years since he'd last done that. Maybe today would be his last. He dismissed the thought. It wasn't worth thinking about. Marcus turned to his troops and raised his spear high in the air.

"Triarii, for Rome, advance!" he shouted. Then he was away storming towards the Carthaginian line. Behind him the trumpeter blasted the signal to attack and a huge cry rose up as two thousand men surged forwards in pursuit of their commander. Marcus ran. A group of Iberians alerted by the tremendous roar turned to face him. Marcus held his spear tightly clasped against his body. Then he opened his mouth in a great roar as the spear point thudded straight into an enemy shield. The force of his charge sent his opponent stumbling backwards taking Marcus's spear with him. Marcus's shield battered into an Iberian's face and Marcus was rewarded by a howl of pain. Then a heavy object smashed into Marcus's shield and he felt the blow travel up his arm. Drawing his gladius he jabbed his sword at the enemy but the blade struck nothing. Another mighty blow hammered into his shield sending Marcus staggering backwards. He heard an angry, snarling noise. He

357

jabbed again and this time his sword glanced of a man's armour. An Iberian loomed over him, his face contorted in fury and hatred. The man tried to rip Marcus's shield from him but as he did so Marcus stabbed him and felt his sword penetrate flesh. With a groan the Iberian vanished from sight. Then to his right and left the Triarii came surging into the enemy line, their shields and spears raised and the shock and massive noise of their attack punched into the Iberian's like an angry bull tearing through a crowded street. Men tumbled to the ground all around Marcus. A man close by was decapitated by an axe which sent a thin spray of blood flying through the air. Another was impaled on a spear, driven straight through his midriff. Someone was screaming hysterically. Marcus had no time to look around. Another Iberian came at him swinging a spiked club. The man was screaming, his face contorted with blood lust. The club smashed into Marcus' shield splitting it into two and sending Marcus staggering backwards under the impact. The man roared and raised his club to finish Marcus off but just as he was about to strike, he was impaled by two Roman spears. A group of seven Triarii surged passed him, trampling the Iberian to the ground. Marcus stared wild eyed at the shattered piece of shield in his hand. Then he was on his feet. He grabbed a discarded shield and charged back into the melee.

The Roman assault on the Iberian flank was causing chaos amongst the enemy. Marcus pushed forward into the fighting line. The Iberians were being attacked from the front by Livius's men and now also from the side and rear as Marcus's maniples wheeled round the end of the Carthaginian line and started to roll the enemy up from behind. Marcus felt a surge of violent joy. They had done it. The enemy would break at any moment. They were going to be slaughtered.

A sharp shooting pain seared up his right leg and Marcus cried out in sudden agony. A sword had sliced below his shield and into his unprotected shinbone. Marcus stumbled backwards and collapsed to the ground. The pain was excruciating. He cried out again and stared down at his leg. Blood was pouring from the wound. His leg looked a mess and he couldn't feel his foot. Then a pair of arms lifted him up and dragged him out of the front line. Marcus cried out again as his leg flopped and jerked as he was dragged roughly across the corpse littered field. Then unceremoniously he was dumped onto the ground.

"Pay attention Sir," the grizzled old face of one of his Triarii shouted as the man ran forwards to rejoin the fighting. There was a disapproving look on the man's face that made Marcus want to laugh out loud. He lay on his back as the pain continued to come in great surging bursts. Marcus grimaced and stared up at the sky. Gods, his leg hurt. Then he heard the cries of Roman voices.

"Hasdrubal, Hasdrubal, there he is, Hasdrubal!"

***

Hasdrubal sat on his horse. His chest heaving with exertion. His eyes flashed wildly as he stared at the battle raging around him. In his hand he held his general's banner. Sweat poured down his face. He had been everywhere, he had done everything he could. He'd shouted at his Africans and Ligurians to hold their line, he had encouraged them, he had threatened them. His very presence behind their ranks had made them hold the centre against the more heavily armoured Roman Legions. The elephants had wreaked havoc amongst the Roman central assault but the beasts had been too few in number to send the

Romans fleeing and he'd watched in helpless despair as the Romans had surrounded and killed them one by one. The Gaul's had proved useless and Hasdrubal's contempt for them had grown and grown. The Celts had been happy to stay in their impregnable position and watch the fighting as if they were spectators. What a farce he'd thought and he had resolved to ignore them completely.

It was on the right that Hasdrubal's hopes had been raised. His trusty Iberians had fought with great courage and skill. They had been driving Livius's Legions back when too late, Hasdrubal had seen the Roman flanking move. He had no idea what had happened to his cavalry. They should have been protecting his flank but they had vanished. They must have been outnumbered by the Romans and had fled. He should have seen it earlier but he'd been too concerned with the fighting in the centre to pay it attention. The mistake had cost him the battle.

Hasdrubal's shoulders drooped. It was all over. He had lost. As he looked on the Iberian infantry on the right began to break and flee. They had been attacked from three sides. No one could stand up to that. The Africans and Ligurian's in the centre had seen the growing rout to their right and the men too had begun to flee. Now as Hasdrubal sat on his horse, his soldiers came streaming past him in great disorganised and terrified masses. Order had completely broken down. The Carthaginians had began to run for their lives. It was every man for himself now. Hasdrubal stared at his men. Behind them, charging forwards in pursuit were the Roman and Italian heavy infantry. The battle was about to descend into a massacre and everyone knew it.

Hasdrubal turned to look behind him. His bodyguards had deserted him and had joined the ranks of the fleeing mob. Only one of his Punic guards had remained at his post. Hasdrubal smiled sadly at the brave, frightened young man. Then he turned to stare at the ranks of the advancing Romans.

"If you survive Bostar and if you make it back to Carthage," Hasdrubal said wearily, "Then tell our people that I, Hasdrubal, did not betray my brother or my soldiers. Tell them that Hasdrubal honoured the memory of the men who have fallen fighting for him. Tell them that I went to my death like a Carthaginian general should when the tide has turned against him."

Then without waiting for an answer Hasdrubal urged his horse forwards into a gallop and headed straight for the Roman line. As he galloped towards the enemy, his fleeing men sprang aside in terror. The Romans, recognising him at last, had started to shout his name. Hasdrubal rode on straight at his enemy and as he did so, in his mind, he suddenly saw his father beckoning to him from the river, just like he had seen him in his dream. There was a warm loving smile on Hamilcar's face and as he saw his father, tears began to roll down Hasdrubal's cheeks. Then, at the last moment, he raised both his arms into the air and crashed headlong and alone into the Roman ranks.

**

The wounded Roman soldiers had been laid out in long lines beside the Metaurus. Marcus lay stretched out, his eyes closed, feeling the warm sun on his face. He was exhausted. A group of army doctors had set up a wooden table beside the river upon which they were busy working on the most seriously wounded

361

men. The cries and shrieks of the wounded was the worst noise Marcus had ever heard. Someone had carried him from the battlefield and dumped him beside the other wounded. The battle was won the soldiers had told him in jubilant voices. The Carthaginians were fleeing. Their army had been utterly routed and Hasdrubal was dead. Now a few hours later Marcus felt weak from a loss of blood. One of his Triarii had bound a Focale, a soldier's scarf around the wound to stem the bleeding and someone else had forced a cup of wine down his throat after which they had left him alone. Marcus had drifted in and out of consciousness. The pain had dulled but it came surging back every time he tried to move. He wondered whether his leg would ever mend again. Would he become a cripple like the poor veterans he'd seen every day in Rome? It didn't bear thinking about.

Marcus opened his eyes. A young doctor was coming down the long line of wounded men. The man was wearing a blood stained white sheet over his tunic. Marcus frowned as he tried to focus on the man. There was something strangely familiar about him. Then the doctor approached him and the young man's face suddenly broke into a furious blush.

"Hello father," Gaius exclaimed.

Author's notes

In this novel I have tried to stick as faithfully as possible to the known historical facts concerning Hasdrubal's Metaurus campaign and the Roman response. In Sir Edward Creasy's famous 1851 book, the battle of the Metaurus in 207 BC is listed as one of the fifteen most decisive battles in history. It certainly was the most decisive battle of the 2nd Punic war for by defeating Hasdrubal and preventing him from bringing reinforcements to Hannibal it effectively ended any chance that Carthage had of winning this, the most pivotal war of the classical age. The second Punic war was a struggle to decide who would rule the Mediterranean world. Rome's ultimate victory meant Latin and Roman culture would dominate Europe for the next seven hundred years.

Placentia was besieged by Hasdrubal early on although he failed to take the colony. Livy tells us that Hasdrubal's two guides did indeed desert him early on in his night march and that this caused him and his army to lose their way during the night. One of the guides is supposed to have swam across the Metaurus.

Livy also tells us that after the battle of the Metaurus, the Consul Nero marched straight back south to his command. He is said to have completed the journey in six days. The first news that Hannibal had of his brother's defeat was when Nero ordered Hasdrubal's severed head to be flung into the Carthaginian camp. Hannibal, Livy tells us, is supposed to have sighed as he gazed at his brother's pallid and distorted features and uttered the words, "I recognise the fortune of Carthage."

The exact site on which the battle of the Metaurus was fought is a long and fiercely debated issue with no clear winner. Three sites have been proposed but no one really knows for certain where the battle took place. In this novel I have opted for the site, on the left bank of the Metaurus near the village of La Lucrezia, the site proposed by General Vaudoncourt in 1812.

The Consul Nero was the forefather of that emperor by the same name who would later be held responsible for the great fire of Rome in AD 64.

Glossary

Amphora, an ancient ceramic container used for the transport or storage of various products including wine and Garum.

Ariminum, Modern day Rimini.

Fibula, A fibula is an ancient brooch. Their practical use was to fasten clothing.

Gladius, The Latin word for sword.

Ides of March, The fifteenth of march.

Infula, A sort of fillet worn by ancient Roman priests and dignitaries. It was generally white.

Liburnian, A small galley used mainly for raiding and patrolling.

Lictor, A lictor was a member of a special class of Roman civil servants. The lictor attended and guarded the magistrates of ancient Rome.

New Carthage, Modern day town of Cartagena in Spain.

Palla, A palla is a traditional Roman mantle. It is similar to a shawl that a woman of today would wear.

Peplos, A body length garment worn by women in ancient Greece and Rome.

Pisae, Modern day Pisa.

Placentia, Modern day Piacenza in northern Italy.

Praetor, A Praetor was a title held by a man who acted in one of two capacities. Either he was a commander of an army and appointed by a Consul or else he was an elected magistrate who was assigned specific duties.

Stola, A traditional garment worn by Roman women.

Made in United States
Orlando, FL
16 March 2023

31065389R00221